SKYTHANE

LIMINAL SKY: THE OBERON CYCLE BOOK 1

J. SCOTT COATSWORTH

Published by
Other Worlds Ink
PO Box 19341, Sacramento, CA 95819

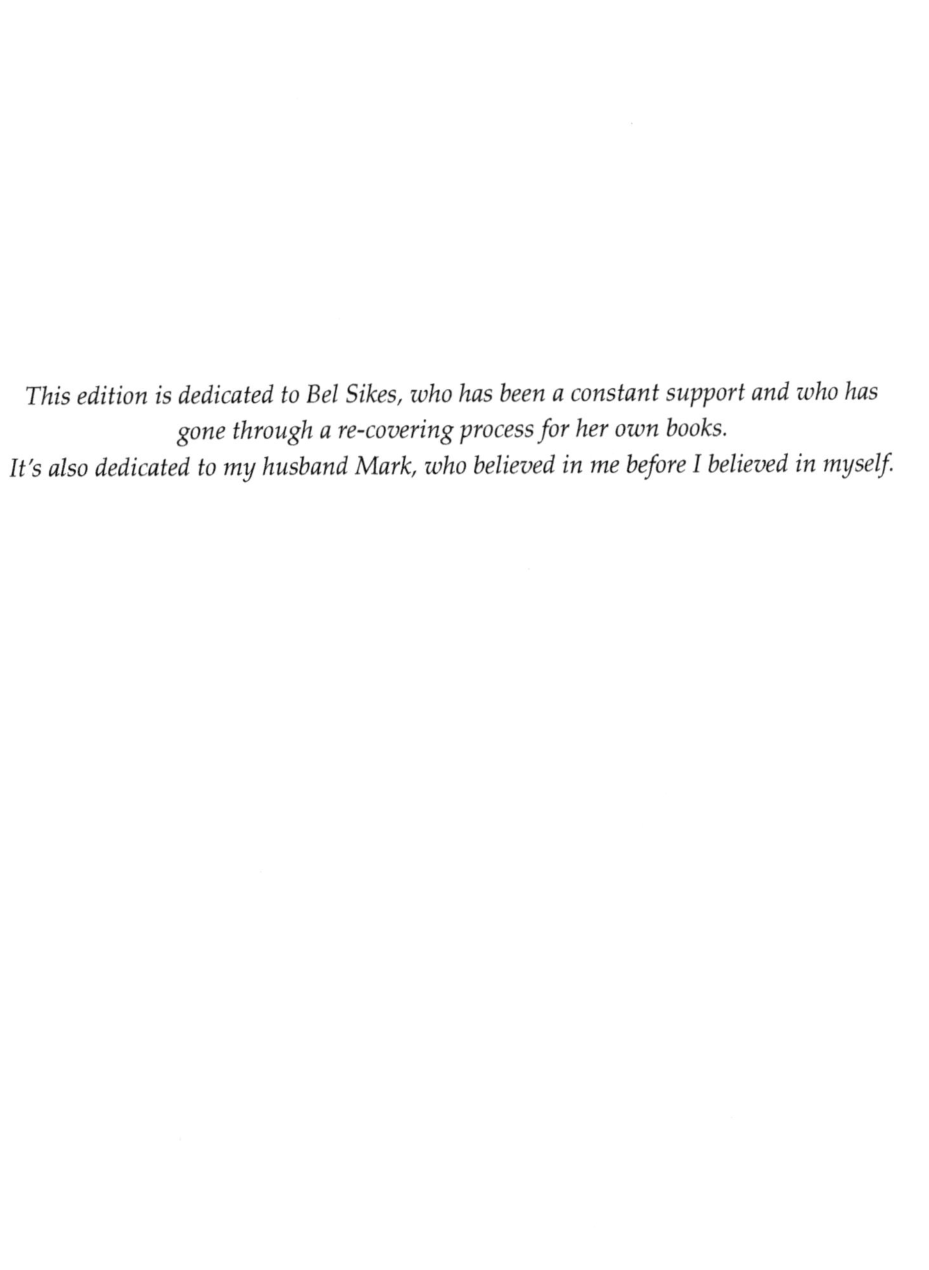

This edition is dedicated to Bel Sikes, who has been a constant support and who has gone through a re-covering process for her own books.
It's also dedicated to my husband Mark, who believed in me before I believed in myself.

CONTENTS

ACKNOWLEDGMENTS

ONCE IN a lifetime, a writer publishes their first novel. This one wouldn't have happened without a kick in the pants from my mom, a kitchen brainstorming session on the weather dynamics of a half world using a cereal bowl with our dear friends Bill and Kathy Cox (which was based on the weather musings of Dave Fragments), and the love of all of my other friends and family. And Kelley York of Sleepy Fox Studio has been amazing to work with for the covers of the second and third editions. But most of all, it took the undying support of my husband Mark, who has (against his better judgment) been steadfast in his belief in me and my writing talent. I love you, Mark!

PRINCIPAL CHARACTERS (GLOSSARY AT END)

Alix Preston (PA Erissa): Xander's ex, a lander man missing for a year

Danielle (Dani) Black (PA Hera): One of the lander enforcers in Gaelan, daughter of Danner Black

Davyn Sléite: Xander's Gaelani name

Jameson Havercamp (PA Angie): Psych from Beta Tau who comes to investigate pith shortage on Oberon

Jessa: Jameson's fiancée on Beta Tau

Kadin Tamain: The chamberlain of the House of the Moon

Lyrin Madainn: Jameson's birth name

Morgan: Mysterious child Xander finds on Oberon

Mylin: Young skythane girl who helps Xander

Quince Farrai (PA Ari): Xander's skythane friend who joins the quest

Robyn Sléite: Queen of the Gaelani and mother to Xander, and Quince's former lover

Rogan Horth: Syndicate boss who has history with Xander

Xander Kinnson (PA Ravi): Skythane who works in Oberon City, embarks on a quest with Jameson

FOREWORD

This is the third edition of this by-now venerable sci-fantasy series of mine. *Skythane* was my first published novel, originally released in February, 2017. It's hard to believe it's been almost ten years!

Since that time, I have gone on to publish thirteen additional novels across six different series, and books fifteen and sixteen will come out later this year.

There are now eleven novels and one anthology in the Liminal Sky universe, of which *Skythane* and the Oberon Cycle are a part.

But *Skythane* is still one of my favorites. In addition to being my first published full-length story, it was also the first thing I ever wrote that reflected my sexuality, with a gay sex scene to kick off the story. Which seemed a bold choice when I wrote the first few scenes of what would eventually become Skythane back in the early Nineties.

I also still love my two main protagonists, Jameson and Xander, and all the supporting cast, especially Morgan.

As the book approaches its tenth anniversary, it seems appropriate to revisit the cover. The initial series covers were overtly gay, beefcake covers that matched what was popular at the time.

When left my old publisher, Dreamspinner, I took the covers in a different direction, emphasizing the sci-fi aspect, with the help of Kelley York from Sleepy Fox Studio.

Now I'm striving for a middle ground, once again with Kelley's help, to help freshen up the series and connect it to a new audience.

I hope you enjoy the cover, and the book!

PROLOGUE

And we fairies, that do run
By the triple Hecate's team,
From the presence of the sun,
Following darkness like a dream.

-William Shakespeare, *A Midsummer Night's Dream*

QUINCE SAT at her desk by the window of her flat, staring off into the distance through the floor-to-ceiling plas window.

Outside, the storm was coming. It had roared out of the Pyramus Mountains that morning, causing flooding all the way down to the Gildensea, and now the vast tempest was approaching Oberon City. Angry purple clouds stretched up to at least 30,000 feet above sea level, and great multiforked lightning bolts lanced down from the sky.

She was tired of everything—the city, the attitudes. A winged skythane woman among all these wingless lander men.

The streetscape of the city spread out below her, thousands of amber lights running in strings along the main roadways where the ground transportation rumbled among the mostly industrial buildings.

In the distance beneath the clouds, she could just make out the blue shadow of the Pyramus Mountains, their peaks a sharp-toothed wall of darkness along the eastern edge of the world. Above them, in a break in the clouds, the stars swam in the deepest night, thickest overhead.

Neither Hermia nor Lysander, Oberon's two moons, was up to challenge the stellar dominance of the night sky. Somewhere out there, Titan Station tracked slowly across the heavens.

She watched it all from her small apartment, perched halfway up one of Oberon's great arcos—ten two-hundred-story residential-commercial habitats that housed most of the population of the city.

In her mind's eye, she could see the waters of the Argent Sea on another world, lapping at the rocks far below her bedroom window, half a lifetime ago.

She closed her eyes and remembered the day it had all begun.

Quince was all alone in the forest just outside Ballifor, searching for hoarberries to take back home to her uncle's house. She walked under the great redoak trees, the sunlight filtering pink through the branches and leafy canopies down to the forest floor.

Something cracked behind her, and she spun around, catching her foot on a root and falling hard to the ground. When she looked up, winded by the fall, the most beautiful creature stood there, looking down on her.

It was a nimfeach. She… or was it a he? It, she decided. It looked like a luminescent butterfly as tall as a human being, its gossamer wings trailing off into a shower of soft sparks, golden in the darkness under the trees. Its features were humanoid, but its eyes were far larger, and its face was heart shaped.

The nimfeach had existed here for as long as humanity. There were legends about them going back to the first skythane settlers. Some said they brought luck; others that they were tricksters.

Quince was unafraid. She stood and approached the creature. Its large eyes regarded her with what she could only interpret as curiosity.

It held out a glowing hand with three fingers, and she lifted up her own so that they met.

Quince.

She nodded.

I have come to find you.

Quince broke contact, surprised. How could such a beautiful creature know someone as lowly as she, let alone want to speak with her?

The voice persisted. There is a task we must ask you to perform. It will not be easy, and it will profoundly change your life.

Quince considered. Her life was dull beyond words, living here in a small village away from Gaelan and the Court. Maybe it was time it changed for the better. She nodded. "What do you want me to do?"

The creature smiled, and Quince was flooded with warmth. When the Queen of the Gaelani calls for you, you must go. She has borne a child....

Shortly after, she had been summoned by the Queen. Apparently Robyn had gotten a visitor too.

A loud crack of thunder startled her out of her reverie. She had been so young then. Sometimes she felt she'd lived a century in these past twenty-five years.

These storms had grown worse these last few months. Her time here was growing short.

The last message from Robyn had arrived in a tube tied to the scaled leg of an imprean along with a vial of pith, a delivery method so antiquated it made her smile.

The news inside had not.

The King was dead. Whether by natural causes or the machinations of the invaders, it wasn't clear. But what was clear was that their quarter-century wait was at an end.

Coincidental or not, the crisis they had anticipated was upon them.

With luck, they would be reunited soon, and the years-long occupation of Gaelan would come to an end. All their carefully laid plans were coming to fruition at last, but there were so many things that could still go wrong.

She tapped the side of her head, activating her cirq. "Ari, where is Davyn?" she asked quietly. It had taken Quince a long time to get used to the tech of the Common Worlds, so different from how simple things had been back home, so inherently invasive, and yet, so convenient.

Her personal assistant responded immediately. "Xander is at home. All vital signs seem normal, though he does appear to be in a state of some excitement." The voice was warm and professional.

Quince chuckled. *I'll bet he is.* "And Lyrin?" *He's finally coming home.*

This time it took longer.

While she waited, Quince went over her contingency plans. She had to get the two of them together, and soon. The fate of both worlds depended on it.

She recited Elyra's prophecy—written seven hundred and fifty years before —that she had long ago committed to memory:

Tempest comes with clash and thunder,
Skies alight with rainbow's blood,
When the sunlight runs to red,

Comes the reaper for the dead.

One with wings as black as night
One with wings of golden light
Spin the worlds back into one
To save them from the murdering sun.

It looked like the end time was finally here.

Ari broke into her reverie. "Jameson is on approach—he has arrived at Titan Station and is expected in Oberon City by shuttle this afternoon at 13:20."

"Thank you, Ari." Everyone said personal assistants were just bioware, that they had no true feelings, but it cost her nothing to be polite. One never knew.

"You're welcome, Quince." Ari sounded satisfied.

Quince closed her eyes and sat back, thinking about all the things that could've gone wrong up to this point. Thinking about Robyn with her long dark hair, her eyes alight with mischief....

She shook her head. This was no time for fanciful daydreams. "Ari, access protocol 'clear screen.'"

There was a slight pause. "Are you sure?"

"Yes, I'm sure. Please run the protocol."

"Running protocol 'clear screen.'"

In five minutes, all record of her time here would be erased from Oberon's grid. Even in the virtual jungle, it was best to cover one's tracks.

She stared off toward the edge of Oberon City for a moment longer. Beneath the approaching storm, the neat, geometric lines of the city scrambled and snarled in the Slander, where the Syndicate held sway.

Quince stood and took one last look around the small, sparsely furnished room. It wasn't much. She had chosen it mostly for the view, which had astonished her when she had first arrived in this thriving, decadent metropolis so many years before. The room held a bed, a small writing desk by the window, and a couple chairs.

There was an open carry sack on the mattress, filled with the few possessions she cared to take with her.

The apartment was impersonal, and yet it had been *hers* for these twenty-five long years.

She closed her eyes. She was tired of fighting. So tired. She sighed, resigned to the fact that her life was about to change once again, but soon enough it would all be over.

She checked the contents of her carry sack once more, then ran her hand over the edge of the bag to seal it seamlessly. She snapped the straps over her shoulders, letting the sack rest between her white-feathered wings.

She closed the door behind her, leaving the place empty.

As if she had never been there at all.

ROBYN SLÉITE sat on the cold stone at the edge of the wide reflecting pool, her hand trailing in the water, creating ripples that cascaded across the still surface to the other side. They disturbed the reflection of the worryingly yellow-tinged sun in the sky above.

The crown sat heavy upon her head today. She was alone with her thoughts in the stone courtyard of the House of the Moon; her husband, the King, lay in state, attended by those lander bastards who had wormed their way into his counsel. She spat out the word in her mind, detesting them with all her will. They had all but taken her city from her, first by guile as "advisors" to the King, and then by force with superior weaponry. She'd been powerless to stop them.

The sun was directly overhead. The day was warm, with fluffy clouds peppering the pink-tinged sky above. Still, she was uneasy.

She had sent her last message upon the death of her husband, four days before. Soon it would reach Quince on the other side, and events would be set in motion that would bring her long pain to a close, if all went as planned.

If not?

She put her palm on the silver hilt of the dagger at her side.

After twenty-five years, she still wasn't sure she had made the right choice, and she had no one here in whom she could confide. Even her own husband had remained ignorant of what had truly happened that day. Theron Sléite would have had her head, queen or no, if he ever found out what she had done, then and with Quince in the years before.

Soon, Quince would be with her again.

She stood, spreading her black wings in defiance. If her husband, the King, had had his way, they would have kept her son there in Gaelan. He would have been killed, and all would now be lost, or so the nimfeach, floating in the air like a phosphorescent butterfly, had told her on that winter day in the forest, so many years past. She had believed it, and it had sent Quince to her side.

She still regretted the day she had sent her lover away to the Erriani.

Robyn's wings settled against her back, and she wiped the corners of her eyes before turning away from the pool. Someone needed to go see what those invaders were doing to her husband. She supposed it had to be her.

Once he was buried and gone, she would clean house and send them all packing.

"Your Highness, a word?"

It was Dani, the leader of the lander invaders.

"I'm busy at the moment."

"It wasn't a request." The woman put a hand on her pulse rifle.

Robyn glared at her. They treated her like a dog, expected to respond to their every beck and call. "What did you want, Dani?" She tried to keep the sneer out of her voice.

"Just come with me, ma'am."

Robyn stood and followed her, her wings shaking with annoyance. Soon. Very soon.

PART ONE
OBERON

OBERON

TITAN STATION

HERMIA

LYSANDER

CHAPTER 1
ARRIVAL

IN ANOTHER APARTMENT in another arco not too far away, the rain hit the plas and ran downward in little rivulets, separating and rejoining like branches of time as the storm whipped itself into a frenzy over Oberon City.

Xander Kinnson lay on his bed, head thrown back, watching the tempest with a laziness that belied his inner turmoil and pain. Alix had left him and gone missing. A year had passed, and still he had a hard time accepting that simple fact.

His dark wings with their jet-black feathers were stretched out lazily to each side of his supine form, their tips extending past the edge of the bed. His chest heaved slowly up and down, and he breathed easily, as if he were utterly relaxed.

Nothing could have been further from the truth. Below the surface, under the deception of skin and sinew, his heart beat at a thunderous pace, and his mind raced for answers to Alix's fate that slipped beyond his grasp.

The handsome trick he'd brought home rested his warm hands on Xander's thighs, his hot mouth engaged elsewhere. Xander smelled the deep, masculine musk of him, slipping a hand absently through the man's dark, tousled hair as the rain increased to a thundering downpour against the plas. The drops glistened, each an individual universe of shimmering light before running quickly out of sight.

A flash of lightning illuminated the room, thunder indicating how close it had been. As the heavy rain pounded against the arco's walls, Xander rode the wave of pleasure higher and higher. Despite himself, he rose quickly toward climax, drawn up on the tide as the trick worked his cock. Unable to stop himself, he thrust his hips almost angrily upward into the man's willing throat. Closer, closer....

He reached the crest, a pleasure so intense it burned through him like phosphorus, a white-hot fire.

Lightning flared again across the wet, black sky, followed by thunder so close it shook the bed. The storm had reached a fever pitch outside, and he arched his back in the air one more time, his wings rustling beneath him. As if in concert with the storm, Xander came, the release of his orgasm radiating from his hips along his spinal cord and down through his toes and the tips of his wings. He held the man's head there while he exhausted himself.

The rush of elation washed away his cares for a few brief moments. Xander shuddered, shivered, and shuddered again, and it was over.

For a while, he drifted in an oblivion that was blessed in its emptiness. The rain fell in a steady beat against the window, and he forgot to wallow in his pain. His mind floated free, with no responsibilities, nothing to worry about for those brief moments between sex and real life. *This* was what he needed. This lack of thought, this pleasurable oblivion where he could *just be.*

When he opened his eyes at last, the nameless trick was staring down at him, expectant.

"You're still here."

"I can do more, if you'd like," the man said with a grin. Like Alix, he had no wings—a lander man.

Xander glared at him, annoyed. He was handsome enough, tall, dark-haired, with blue eyes and a light complexion. Strangely, he reminded Xander of Alix. The hair and eyes were wrong, but there was something about him, and that annoyed the hell out of Xander, for reasons he didn't care to examine too closely. "Get out," he said with a dismissive wave.

The man frowned. "I thought—"

"Oh right, your pay." Xander took the man's arm and slitted him a hundred crits from the wrist reader embedded in his own. Then he waved the trick away. "We're square. Now get the fuck out of my flat."

The man gathered his own clothes, but Xander didn't give him time to put them on. Instead he hustled the trick out of the irising door, palming it closed on his hurt and angry expression.

I really have become a bastard, he thought, staring at his dim reflection in the shiny black door. It had been a long year.

He tapped the cirq in his temple with his left hand, and called out to his PA. "Ravi, any messages for me?"

Ravi's smooth voice spoke in his head. "Just one, from OberCorp. A reminder to meet the psych who's coming in from off-world at Immigration tomorrow morning."

Xander pulled off his boots, leaving himself naked, and strolled over to the window to look at the storm. "What's his name again?"

"Jameson Havercamp, from Beta Tau."

"Image?" He closed his eyes and saw the man's face in his mind's eye. The man had to be in his midtwenties, close to his own age, with a shock of tight-cropped red hair, brown eyes, and light freckles across the bridge of his nose. He had that kind of schoolboy sexiness that appealed to Xander, looking very much like a younger version of Alix.

Quince had set him up to play tour guide to earn extra cash—one of Ober-Corp's side jobs.

He was cute enough—slender, not effeminate, exactly, more… refined. Just Xander's type, like Alix. But Havercamp seemed a little conservative for Xander's taste, dressed in a tailored suit and one of those rigid white Beta Tau collars. No matter. A few days in this hellhole would loosen him up.

The raindrops increased, the storm once again picking up steam. It was the strongest tempest Xander remembered seeing in years, and the winds shook the sturdy walls of the arco enough to make him worried. Hopefully the worst of it would have passed before he had to leave to pick up his guest.

"What am I supposed to do with him?"

"He's here to find out why pith production has dropped off. You're to ferry him out to these coordinates." Ravi's voice had just the slightest hint of disapproval, an *I already told you this* tone. A map appeared, with a point in the Pyramus Mountains flashing blue, along with a contract.

Xander ignored the attitude. After all, Ravi was just gridcode.

OberCorp had hired him for off-the-grid jobs like this before. It was a clean one-shot contract. He'd have to thank Quince later.

Xander had spent a fair amount of time in the wilds outside Oberon City with Alix, in the vast inland forest that was mostly uninhabited and little explored.

Alix. The man who had pulled Xander out of the gutters of the Slander, and had shown him that he was more than just a trick or rent boy. That he *could* be more. He'd shown Xander that someone could love him.

His one-time lover had vanished into the Outland a year earlier while on a hunting expedition with friends. Xander had been concerned when he hadn't come back after a few days, and later he'd panicked when Alix failed to return altogether. He'd been out of range of Oberon's grid—too close to the Split, where electronics often failed. Xander had gone out to look for him, spending two weeks on his trail, to no avail.

Xander sank down on his couch, his wings fluttering behind him anxiously. He waved his hand across the tri-dee, activating the screen in the wide table. "Ravi, playback, please. Alix, Deca 7."

"Playing."

Soon the projection of Alix's body appeared above the tri-dee, rendered in almost lifelike precision. Only the slightly see-through quality of the image betrayed it as a holo-vid. Alix's long red hair was swept behind his ears, and his brown eyes seemed to look directly at him, more perfect than he had ever been in real life.

How many times had he watched this? He'd lost count.

"Hi, Xander. We're out here in the Pyramus Mountains." He grinned, showing off his beautiful smile. Static shot through the image. Alix had been on the edge of the e-zone, where electronic transmission was barely possible. "Tomorrow we're heading up into the mountains and...." He turned to look over his shoulder. "What?"

Xander knew every word by heart—he'd watched this a thousand times. He mouthed the words as Alix spoke them. "Dani says she's got dinner ready. It's amazing here, Xan. One of these days I'll take you out this far. Gotta run... love you." Alix blew Xander a kiss, and then reached forward to shut off the video.

Xander got up off the couch and paced back and forth, nervous energy fueling him. He held back a barely pent-up rage. *Why did you leave me?* he wondered. A year had passed in waiting.

No more. Xander was done with this obsession.

This trip was just the thing he needed to take his mind off Alix, to put the whole sad thing behind him. *I can't wait for you forever.*

He grabbed a carry sack and filled it with the things he'd need on the road. He'd be meeting the psych the next day, and would bring Havercamp to his storage unit to pick up a few more things. Then he would haul the man out toward the Split. It would be good to get away from everything here that reminded him of Alix.

He finished packing, too tired to even think anymore. He dropped down onto his bed, exhausted. He closed his eyes, but sleep refused to come, and he tossed and turned for another hour.

At last he sat up, frustrated, and ordered a sleeper from Ravi. It dropped out of the replicator slot, and he slapped the patch onto his wrist and lay back down, waiting for the drug to take effect. He needed to be fresh tomorrow.

It coursed into his system through his skin, and he fell almost immediately into a dark and dreamless sleep as the rain continued to fall unabated outside.

JAMESON HAVERCAMP stood on the observation deck of Titan Station, the floor transparent beneath his feet. He stared down at the strange world that spun slowly below him, trying to contain his unfounded fear. His mind told him he was perfectly safe, that this "window" beneath his feet was thick enough to hold the void outside at bay.

His body told him to run.

"It's quite a sight, isn't it?" someone said behind him.

Jameson laughed. He turned to the speaker, a man a little older than he was who was holding a boy's hand. "Yes, it is."

"We're here for a conference. Brought this little bugger along because, really, how often do you get to see one of the wonders of the galaxy?"

Jameson had to agree. Split was its slang name—it was more properly called Oberon, and it rotated below them, almost a perfect half sphere. The "round" side was a picture-perfect normal, Earth-analogous world, green and blue. It turned under the sunshine as the station swung around from the north to the south pole.

The other side, barely visible from this vantage point, was a nightmarish tangle of broken, melted rock, evidence of whatever had torn this world in two. His reading had informed him that the backside of the planet was called "The Split."

Only no one knew what had actually happened here, where the other half had gone, or what force kept the remainder of this world from crumbling into a rocky ball. Some theories posited that the other half was still there, perhaps converted to dark matter, but no one had been able to prove it.

"My name's Jameson." He held out his hand. "I'm here on a mission from Beta Tau." He pulled at his stiff collar. He longed to be free of it, but formality insisted that he be properly dressed when he met the company representative.

The man shook hands with him, smiling. "I'm Zefron, and this is Davis. We're from Pleiades II. Have you ever been?"

"No. It's my first time."

There was a loud chime. "Passengers on the Oberon City shuttle, please come to hanger three. Departure in fifteen minutes." The station used Earth-Standard measurements, something he was going to have to get used to. Beta Tau was bigger than Earth, with a slower rotation, so he was used to days about two hours longer than Earth's, and the Oberon "day" was two hours shorter than that.

"Good luck at the conference!"

Zefron winked at him. "Thank you. Good luck on your mission."

Jameson shook his head. He was always getting hit on by other guys. It didn't offend him, but everyone seemed to think he liked men. He didn't. He couldn't. His parents would have his head if he ever so much as showed the slightest inclination toward that sort of thing. They were Christianists, and Beta Tau was a Christianist world, where men married women. Period. Where men were supreme, and women kept a nice kitchen—or mansion, in his mother's case.

Still, it was nice to be noticed.

Jameson picked up his suitcase and followed the other passengers toward the shuttle bay. This was his first research mission for the Psych Guild. The Guild had its fingers in a number of planets and industries, from the psychological treatment of billions to the pharmaceuticals that treatment required.

He still wondered why he had been chosen for this mission. He had just three years of experience, most of it treating miners on Tander's World with pith addictions. The pharmaceutical originated here on Oberon and had a variety of legitimate uses, including inducing a useful dreamlike trance at low doses that had been a great aid to therapy. It could also be used as a kind of aphrodisiac in higher amounts.

The pharmaceutical supply had dried up over the last six months, something of great concern to both the therapeutic community and to addicts across the Common Worlds.

They should have sent someone with more experience. *I have no idea what the hell I'm doing here.*

And yet, here he was.

He hoped the company representative would be able to provide some guidance.

He sighed and settled into a seat, letting it strap him in for the ride down to planet-side.

CHAPTER 2
PSYCH

XANDER'S ARM *was outstretched toward a winged stranger as he plummeted toward the ground. His own left wing hung limp and burned as red bolts of molten lightning rained on the landscape below like hammers of God.*

The arcos were crashing down to ruin, one after another, adding a terrible grinding crash to the chaos of the red afternoon. They ruptured as they collapsed, and hundreds of bodies fell out, people screaming as they plummeted toward the ground.

Xander awoke in a pool of sweat, the sunlight touching his lithe form through the thick plas, warming his face. Everything was quiet and calm, and the arco was still standing.

He glared at the sunlight; it seemed strange. Dimmer? He remembered the trick blathering on the night before. *Something about sunspots.* Xander hadn't really been listening.

He stood and stumbled over to the wash stall, slipping himself inside the small cubicle with some effort. He tapped his cirq. "Bathe." The warm ionic spray blew over him, covering his shoulders, his chest, his wings. Xander stepped out a moment later and slipped into his riding armor, a black plas-faced jumpsuit that covered his arms, chest, and legs, protecting him from Oberon's harsh daytime glare and the knacks and wereverens who loved to bite the unprotected for a quick blood snack. He slipped fingerless black leather gloves onto each hand.

"Breakfast," he mumbled, and a moment later a tray slipped out from behind a small hatch in his eating nook. The smell of cafflite and eggs filled the room. He downed the meal hungrily, his nerves tingling from the stim he'd taken the night before, a mix of pith and uppers.

Xander wasn't even sure it *was* pith. That shit was harder to come by than an Oberon City virgin these days.

Shoving the dishes into the recycler, he grabbed the carry sack he'd packed the night before and pressed his palm up against the clear plas of the window, feeling the cold from outside. The storm had largely abated overnight, reduced to tattered clouds with some flooding down in the streets below.

The pattern recognition system matched his palm print, verifying his identity. Twin doors slid aside in the floor, and his hoverbike, a sleek, black machine all darkness and sexy lines, slid up into view. The doors sealed shut below it.

Xander slipped into his riding chaps, pulling his custom-made jacket around his wings and fastening it to keep out the cold, leaving his wings free. There were few enough skythane, or wing men, here in the city, and it was hard to find clothing made for someone like him.

In public, many people threw him dirty looks because of his wings. Wing men were a breed apart from "normal" humans. The skythane—first-wave colonists like him—were often called barbarians by the landers, the second-wave human colonists whose bodies more closely matched the galactic norm. *Jealous bastards.*

The company had tried to eradicate his people, once upon a time, and even now it wasn't so uncommon for people to spit on him and call him a *native bastard.* Xander ignored them; he had grown a thick skin in his adolescence, after his adoptive parents had died and he'd been forced to live out on the streets. Before Alix.

He pulled on his black riding gloves. "Ravi, open the doors."

"Acknowledged."

The plas window directly in front of the cycle split apart, a straight hairline crack that spread from the base of the window up to six feet off the floor. Clear doors formed in the plas, and then they opened outward, letting in the chill. The storm had passed.

Xander climbed onto the bike and palmed the power key. The machine roared to life underneath him. He powered up the bike's amalite drive and released the brake, soaring out of the arco into the open air. The wind whistled past him, and he spread his wings to slow his velocity, thrilling in the drag as the cool air flowed past. The breeze buffeted him as the bike descended toward the personal air transportation level a hundred meters above the ground, and he felt free for just a moment.

The whole of Oberon City was spread out before him. The streets far below were still glistening from the rain. Xander breathed in deeply, smelling the scent of the Outland forests, pulling the moisture-laden air deep into his lungs. He loved being outside after the rain. For a few hours, the air was fresh and clean, without the usual nasty, metallic tang of the city.

For all that he'd grown up here, sometimes he still felt like he didn't belong. He loved instead the wide open spaces of the Outland, beyond the city confines.

The ground below sped toward him, a landscape dotted with factories and feeder tubes and causeways thick with traffic. Heavy supply tractors lumbered up to the base of the tower, laden with foodstuffs from the farms at the edge of the city or amalite ores from the Split.

Behind him was the row of two-mile-high arcos, anchored to each other by massive, silvery blue metallic trusses a hundred feet across. The arcos ran in an ordered row along the waterfront.

Beyond them were factories and warehouses where those prized ores of Oberon were refined and prepared for out-system shipment, and past that, the criminal warrens of the Slander began, a never-ending maze of haphazardly constructed warehouses, shantytowns, and Syndicate strongholds like a creeping blight, home to hustlers of all kinds, Dark Market dealers, and anyone who didn't want to be found by the law, such as it was. His home in a previous life.

In the distance, the Governor's residence sat in a massive park-like district off to the east. The upper class of Oberon City had country homes out in the hills beyond the city, including the man who was, in title at least, in charge. Everyone knew OberCorp really ran things here.

Everything below him grew rapidly larger, then skewed out around him as the bike leveled off. Now other structures rose up on either side of his bike, from industrial plants to commercial buildings splashed with the logos of some of Oberon's own companies, as well as several multi-world conglomerates.

Xander was over the Midcity now, following an invisible rail as the grid assigned him a flight path. He folded his wings behind him.

This zone was reserved for individual traffic. Delivery trucks and trains used the crowded streets below, which were finally beginning to dry out from the storm.

Xander's destination was the spaceport on the northern edge of the city, where he'd meet the incoming shuttle from Titan Station. He veered onto a northbound connector, his guidance system selecting the least busy path.

Soon he was merging onto one of the main air causeways, riding out of the central city on a path that would take him out to High Slopes. He pulled his wings in tightly and gunned the engine, determined to move forward.

THE SHUTTLE blasted away from Titan Station, moving at a serious clip. It swung in a wide arc, eventually turning around to give Jameson a view of the donut-shaped installation. It was not the largest station he had ever been through, even in his short lifetime. Transfer Station, anchored to the elevator cable that touched down on the equator in Earth's South American quadrant, had that honor. Jameson had passed through Transfer a year before, when he'd gone to San Francisco on old Earth for his Masters training with the guild. It was as big as a city, six tori stacked upon one another, each one as large or larger than Titan, and they were expanding it yet again now.

As the shuttle veered around, Oberon came into view. The shuttle shot out past the ragged edge of the world, over the rim wall that encircled it a half mile high.

Zefron and Davis were in the seats in front of him. The boy's hands were pressed against the cool plas window, his eyes wide with wonder.

Jameson was about to say something when the shuttle banked, coming back around toward Oberon and giving him his first real view of the backside of the world. The Split.

The landscape, if you could call it that, was half in sunshine and half in shadow. The part that was illuminated was a nightmare of shattered stone, although much of it was hidden under perpetual cloud cover. A great storm circled the center of gravity like water around a drain, throwing off periodic tempests over the rim of the world, smaller storms that spilled over the mountains like the fog over the old Golden Gate Bridge, back on Earth.

The fact that he could make out details at all at this distance made it clear the huge scale involved.

Out toward one edge of the Split, a patch of light glowed.

"That bit of light out there? That's Alpha Camp," Zefron was telling his son. "That's one of the places where they mine the ores. It's all done manually, because electronics don't work out there. There's too much interference."

"Then what are the lights?"

"Smart kid." Zefron glanced back at Jameson and grinned. Jameson gave him the thumbs-up. "They burn oil. That's a huge chimney that lights up the area and carries off the residue up into space."

Jameson activated his cirq. "Angie, I want to review my notes on Oberon." Angela was his mother's name. It had just seemed natural to use it for his PA too. His parents frowned on bioware because it "subverted God's plan," but it had been invaluable in his career, and this was his way of making it okay.

"Here you go," Angie said in a voice that was eerily similar to his mother's.

He closed his eyes and the documents appeared in his mind's eye.

Discovered by AmSplor in the second wave in 2857, Oberon's unique geology had provided a raw ore called amalite, a compact power source useful in many areas of the Common Worlds' far-flung economy. For two hundred years afterward, OberCorp had run the planet as its own personal fiefdom until it was brought to heel, forcefully, by the Common Worlds.

The corporation still held sway here, unofficially. The Syndicate, an organized crime ring, was also a factor.

Interesting. There'd been two waves of human colonization here, not just one. The first had been from a life ship that had reached the planet five hundred years before the first FTL ships. The skythane, as they were called, had created their own culture, and their language drift had made early interactions with the landers, the second-wave colonists... difficult. There were rumors of a virtual genocide of the original population.

The shuttle started to tremble. They were entering the planetary atmosphere. Jameson opened his eyes and looked out the window—they were about to pass over the edge of the world once more.

"Attention, passengers, in about thirty seconds, we will lose power. It's nothing to be alarmed about. We're coming close to the interference zone. The shuttle was built for this, and we will be past it in just under a minute."

Easy for you to say.

About twenty seconds later, the power dropped down to nothing. The g-force created by the thrust was there, and then it wasn't, and the cabin lights went dark.

Davis started to cry in the darkness.

"Hey little guy," Jameson said in his best singsong voice. "Let's play a game. Let's see if we can hold our breath until the lights come back on. What do you say?" He demonstrated.

Davis looked back at him in the dim planetary glow and nodded. The boy took a deep breath.

Jameson counted off the time, and Davis did too, though his counting was off.

Zefron shot him a thankful look.

Just when Jameson thought his lungs would burst, the lights came back on. He exhaled forcefully and took a deep breath.

Davis laughed. "Let's do it again!"

Jameson shook his head. "Sorry, but you're too good for me!"

"You're great with kids." Zefron smiled.

"I'm a psych." Jameson grinned back. "I worked with a bunch of them during my training." He glanced out the window. The ground was rushing up toward them, the waters of the Gildensea reflecting the light of Oberon's primary. The clouds were dissipating.

Oberon City sat at the edge of the planet's only continent, bounded on the west by the Gildensea. The city spread out from the edge of the water like a complex spiderweb. As the shuttle descended, Jameson could see the spine of the arco towers that housed most of the residents of Oberon.

"That's Oberon City," Zefron said to his son, pointing to the towers below as morning swept over the coast. They grew steadily, ten of them running in a long row, all identical, built by the OberCorp to house most of the city's tens of thousands of permanent residents.

"How many stories?" Davis asked.

"About two hundred."

Causeways led out of the core of the city into the other cities along the coast on the "smooth" side of the world on Oberon's only continent. The rest of the world was wild—the Outland, the locals called it, at least according to the dataset Ober-Corp had slitted him. Old Oberon, as he thought of it, mostly untouched since before the current wave of mankind had come here five hundred years before.

Outside the city core, lower buildings spread out, in some areas fairly well organized along a standard north-south street grid, in others a vast shanty-town spread out like a cancer. The Slander. He'd read about this lawless zone at the city's edge, but the reports didn't do it justice. It was vast.

In the distance, he saw the Pyramus Mountains, apparently thrust up when the world had been so violently sundered in two.

The shuttle veered away from the city, g-force pushing him back into the padded chair, and banked toward the landing pad that sat on the metropolis's outer edge. A company representative would be waiting there for him. Perhaps he could convince them to give him a tour of the Split, and maybe even show him the source of the psychoamoratic drug, pith.

He wondered for the hundredth time why he'd been chosen for this partic-ular mission. There were thousands of pith specialists in the Guild, a number of whom had half a hundred years of experience or more. Perhaps they didn't want to be sent to this backwater end of the Common Worlds?

He was inordinately grateful for the opportunity, though, having spent the last three years in virtual oblivion on Tander's World, counseling lonely miners on that desolate outpost. Here at last was civilization, of a sort. Though he doubted they had a ballet, or even space opera.

The shuttle braked with an intense, ear-splitting whine, the g-force pressing Jameson back into his seat once more. It lasted for about ten seconds, and then just as quickly the pressure eased. The shuttle settled down on the concrete landing pad with a shuddering sigh.

"Welcome to Oberon City," the pilot said over the intercom, and the door irised open, extending stairs to the ground below. "Please be sure to take all your belongings with you, and enjoy this beautiful day."

Jameson gathered his suitcase from beneath his seat, brushing some stray lint off his jacket, and clambered down the stairway into Oberon's gilded light. He breathed in deeply. The planetary air smelled amazingly fresh after years of being locked up in tin cans, first on Tander's World and then in the Arcatus on the trip here.

The wide-open horizon was intimidating too. He was disoriented by the broad expanse of green-tinted sky. This was all going to take some getting used to.

Hopefully he'd be safely back inside shortly.

Xander leaned back against his bike, stretching his arms and wings and enjoying the warmth of the sun that had finally peeked through the clouds. It was a beautiful day, a sharp contrast to the heavy rains of the day before.

He'd watched the shuttle land half an hour before, descending to the concrete pad just beyond the short squat rectangle of the immigration center and kicking up a cloud of dust.

Beyond the landing pad, one of the Rentz Class cargo carriers thundered into the sky on a tower of smoke and fire, carrying a load of amalite up to the waiting interstellar ship.

Xander called up Jameson Havercamp's face again. His first impression had been right—the man was handsome enough. He needed to lose the suit and tie, but there was something about his brown eyes….

A few days on the dark side would shake him up.

At last, the doors to the immigration center irised open, and Havercamp came out, looking around at his destination, a twin to his photo. He looked as if he had just stepped out of an office instead of off a station shuttle.

Cuter in person. Xander strode forward to meet the psych, extending a hand. "Jameson Havercamp? I'm Xander Kinnson, at your service."

"Hello, Mr.... Kinnson, was it?" He shook Xander's hand with a nice firm grip while staring openly at Xander's wings. "Yes, I'm Jameson Havercamp. So nice to meet you."

Xander grinned. This one was going to need *a lot* of shaking up.

He took the other man's suitcase and secured it to the rack on the back of his bike. "Hop on. We've got a lot to get done today."

"Where's the company transport?" Havercamp looked around, seeming confused.

"You're looking at it." He powered up the engine and gestured for the psych to climb on behind him.

"I've never ridden a hoverbike before." He said the word as if he'd just stepped in something that was never going to come off his shiny leather shoes.

"If you'd rather walk...." Xander pointed off at the line of arcos on the horizon.

Havercamp heaved a sigh, but he complied, climbing up behind Xander.

Xander gunned the engine, just for the thrill of it.

The bike lifted up into the air and sped back toward the heart of the city.

CHAPTER 3
EXIT PLAN

XANDER'S BIKE flew over the crowded streets of Oberon City. It was midmorning, as far as Jameson could tell from the slanting rays of sunshine over the city.

The wind whipped through his hair, making a rat's nest of it. He was going to look a mess when he arrived at the OberCorp Headquarters, but there was nothing to be done for it. He mollified himself with the thought that it was the company representative's fault.

Jameson clung to Xander's waist, uncomfortable at being so close to the other man, but terrified all the same to loosen his grip. The man's wings settled in around him like a feathered blanket.

Xander Kinnson had *wings*—he was a skythane man.

Sure, the whole wings thing had been in the briefing, but reading it and seeing it in person were two very different things. They were beautiful, running up from his shoulder blades into the sky when he had them extended, and powerful. The dark feathers glimmered with an iridescent sheen in the sunlight.

Jameson didn't think he would have the courage to fly—hoverbike flight was unnerving enough. And yet... wings.

They whipped past heavy armored transports and automated delivery trucks that rode the streets below them, mixed in with pedestrians and even some wagons and rickshaws, as strange an assortment of traffic as he had ever seen in one place.

"We're going to Oberon Corp Headquarters, right?" he shouted at Xander over the noise. He *hated* shouting.

"What?" Xander shouted back.

"OberCorp Headquarters?"

"Sorry. Can't hear you!"

Jameson gave up. He settled in to observe the city around him.

The huge arcos formed a virtual blue metallic wall ahead that began to block out the sunlight as the hoverbike moved closer. They were impressive in their uniformity, reminding him of the statues of Easter Island he'd visited during his trip to Old Earth.

From this vantage point, the city seemed much bigger than it had looked from the shuttle flying in, but outside of the impressive architecture of the arcos, the rest of Oberon City was made up of much less impressive, shorter buildings, with the tallest of these topping out around fifteen stories. They were in varied states of decay, with broken windows and rusted stanchions, some of them overrun by wild vines. The city looked like it was badly in need of an urban renewal project—a few buildings were in such bad shape that Jameson was amazed they hadn't already collapsed under their own weight.

After about fifteen minutes, Xander's bike slowly dipped down to the ground, coming to a landing between a couple of low buildings. They arrived at a nondescript three-story, concrete-slab structure that would have fit into almost any urban cityscape. It was made entirely out of prefab plascreet panels like all the other ugly buildings around it.

Xander palmed a sensor next to the metal roll-up door and it chugged up noisily, revealing a storage space maybe three meters wide by about three times that length deep. He pulled the bike inside and parked it, beckoning for Jameson to dismount.

Jameson did as he was told, though he was starting to get worried. When it came right down to it, he knew nothing about this man, having taken Xander at his word that he really was a representative of OberCorp.

How could he know for sure?

The idea nagged at him.

The man might be a pirate who preyed upon unsuspecting arrivals at the immigration center. He certainly fit the profile—standoffish, antisocial, certain he was always right. Jameson had seen that many times before in his practice. Then again, most sociopaths were more social.

At least he'd made it to the city now. It might be best to get out of here and find his own way to OberCorp.

Jameson started to back slowly out of the storage unit, away from Xander. He could make a run for it.

"Stay right there," Xander said without turning, his voice sharp. "This is a bad part of town. It's dangerous, especially for off-worlders who don't know any better."

Jameson looked out onto the street nervously. Oberon City was a lot grittier at ground level than it had appeared from the shuttle—the pavement looked petrochemical based, and it was uneven and black, so different from the beautiful marble streets back on Beta Tau. Some dark fluid flowed in fits and starts down the gutters, and it gave off a nasty smell: part urine, part hydrocarbons, part rotting food.

He *was* overdressed for such squalor. "Are there any *good parts?*" He stepped back inside with a sniff.

Xander snorted. He'd set aside Jameson's suitcase, and was now rummaging around through some plas containers at the back of the storage unit. He pulled out something and threw it over the back of the bike.

It looked like the saddlebags that Jameson's parents used with horses on their estate to carry supplies or foodstuffs for picnics or hunting trips into the Holywood.

Xander pulled out a knife and used it to pry open Jameson's suitcase, setting off the luggage's alarm. Xander snarled and kicked it until the sound died down to an irritated chirp.

"Hey… what are you doing?" Jameson reached out to stop him, but Xander pushed him back, knife in hand. "You can't wear *that* where we're going." He indicated Jameson's clothing with the same disdain Jameson himself had used for the hoverbike. He rummaged through the clothes in the suitcase. "None of this will do." Xander turned to size Jameson up, head to toe. "I think I have something that will work." He returned to going through the bins at the back of the unit.

"What do you mean, this won't do? I've met with upper-level management in the Psych Guild on numerous occasions, dressed just like this—"

"We're not meeting with management." Xander returned with an armful of clothes. "Here, put these on."

"I must insist that you take me to OberCorp Headquarters right now and—"

Xander dropped the new clothes on the dirty floor and ripped Jameson's button-down shirt right up the middle, exposing his bare chest. His wings flared out behind him, and he gave Jameson an evil grin. "Change. Now."

Jameson tried to stare him down, but there was an angry gleam in the man's eyes that he decided he didn't want to challenge. He lowered his eyes and picked up the new clothing. "Is there a place for me to change, at least?" He was *not* getting naked in front of this barbarian.

"Over there." He pointed to a small door near the back. "If you need anything else from your suitcase, throw it in the bags."

Jameson opened the door and found a small sanitation room, not so different from those on Tander's World—a metal toilet and a small sink. He changed into the new clothes, pulling on the thick gray work pants and a nondescript white, long-sleeved shirt. There was a heavy black jacket with a hood and a pair of black work boots. They all fit him well enough, though the boots pinched his toes.

He was six inches shorter than Xander. He wondered who these clothes had belonged to before.

Jameson didn't want to go back out there to face Xander. He tried not to think about those wings. Jessa was waiting for him, back on Beta Tau.

He tapped his cirq. "Angie," he whispered, "connect me to OberCorp Headquarters."

There was a pause. "I'm unable to establish a connection to the local grid at this time," Angie said in his ear.

Fuck it all. "Keep trying." He washed his face to kill a little more time, staring at himself in the mirror. He looked strange in this work garb. More like one of the miners he used to treat than a well-respected psych.

At last he stepped out of the little room with a sigh, and looked out again at the city. This place was nothing like Beta Tau, a fully terraformed and pastoral world where no day was anything less than pleasant. His time on Tander's World, while not without its own dangers, had been in the wilds, working with men in a mining camp on a world with an unbreathable atmosphere.

Jameson had never spent any appreciable time in a large city, and this one and the wing man currently holding him all but hostage were starting to scare him.

"Let's see," Xander said to himself, "we'll need enough food for two weeks in the Outland, a few weapons, some more clothing...."

Jameson stared at him. He was fascinated by Xander's wings. Where Jameson came from, only angels had them, and though he'd been taught to believe in them by his Christianist parents, he'd never actually *seen* one.

Xander looked the part of an angel. Or at least a fallen one. His body flowed as he worked, his face intent. He wasn't handsome, exactly, though he certainly wasn't ugly. He was filled with confidence, moving with a sure sexual grace that was more akin to a jaguar than an eagle. He pulled at

Jameson simply by being in the same room—and because of that, he was beautiful.

Jameson shook his head to clear away the image. He thought instead about his fiancée, Jessa, awaiting him back home. They were set to marry next year when his internship ended, an arranged betrothal between two of the founding families on Beta Tau. He liked her well enough—they'd been friends since childhood, and she was whip-smart, with long blonde hair and blue eyes. He supposed she was pretty.

Jameson decided to try one more time. "This really seems irregular to me. I was told that I would be meeting with the people from OberCorp." He was starting to sound whiny, even to himself. "Wait, did you say 'the Outland'?"

Xander grunted. "Yes. The company farmed this out to me, and I'm going to take you out to where pith comes from. At least, where they *think* it does."

"But I haven't even had time for an ionic shower," Jameson complained.

"Oh, I wouldn't worry about that. There are no showers where we're going."

Jameson was starting to panic. Bit by bit, he was losing control. He was a control freak—he knew that—but knowing it and doing something about it were two different things. "Wait, what do you mean 'where they think it does'?"

"That's what my contract says," Xander replied curtly. "I don't make the rules."

Though I'll bet you know how to break them. Jameson tore his gaze away from Xander and pulled a few things from his suitcase. He put them in the bag, including a holo of Jessa's smiling face. She'd given it to him when he left. It wouldn't be right to leave it behind—they were bound to be married, after all.

He wondered if he would ever see her again.

Xander was getting tired of the constant interruptions by his new client. Jameson was clearly a prude, and maybe a rich, overly pampered idiot besides. Although he looked a lot like Alix—and that *did things* to him—his attractiveness was quickly waning in Xander's eyes.

Xander had learned long before to always have a ready stash of supplies and an exit strategy. Even his time with Alix had done nothing to change that. You never knew when things were going to change, and in Xander's experience, change was almost never good.

He kept this storage unit filled with everything he might need should he have to get out of town quickly.

He packed enough camping meals for the trip, along with the camping supplies they'd need to get by in the Outland, including a sleep sack each and a few collapsible pots and pans and fire-starters.

Now for the weaponry. Xander opened the crate that contained his small selection of arms. He pulled out his two pulse pistols, then cursed. The power level on one of them had dropped to almost nothing. He threw in a solar cell as well—he could always charge it on the road, but it would do him no good in the meantime. The depleted one might be good for a shot or two before it was wiped out.

He ignored the shocked look on Jameson's face as he packed the weapons. "Welcome to Oberon," he said with a grin. "We're more rough-and-tumble here than on… where did you say you were from, again?"

"Beta Tau."

"Than on Beta Tau." The man had to learn that things could get messy out here on the frontier of the Common Worlds.

Satisfied that they had everything they needed, he was closing up the saddlebags when the light in the storage unit darkened. He turned to see a shadow descend outside the roll-up door.

Xander stepped up to the entrance, pushing Jameson forcibly behind him.

A small, unmarked matte black hoversport was descending from above, its rounded shape bristling with pulse rifle barrels. "That's not good," he muttered under his breath. Someone at OberCorp had sent a team of enforcers —the company's black ops division—to find them. Which was curious, since he was supposed to be working on contract with the company. Or were they Syndicate men?

"What is it?" Jameson asked.

"I'm not sure," he lied. "Just stay behind me and keep quiet."

The hoversport alighted just outside the unit. The lift door groaned open and three enforcers stepped out, all wearing matte black body armor. Two of the men were holding heavy pulse rifles.

Xander stepped out into the sunshine, all smiles. "Greetings, gentlemen. What can I do for you today?"

"Xander Kinnson?" the lead man asked, flipping up his visor.

"I might be. Who's asking?"

"Please come with us." Xander glanced at the other two men and their weapons. This was clearly not an invitation.

"Understood." Inside, he was thinking furiously. These men reeked of OberCorp, from their smartly tailored black uniforms to the company-issue guns they carried. The Syndicate had firepower, sure, but the criminal organization was a maze of different bosses and rival groups, nothing so militarily precise as this. Something smelled fishy. "Let me just grab something from my bike."

The leader frowned, but nodded. "Make it quick."

Xander stepped back carefully, reaching into his saddlebag. "Get down," he whispered to Jameson. In one smooth movement, he grabbed the blast pistol that was low on charge and fired at the three men who'd come for him. The blast wave knocked them off their feet and pushed them back into the street, slamming them against the hard, unyielding shell of the hoversport. That gave him a precious few seconds to slam the emergency control on the storage unit door. As the armored metal door came rolling down the men started to get up.

They had little time to escape.

Always have an exit plan. Xander grabbed the other blast pistol, sealed up the bags, and hopped onto the bike. "Get on."

For once, Jameson didn't object. He climbed on the bike behind Xander, wrapping his arms around his waist.

Xander could hear the men pounding on the outside of the storage unit door.

If they were Syndicate men, they had probably been sent by Rogan. Xander suspected that Rogan had sent his men after him because the Syndicate boss was afraid he was going to cut and run. Which he was. He had no intention of being taken back there.

The last time had almost destroyed him, body and soul.

Xander had chosen this particular storage unit for a reason. He pointed the blast pistol at the back of the room and fired, and the wall burst outward where he had weakened it years before, sending his storage bins flying everywhere. He threw his arm over his head, blocking the debris. When he looked again, there was a gaping hole, giving them access to the unit behind his, which opened out onto the next street.

"Ravi, I need you to open the door on the unit in front of us."

"Affirmative. Give me one moment."

Xander had upgraded his PA with a shitload of blackware, including some handy hacking tools. He eased the bike through the new hole in the wall. "I don't think we have a moment, Ravi." Behind him he could hear his assailants taking a laser cutter to the door.

"Deciphering the passcode now," Ravi said.

Xander glanced over his shoulder. A line of bright white light was coming through a new seam in the roll-down door. In another moment or two they'd be through. "Come on, Ravi."

Jameson squeezed his arm.

"Access granted."

The door of the new storage unit slid open just as the remnants of the door behind them crashed to the ground. Xander gunned the engine again and they were out of the storage unit and back into the air, a pulse beam singeing the right sleeve of his jacket as he pulled away. They weren't out of danger yet, though. "Ravi, chart me a course out of the city. Going east."

"Do you want me to assume guidance?"

"Yes." He glanced over his shoulder again, seeing the black hoversport rising up over the top of the storage building behind him. He hoped the second pulse pistol had a decent charge in it.

The hoversport slowly closed the distance between them as the city flew by on either side. Ravi ran them on a crazy course between the buildings, up and down and around until even Xander's stomach felt a bit squeamish. "You okay back there?" he asked Jameson.

"Not really." The man's hands squeezed Xander's waist tightly.

"Well, hang in there. We'll either be out of this or dead soon." He glanced back. The hoversport was almost upon them.

The bike swung hard left into a narrow canyon between two buildings and he turned and aimed to take the shot. He pulled the trigger.

Nothing happened. The charge gauge must have been faulty.

"Oh crap. We're going to have to outrun them."

"On a *hoverbike*?" Jameson's disbelief was evident.

Xander nodded, his mouth set in a hard line. "Ravi, pass me control."

"Done, Xander."

Xander poured on the speed, leaving the hoversport behind. Buildings whipped past him on the left and right in a blur.

Xander grinned. "See?" He glanced over his shoulder. "That wasn't so hard."

Jameson pointed ahead wordlessly, his mouth working to speak.

There was a crowd of traffic in front of them. "Dammit," Xander said, glancing back over his shoulder again. The hoversport was catching up again. "Hold on."

Jameson's arms contracted even tighter around his waist. He pulled the bike up hard and flipped it over the top of a building, violating about a dozen city airspace traffic rules in the process.

"Oh shiiiii—"

Jameson's exclamation was cut off as Xander swung them hard to the right, taking them in a ninety-degree angle over the building.

The hoversport flew past but swung back around and was on their tail again. *Why haven't they fired?* As if in answer, there was a loud *boom*, and Xander waited to die. *It was a good run.*

Suddenly the hoversport behind them was careening out of control, slamming into one building and then off into one on the other side. It spun past them end over end in a tumbling ball of fire, taking out the corner of the building ahead of them. Debris pelted them, creating a nasty racket as it strafed the bike, and then they were past it.

"Hold on again." Xander pulled back hard on handlebars, lifting the bike up at a vertical angle into the air. They soared out of the way as the hoversport hit the ground below, sending up a cloud of smoke and flame.

Xander had no time to concentrate on what had just happened.

He brought the bike level and then dived back into the canyons of the city, using his wings to slow them down. The auto avoidance routines shuttled an approaching cyclist into a new direction just in time to miss a collision.

"Someone is requesting contact," Ravi said in his ear. "Communication flagged urgent."

"Split it," he cursed. "Okay, put it through."

"Nice maneuvering there, hotshot." It was a woman's voice.

Xander blinked. "Holy crap, Quince, is that you?"

"The one and only. Down your left."

He glanced down. Another cyclist was paralleling them below, silver hair flying in the wind. "Was that your shot back there?"

In response she held up a pulse pistol and blew imaginary smoke off the end. "Follow me. I scrambled the local grid for a bit, but we have to get you two out of town."

CHAPTER 4
QUINCE

QUINCE LED Xander and his passenger on a torturous course through the Oberon cityscape, trying to avoid spy drones and other hostiles. Ari guided her, utilizing the ferret program she'd carefully infiltrated throughout the city's network over the last twenty-five years. She'd worked toward this moment for more than two decades, and she didn't intend to blow it now. There was too much at stake, and Robyn was counting on her.

At last, they reached the edge of Oberon City proper. She had taken them on a roundabout course, skirting the Slander. Now they slipped down onto the streets of the makeshift criminal district at ground level, and she led them down a long, dark alleyway.

The city sang to her. Her augmented senses picked up all kinds of things she was sure her companions missed—the sounds of people behind the thick walls, talking, laughing, fucking, maybe sometimes even dying, all mingled together in a sensory soup that her ears processed and disregarded unless something seemed to represent a direct threat.

Data streams flowed through the air like multicolored ribbons, slitting information from one part of OberCorp to another, or from one Syndicate boss to another.

Even the smells of the city streets told a tale: someone stir-frying arracha, a water main break in the Central City, dead vermin in one of the city's sewer drains.

That vermin was human, as often as not.

They needed an undercover way out of the city that no one would suspect, so she'd turned to the last person anyone would expect to help them. She was sure she could convince him.

At least, she hoped so.

AROUND JAMESON, the character of Oberon City shifted. The prefab structures had ended as suddenly as a crash, and instead the street they followed, if one could even call it that, was surrounded and covered over with all manner of building materials, from corrugated metal panels to old rusted cargo containers. They passed under the conglomeration, and Jameson looked up in wonder.

A faded advertisement for something called Mugjuice graced the side of one of the more permanent structures. Some of them looked like old warehouses, while others were too ramshackle to even be called buildings—and pipes and wires stuck out here and there at odd angles.

The stench grew worse, if that were possible—thousands of people lived down here with no real plumbing or sanitation. As he looked around, he realized he was being watched. Eyes peered out and down at him from up among the conglomeration of debris above.

He shivered.

Trash heaps were piled up on either side of the street like fetid banks of snow, in some places nearly twice Jameson's height. Something rustled under one of them, and he looked quickly away.

The odors, which had been intermittent in the normal city streets, were pervasive in the Slander, and he put his forearm up against his face to ward off the worst of the smell.

He cast a nervous glance backward at the disappearing light behind them. It felt like the descent into hell his mother had been so fond of warning him about. Indeed, the heat was becoming oppressive; sweat dripped off his brow, and he tried to wipe it off, mostly unsuccessfully, with his sleeve.

He decided that he *hated* cities.

The street was empty of traffic except for the three of them. "Do you know where we're going? This whole thing seems a bit irregular."

Xander laughed harshly. "Not exactly. Ask her."

"Who is she?" He glanced at Quince, riding ahead of them, her white wings tucked in behind her. Like a rock and roll angel.

"An old friend."

Jameson was getting tired of being spoken to in such vague terms. He wasn't used to being treated this way. Did this guy even work for OberCorp? He felt odd in these absurdly casual clothes. "Oh, come on. I'm an official representative of the Psych Guild. You shouldn't be keeping me in the dark like this…."

Xander turned to glare at him over his shoulder, and Jameson shut up. None of this was going as he'd planned. Trapped as he was on the back of Xander's cycle, though, he wasn't in much of a position to do anything about it just yet.

Quince turned down yet another side alley, and Xander followed. Though Jameson was not a good judge of such things, this area looked even seedier than the part they'd just passed through. The buildings were mostly rusting, corrugated metal, and the walls sagged on both sides. In fact, few stood at anything like a right angle to the ground.

Oily liquid pooled here and there, covered over with some kind of algae that was a dark purple and vivid orange.

They threaded their way through the narrow space around stacked piles of debris. When he looked up, he saw Oberon's green-tinted sky above, just visible between the buildings.

At last, Quince stopped, climbing off her bike and palming an unassuming door. It looked new—strangely out of place in this run-down district. It slid open, wide enough for her cycle to pass through, and she slipped inside with the bike, gesturing for Xander to follow her. Xander steered it inside after her.

As the door slid closed behind them, the room lit up, revealing a large, white space. Jameson felt Xander's body stiffen. Following his gaze, he saw the group of men standing on the edge of the room, waiting for them.

The building was an old warehouse, but it had been cleaned up and modernized inside. Plas pallets were neatly stacked in one corner, and the building boasted a wide-open floor plan with new cement floors and a large roll-up door on the far end.

He returned his gaze to the four men. They were all sharply dressed. Like mafia guys in the Old Earth serials.

"What the hell is *he* doing here?" Xander hissed as his bike settled to the ground. He glared at the man across the room, his whole body tense.

"Relax, Xander." Quince put a hand on his shoulder. "We need him."

Xander spat. "I don't like it."

Quince gestured at him to stay put and strolled alone toward the group of men. "Gentlemen, thank you for meeting us here."

The biggest of the men, a giant guy with red hair and a full bushy beard, stepped forward to shake Quince's hand. "Your message said you had something of interest to us. I had no idea it was something so valuable." His brown, close-set eyes looked directly at Xander. He looked *hungry*. "I've missed that one."

Quince shook her head. "I'm sorry, Rogan, but he's not on offer." She ignored his muted growl. "I've got something even better for you."

Rogan's eyebrow arched. "It would have to be *much* more valuable to make up for such a loss." His gaze remained fixed on Xander, who squirmed.

Jameson wondered what exactly this man had done to Xander to make the self-confident ass act so squirrelly.

Quince glanced back at them and grinned. "Yes, he is quite a catch," she acknowledged. "But what if I could get you back in on the pith trade instead?"

Rogan's attention snapped back to her. "Don't play games with me," he growled. "Pith is dead. No one's run any in the last three months."

His men shifted as one, reaching for what Jameson assumed were weapons. "Oh crap," he whispered and looked around wildly. There was nowhere to run.

"Correction." Quince put her hands on her hips, looking as confident as Jameson didn't feel. "It *was* dead. Things are going to change soon, and someone's going to make a helluva lot of money when they do."

Xander was looking at Quince as if he'd never seen her before.

Rogan registered a flicker of interest. His men put their hands back in their pockets. "Why should I believe you?"

"Because I brought this for you." Very slowly, she reached into her own pocket and pulled out a small plastic box about a hand's width wide. She placed her palm on the surface, and the device hummed and split open. She took out a sealed vial filled with an inky black liquid and handed it to Rogan.

He took it reverently, looking down at it, his mouth dropping open.

"What is it?" Jameson whispered. It was small, dwarfed by the size of Rogan's hand.

"About a quarter million crits' worth of pith." Xander whistled softly, staring at Quince. "Who *are* you?" he asked, low enough that only Jameson could hear him.

"That's yours, with plenty more to come," Quince said. "But only if the three of us walk out of here alive, with anonymous transportation out of the city."

Rogan stared down at the pith for a moment more, seeming transfixed. Then he looked up, nodding slowly. "Whatever you need." He didn't even look at Xander. He turned to one of his men, a short gentleman who looked more like a majordomo than a common thug. "Dawson, make sure this woman gets everything she asks for." He nodded at Quince.

"Your assistance is much appreciated." She flashed him an insolent grin.

Rogan held up his meaty fist in her face. "I warn you. Fuck with me and I'll string you all up and bleed you dry. Even that one." He pointed at Xander, who paled. Then Rogan turned and beckoned for the rest of his men to follow him out the door.

"So what can I get for you?" Dawson asked. The man was short, with carefully trimmed graying hair and a sharp, rat-like face. *Probably an accountant.*

"I have a list." They touched wrists, and she slitted the information over to him.

He closed his eyes to review her requests. He blinked and nodded. "I'll see to it." Then he followed the others out of the room.

Quince turned back to find Xander and Jameson staring at her with mouths open wide. "What?" she asked, frowning.

"What the hell was that about?" Xander asked, dismounting from his bike.

"We needed a safe way out of here, so I made a deal."

"We couldn't just ride out? You had to go to *him*?" Xander looked like he was ready to spit. "We were just attacked by a Syndicate hoversport. Or maybe they were OberCorp? This is fucking insane."

Quince shook her head. "Just a minute." She rummaged through her saddlebags and pulled out a little black ball about the size of her thumb. She rubbed it between her palms and then threw it into the air. It bobbed about a foot and then stopped, hovering above them, spinning and giving off a flickering silver light. "Okay, now it's safe to talk. No one can listen in on us under the distortion field," she explained to Jameson. "Those men who attacked you weren't Syndicate—they *were* OberCorp. We need a way to slip out of the city that won't trigger any of their alarms, and the Syndicate can provide that for us."

Jameson was confused. "OberCorp brought me in to investigate the pith shortage. They sent Xander to meet me. Why would they attack us?"

Quince shook her head. "OberCorp didn't bring you in. I did."

Xander frowned. "So there never was a 'job'?"

Jameson watched them go back and forth, a frown on his face.

"Not in the sense that you mean, no."

"And how did you come across so much pith? I know you don't make that much crit in a year."

"Let's just say I have my sources."

Jameson grew tired of waiting to ask his own question. He pushed them apart. "Enough! I think I'm entitled to ask what the hell is going on here too. I arrive on-planet, and you"—he jabbed a finger at Xander's chest—"pick me up at the immigration station, claiming to be an OberCorp representative. Then you take me on a wild ride to some storage unit in a godforsaken part of this crap town."

"I thought—"

"I don't want to hear it." He dismissed Xander with a wave. "In no time, we are besieged by a bunch of armed hoodlums shooting at us with pulse pistols."

"Actually, I was the one with the pulse pistol—"

"Shut the f...." He took a deep breath and recovered his composure, straightening his missing jacket out of habit and dismayed to find it wasn't there. "Just. Let. Me. Finish. Then you—" He spun around to face Quince. "—come riding in like an old-fashioned cowboy posse and take out an entire freaking hoversport like it's no big fucking deal. Now you tell us you orchestrated this whole thing? Who the hell were those people, and why did one of them look like he wanted to eat poor Xander alive?"

"You done?" Xander asked, his voice sharp.

"Yeah, I guess so." It had felt good to blow off a little steam. He *never* let himself go off like that. Once when he'd tried at home, his father had given him forty lashes with a riding crop. He'd bottled up his emotions ever since.

"First off, I'm here because I was told that OberCorp had sent me to pick up your sorry ass." He glared at Quince as he poked Jameson in the chest, pushing him backward. "You're damn lucky you got me.

"And second, you should be down on your knees thanking this woman for saving both of our asses out there." He gave Jameson a withering look and turned back to their aforementioned savior. "Quince, seriously, what the hell was that?" He waved at the door, where Rogan and his men had made their exit.

"Xander and I go way back," Quince said with a wink to Jameson. "I knew him when he was just a babe in swaddling clothes."

There was a mental image Jameson couldn't un-see.

"*That,*" she said to Xander, "will get us out of here alive, with everything we need to help Jameson on his little quest."

"So there *is* a quest?" Jameson asked. "I thought you made this whole thing up out of thin air." He frowned. "How did you know my name? We just met."

Quince smiled her infuriating grin once again. "Oh, this isn't the first time that we've met, little Jameson, but we don't have time to go into that right now. Suffice it to say that you and I have a history of our own."

Xander and Jameson shared a perplexed look.

Jameson decided that Xander looked pretty damned good when he was angry.

As they waited for Rogan's man to return, Xander went back over the contents of his saddlebags.

Quince handed them each a bottle of water from her own bags. "Drink up. Don't want you getting dehydrated out there."

Xander was sure that was meant mostly for their little off-world friend, who didn't look like he had much wilderness experience, but he drank his anyway to set a good example.

After looking uncertainly at the two of them, Jameson shrugged and drank his own.

He'd been rushed back at his storage unit, with the attack and all, so he'd missed a few things he would've preferred to take. He rearranged everything to his liking, aware the whole time that Jameson was staring at him.

The man was cute when he was angry. A pompous ass, for sure, but still adorable.

"What are you looking at?" he asked finally, without bothering to turn around.

"I've never seen anyone with wings before." There was a hint of awe in Jameson's voice.

"Haven't traveled much, then, have you?" Xander put everything back into the bags as compactly as possible and sealed them up.

He was used to being an object of derision because of his wings, which he'd had since he'd hit puberty—like a really bad case of acne that you could never hide. He couldn't remember his parents, or even if they'd had wings themselves. Surely at least one of them must have. There had to be first-wave colonists in his family tree, somewhere. "So what do you want to know?" He turned around and leaned back on the bike, spreading his wings out behind him dramatically.

Jameson was quiet for a minute, apparently considering what he wanted to say. "Do they ever, you know, get in the way?" he asked, finally.

"What do you mean? Like when I go through a doorway?"

Jameson nodded. "Or other things...."

"When I have sex?" He stepped toward Jameson, who scrambled backward.

"Hey, I didn't mean...."

"Are you wondering what it feels like to fuck someone with wings?" He was right in Jameson's face now. He wrapped his black wings around the other man's back, preventing further retreat. He cocked his head sideways. "Is that what you wanted to ask me?"

Jameson shook his head, blushing all the way to the tips of his hair. "No. I mean… I have a fiancée. I'm an upstanding Beta Tau citizen…."

Xander could practically smell the lust on him. He snorted.

"Break it up, boys," Quince called.

Xander glared at Jameson, then reluctantly stepped backward. The little shit would have to learn not to mess with him.

"You guys about ready to get out of here? Our ride'll be here shortly."

Xander stared at the woman who had been like a mother to him, wondering what else she might be hiding. It seemed as if he'd always known her. Quince's beautiful white wings were a counterpoint to his own black ones, and she'd always seemed like an angel to him.

He'd never seen her so overtly aggressive, *and* she had ties to Oberon City's criminal underworld.

How had she found them at just the right time, out there in the city?

Those were questions for later. There was clearly more she wasn't telling them.

QUINCE SENT Xander and Jameson to opposite sides of the warehouse while they waited for their ride. They were acting like hormonal teenagers, and she didn't have time to deal with them. First things first.

She had to get them out of the city, and fast. Despite her best efforts, someone at OberCorp had apparently figured out that Xander was key to the whole pith shortage mess. She only hoped that they didn't know about Jameson yet. She'd planned to catch up with them outside the city, but plans had a way of getting scrambled. She'd had to make the best of it.

The faint rumbling of an engine came from just outside the big roll-up door. "We have company," she announced, glancing over at her two charges.

The back door swung open, and Dawson reappeared. "Your transportation is here," he said with a sneer, putting his palm against the wall. The roll-up door lifted slowly, revealing a narrow street outside. There was a big ground truck parked there, waiting for them.

She had to take it on faith that Rogan would keep his word. She had seen the greed in his eyes when she had handed him the vial of pith. If he truly believed she could bring him more of it, they would be safe. But if he thought she was lying….

There was no other way forward. "Okay, boys, let's go. Our ride's here."

Dawson pulled down a loading ramp from the back of the truck. "Your requested supplies are inside." Quince climbed on her bike, starting the engine, and rode it out of the warehouse door. She drove up the ramp into the back of the truck, and climbed off the bike to secure it to the wall.

Xander followed her, with Jameson walking behind. Within a minute, they were all inside and ready to go.

Xander attached a solar power cell to the back of the truck and connected it to one of his pulse pistols in his saddlebag. "Just in case."

Quince nodded. She peered down at Dawson, standing in the street. "We'll be gone a week, maybe ten days in the Outland. Tell your boss that once we get back, I'll contact him with details about the pith supply."

"You might have Rogan fooled, but I think you're full of shit." Dawson glared up at her. "Don't fuck with him. He'll track you down to the Split if need be, and cut you and your friends into little pieces for the wereveren to eat."

Quince jumped down from the truck, her wings spreading with a whoosh to slow her fall. She took Dawson by his collar and pushed him up against the wall of the warehouse. "Don't threaten me, little man." He tried to push her off, but she just pushed back harder, forcing him up against the rough concrete wall of the warehouse. "You're not Rogan, and he's not here to protect you. I'll keep my word. I always do. Not because some little shit like you told me to." She let him go and climbed back up into the truck.

Dawson looked shaken. He didn't say anything more, just put up the ramp and closed the door to the truck.

Quince grinned. That had felt *good*. She needed to work out her nerves from time to time.

This motor-driven transport truck was a lot more primitive than what she was used to, but they had a better chance of flying under the radar in it. Trucks like this came in and out of the city all the time, laden with merchandise bound for the other cities along the coast or the outer suburbs, and no one gave them a second glance.

She pulled a glow sphere out of her pocket and spun it up, hanging it in the air in the middle of the truck's cargo hold. The engine of the petrochemical-fueled truck started up, and the vehicle began to rumble forward through the city streets.

"Where are they taking us?" Xander asked.

"Out of the city. I made arrangements for them to drop us at the edge of the Outland, where we're least likely to be seen and tracked." She set about transferring the supplies from their crates in the back of the truck into her saddlebags.

"By OberCorp?" Jameson asked.

Quince looked at Jameson, really *looked* at him for the first time since she'd caught up to the two of them. This man, who she had known as a small child so many years ago.

He didn't even remember. How could he?

Now he was grown to adulthood, sturdy and handsome, if a bit bookish and stuffy. The next few days would shake most of that out of him. "Yes, Ober-Corp. Or other parts of the Syndicate."

"They seem to be after Xander in particular." Jameson glanced at his rival.

Quince nodded. "For reasons which I'll explain later. Right now we need to deactivate anything they might use to track us."

Xander frowned. "What do you mean?"

"This." She pulled out a disruptor tool from her saddlebags. She charged it and applied it to her right wrist.

"What the hell are you doing?" Jameson said. He reached to stop her, but he was too slow. She activated the disruptor, and pain seared through her arm. The circuits fried under her skin, and a puff of acrid smoke rose from her wrist.

When she opened her eyes, she was sitting on the bed of the truck. Pain still pulsed through her arm, but it had subsided a little bit.

"Are you insane?" Jameson asked, his eyes wide. "There is no way I am going to let you short out my interface or my PA."

She could see he was trying to get a message out onto the grid. "Won't work. I've had you blocked from grid access since you landed."

Jameson's face turned red. "You had no right."

"Quince's correct. It's the only way," Xander said. "I was one of Rogan's kept boys for years. He gave me these." He lifted his vest to show part of his back; it was scored with angry scars. "She showed her hand with that vial of pith. The story is out. Even if Rogan keeps his word, there are others who have every incentive to come after us, and no reason to be gentle about it."

Quince nodded. "I'm going to need your help to do my cirq."

Xander took the disruptor and put it up to the side of her head, against her temple. "This is going to hurt. I'm sorry."

Quince nodded again. She sat down, with her back against the wall of the truck. The shock would likely knock her for a loop. "Do it."

Pain even worse than before lanced through her skull, like lightning racing through her head. This time she smelled smoke, and felt as if someone had shoved a white-hot poker through her temple. "Damn, that hurt." Quince rubbed her still-warm temple.

She returned the favor, shorting Xander's wrist and temple units. "Fuck, you weren't kidding." They both looked at Jameson.

"Your turn."

JAMESON BACKED up against the corner of the truck. "No. No goddamned way. I won't let you." He'd been systematically stripped of his clothing, his mission, and his dignity. This was a step too far. If he didn't push back now, when would he ever?

The truck was still rumbling along, presumably through the Slander or along the streets of the city proper.

He tapped his cirq. "Angie, call OberCorp's emergency line." Maybe Quince had been lying.

"I'm sorry, Jameson. I am unable to connect to the grid."

Xander shrugged. "Any luck?" he asked with a sardonic grin.

"No. But can't we talk about this—"

Xander was on him in an instant, pressing the disruptor against his head. The pain in his temple burned through his mind. He squeezed his eyes shut, willing the pain to stop as a white light seared his vision. *Sorry, Angie....*

Slowly it ebbed, and he opened his eyes, only to feel the pain flare up again, this time in his wrist.

"Holy craaaaap," he shouted, shaking his wrist. "What the fuck is wrong with you people?" All sense of decorum gone, he banged his aching wrist against the side of the truck again and again until it started to bleed. It helped distract him from the pain of the disruptor burn.

"We're being hunted," Xander said, with no sympathy in his eyes for Jameson's pain. "I'm not leaving your link open just so you can check on your stock portfolio back on Beta Tau."

The pain of the wrist short-circuit was subsiding, though now his hand ached from the repeated blows. Jameson's mind was strangely empty. Angie's voice wasn't in there anymore.

He sank down to the floor of the truck and put his hands over his head, wishing the whole universe would just go away and leave him alone.

He'd been dragged along on this dangerous adventure, when by all rights he should have been in an office at OberCorp talking to someone about a civilized expedition to the pith plantations. Or wherever the hell the drug came from.

Apparently even that was a lie.

"Look, I'm sorry." Xander knelt next to him, a warm hand on his shoulder. "It had to be done."

"Leave me alone." He knew he sounded like a petulant five-year-old, but at the moment he really didn't care.

CHAPTER 5
SPLIT

XANDER WAS LIMPING *through the streets of the Slander, his left leg still pulsing with pain from what Rogan had done to him the night before. The man was twisted and used Xander's body to bring himself pleasure in ways that were often both painful and humiliating for Xander.*

His back was on fire between his recently sprouted wings. Rogan had given him ethilium, the hormone that triggered the growth of wings in the skythane; he seemed fascinated by the possibilities for sexual adventure they provided.

Xander had grown used to Rogan's "attentions" over the years. The lash was one of Rogan's favorite things; he loved the way it left his mark on whatever he owned.

Rogan had sent him to hand carry a delivery to one of the other Syndicate bosses on the far side of the Slander. Xander held the parcel under his arm, glancing warily about to make sure he wasn't being followed. He looked up at the tall silhouettes of the arcos that ran across Oberon City, far above. He dreamed of escaping this hellhole to one of those luxury towers, of getting out of Rogan's clutches, but the man had wired an explosive charge next to his brain, under his skin and linked to his cirq. At any moment, at Rogan's command, death and oblivion could take him.

It was Rogan's way of controlling his slaves.

Xander wasn't paying close enough attention to his path, and he tripped on a pothole in the street. He sprawled out onto the hard pavement, the package flying out of his hands. "No, no, no!" He scrambled up to go after it, ignoring the bloody scrapes on his palms.

Someone picked up the package and reached out a hand to help him. Xander looked up.

It was a man, taller than him, with red hair and warm brown eyes. He was wearing a long black trench coat, and looked like he had money. "You okay?"

It was strange that someone like this would be walking around the Slander. Maybe a john?

Nevertheless, there was something… kind about the way he looked down at Xander. Xander took his hand. "Yeah, I'm okay. Just clumsy, that's all."

The man laughed. It was a nice sound. "Here you go." He handed the package back to Xander. "I'm Alix."

"Thanks. I have to run. I'm late with this." He took off down the street.

"But wait, I didn't even get your name!"

"Xander!" He kept running. Rogan would kill him if he was late.

XANDER MUST have dozed off while they waited for the truck to make its winding way out of Oberon City. He sat up slowly, touching his temple. It was strange knowing that Ravi wasn't there anymore. Alix had paid for the bioware implant when he'd taken Xander off the streets, ten years before.

Xander was sure that Alix must be dead by now.

It was time to move on.

He stared at Jameson, asleep on his side, and was struck again by how much he resembled a young Alix. Same red hair, similar features. He looked like an angel when he slept, without the wings.

"How are you feeling?" Quince was sitting next to him, rubbing her own temple.

"Not so hot. It feels weird to be disconnected from everything." He stood up unsteadily, bracing himself against the side of the truck. "Is Jameson out?"

Quince snorted. "He seems to be. He was snoring a little while ago." She pulled her silver hair back behind her ears and rubbed her eyes.

"How long was I asleep?"

Quince shook her head. "I don't know." She tapped her temple. "I have no way to check now, remember?"

He laughed. "Yeah, this is going to take some getting used to." He closed his eyes, remembering the dream, and the pain. "Look, can I ask you something?"

Quince nodded. "Anything."

"You were the closest thing to family that I had after my parents died. Why didn't you come looking for me? When—"

"When Rogan took you?"

He nodded. "I always wanted to ask." He stared at the wooden floor of the truck, afraid to look at her. "I was afraid of what the answer might be."

"It wasn't for lack of trying." She sighed. "I did look for you. For years. When Rogan's men snatched you, you disappeared from the grid. When I finally found you…."

"It was too late."

She nodded. "He had you wired. I didn't know how to get you out."

Xander barely remembered her from when he'd been a child, before his parents had been killed. She had been 'Auntie Quince,' though he was certain they weren't actually related.

He looked up at her. Her lips were a tight line across her face, and up close like this, he could see the age lines next to her eyes. "When you were fourteen, I made sure you got the ethilium to help your wings grow."

"That was from you? I thought Rogan did that… just so he could play with my wings."

"He treated you horribly. I'm so sorry, Xander."

"It wasn't your fault. It's over now." He could still see the way Rogan had stared at him, back in the warehouse. "Thank you, I think." He flexed his wings. "I've been grateful for them, most days."

She turned to him, and her eyes were wet. Quince was in real pain, kept hidden beneath the placid surface.

"You were there when it counted. Afterward. I needed you then. You were like the big sister I never had, and Alix…." He closed his eyes. It still hurt to think about him. "Alix felt that way too."

She shook her head. "I'm so sorry, Xander. I should have done more to protect you, to prevent what happened to you. I was young, and didn't understand what a great responsibility I had undertaken."

"Responsibility?"

Jameson groaned.

"Later. It looks like he's coming around."

Xander nodded. He'd been impressed by the way Jameson had held it together during the fight and flight, and by how he stood up for himself back at the warehouse. Maybe he wasn't as weak as he looked. Not that he'd say anything of the kind to the off-worlder himself.

"What hit me?" Jameson lay on his side, squinting up at them. "I feel like I've been run over by a truck, not like I'm inside one."

Xander helped him sit up. "Yeah, it hit us all pretty hard." He grabbed a bottle of water from his saddlebags. "Here, drink some of this."

Jameson took it and swallowed some of the lukewarm liquid. "Thanks." He handed it over to Quince, who took a drag. "Not that I get any say in this, but what happens next?"

"We should be at our drop-off point soon," Quince said. "Once we get there—"

The rest of her sentence was cut off by a deafening boom. The truck shuddered, and ground to a halt.

"What in the hell?" Xander shouted as the ceiling of the truck popped off and the walls peeled away on either side.

"Damn it all to hell, they found us again." Quince hopped onto her hoverbike.

Two black hoversports like the one that had chased them through Oberon City were settling to the ground like enormous beetles behind them.

"Xander, you lead one of them off. Divide and conquer." She tossed him a pulse rifle.

He nodded. "I'll take Jameson with me." The man was his responsibility, after all, and he looked completely unable to take care of himself out in the wild. He jumped on his own bike as the doors to the two hoversports started to open and enforcers poured out.

Quince shook her head. "He goes with me. We can't have both of you taken together. No arguments." She took a pulse rifle from her saddlebag and shoved it under her arm.

Xander glared at her. "Why? What aren't you telling me?"

"No time. They'll be on us in a second."

He glanced over his shoulder and nodded. "Where do we meet?" He shoved the pulse pistol into his pants. The solar charger was nowhere to be seen.

"Where you and I went camping last summer, by the Theseus. Remember it?"

"Got it. See you there." Then he was off along the road, heading south at a rapid clip. He glanced back to see Quince's bike lift off the ground and take off in the other direction into one of the boxcorn fields that fronted the railroad.

Behind him, their assailants jumped back into the hoversports, which soon rose into the sky in pursuit.

JAMESON HELD on for dear life as Quince steered her cycle off into the fields on the right side of the road. The bike raced along about five feet above the ground, the leaves of the plants whipping his arms and face as they rushed by.

They were riding up the row between two tall stands of what looked like boxcorn, the plants heavy with square ears of the industrial vegetable.

He glanced back. Xander's bike zoomed down the open road, racing off in an entirely different direction. "He's a sitting duck on the road," he said to Quince, shouting over the sound of the engine and the wind, jabbing his finger in Xander's general direction. Though why that should bother him was beyond him. The man was a prick.

"He can take care of himself," Quince shouted back. "Right now I have to worry about your ass."

He looked down at the ground moving past—they weren't going too fast yet. He could jump off the bike and run into the field. With any luck, he'd be able to lose himself among the corn plants and maybe find his way back to Oberon City, or maybe flag down the hoversport.

Behind them, one of those hoversports had risen off the ground and was following them doggedly. He prepared to jump, but then Quince poured on the speed, and his moment was gone.

He'd have to wait for a better chance. "And what about you?" he shouted. "Who's watching your ass?" He glanced backward worriedly at the hoversport that was coming after them. It was quickly gaining ground.

"I'm not worried about me."

As he watched the hoversport, it fired off a shot that burned away a half a dozen boxcorn plants to their left. "Holy crap. They're trying to kill us." He shuddered. There was no way he was bailing on the hoverbike now.

"Not if I can help it." She turned halfway around, holding a pulse rifle, and got off a shot in the general direction of the hoversport. It evaded the blast easily.

The bike, however, veered slightly, sending a sickening shudder through Jameson's stomach and taking a chunk out of the neat and even row of boxcorn.

"Give it to me." He was *not* going to be killed in some stupid accident in a field in the middle of nowhere.

"Do you know how to use it?" The hoversport was almost on top of them now, and Jameson imagined he could see the pilot glaring at him from behind the dark plas window.

"Yes, I learned how to use one on my last posting on a mining colony. Sunday afternoon entertainment. Now give it to me."

She nodded and handed the pulse rifle back to him. He grasped it and slipped his right hand around the grip.

With one hand around Quince's waist, he turned and got off a quick shot. He winged the hoversport but it seemed to shrug off the blast.

"It's shielded," she said. "You have to hit it when the pulse laser fires."

"Pulse laser?" He looked back at the approaching hoversport. Something that looked disturbingly like a gun turret was descending from the underside of the hoversport. "You're kidding me." He turned back to Quince. "They're going to shoot us!"

"Hold on."

He held on to her as best he could with his arm encumbered by the rifle. She veered through one of the rows of corn, the leaves slapping at them as if trying to pull them off the bike. There was a thunderous blast behind them as several of the corn plants seemed to spontaneously burst into flame.

"Hit 'em now!" Quince called back.

He turned and fired at the hoversport, but he was too slow. The pulse bounced off the shields harmlessly.

"They're trying to kill us," he said incredulously. "Oh my God, they're trying to kill *me*." He started shaking uncontrollably. "Why would they want to kill me?"

"Pull it together, Jameson," Quince said. "I'd slap you if I could, but you're going to have to do it yourself."

Jameson's gut twisted. No one had ever actively tried to kill him before. His parents were pacifist Christianists, so even his home life had been calm and quiet. Mostly.

"Hold on again, and get ready to fire."

Jameson took a deep breath and steeled himself. There would be time enough to freak out later, if they got through this alive. He gripped Quince's waist tightly with his left hand and turned just as the gun mount pulled back to deliver another laser pulse. He shot two blasts at the hoversport as Quince veered again, this time to the left. He glanced back to see one of them connect with the turret.

A blue lightning bolt spread out like a spiderweb, a hair-thin tracery spreading across the belly of the hoversport. Electricity raced around the top of the ship, sizzling in the afternoon air. Then it split the hoversport apart like an egg, the whole thing exploding and showering debris across the sky.

Little bits of burnt plas hit his back, and then the remnants of the hoversport were behind them as the cycle sped away.

"I did it." He started to laugh, flushed with adrenaline. "I *fucking* did it!" He *never* cursed—well, hardly ever—but the force of the moment overrode his normal composure.

"Congratulations," Quince said dryly.

Then the import of what he had done hit him. He'd taken a human life. Probably several. The sickness in his gut returned in force. "Stop the bike."

"We should keep going," Quince said. "There may be more of them coming."

"Stop the goddamned bike!" He was going to lose it.

Quince braked to a halt, settling to the ground roughly and kicking up a cloud of dust.

He jumped off and fell to the ground, throwing up violently, expelling the contents of his stomach on the damp ground. It went on for what seemed like an eternity, and his world was reduced to the cramp in his gut and the vile taste in his mouth.

He felt soiled, dirty. Reduced to an animal state.

Eventually there was nothing left to come out, and he lay on his side, his breaths heaving in and out of his chest.

Quince put a hand on his back. "First time?"

He nodded, not trusting himself to speak just yet for fear he would kick off another bout of vomiting. His mouth tasted foul.

His back chose that moment to start itching, and such a mundane reaction made him laugh harshly. He sat up and took a deep breath.

Quince knelt beside him. "I remember my first time too. Hardest thing I ever did, even if the bastard deserved it."

Jameson looked up at her, searching her eyes. "You killed someone?"

She nodded. "It was shortly after I arrived in Oberon City. I was walking through the Slander—I didn't know any better back then. A man assaulted me, probably wanted to swipe my crits. I would've let him, if I'd had any, but then he wanted more. I was all alone, but I wasn't helpless." Her eyes took on a faraway look. "I broke his neck."

He looked up at her with newfound respect. "It didn't bother you?"

She snorted. "I was sick to my stomach, like you were. Then I went home and cried about it for three days."

"But you got over it?" He'd counseled people before with difficult issues, and he had always told them that it took time to heal their wounds. Now he was starting to wonder if he had been a total idiot. This didn't feel like something that would just go away, no matter how much time passed.

Quince thought about it. "Mostly. I hope to, one day." She stood. "It's good that it hurts, though. It means you're still human." She offered her hand.

"I guess that's something." He took her hand and stood up, wiping off his mouth with the back of his arm. "Let's go."

"Are you ready?"

"As ready as I'm going to get." *How did OberCorp track us down?*

He hopped back on the cycle behind her, and they took off toward the line of trees in the distance.

XANDER RACED away from the destroyed truck, his cycle tracking the road out of Oberon City. Behind him, one of the hoversports followed, its gun turrets bristling menacingly. Quince and Jameson had taken a different direction, off southeast into one of the boxcorn fields. It would slow her down, but it also gave her some cover. He hoped the two of them would make it out of this all right. Whatever *this* was.

Right now, he had himself to worry about.

He poured on the speed, temporarily leaving the hoversport in his dust. On his right, the cornfields stretched off into the distance. On his left, the tall, silvery green gumba trees waved in the breeze, helping to block the worst of the winds from the fields beyond them.

His speed was approaching 300 km an hour, but the hoversport was starting to catch up. He thought about dropping down into the fields too, but he didn't want to bring "his" hoversport in Quince's direction. He eased the pulse pistol out of his pants. "Ravi, take the wheel," he said, tapping his cirq, but then he remembered that Ravi was gone. At least until he was able to return home and get a new cirq installed.

It was strange not having a connection to the grid. He had gotten used to it over the last five years, and now he couldn't decide if being without it was liberating or maddening. It would have been handy to have Ravi to autopilot for him right about now.

He fired a shot over his shoulder, hoping to hit the hoversport, or at least make them drop back.

When he glanced at it again, it was still right on top of him. He considered his options.

They continued on like that for a couple minutes, a strange pair racing toward the Outland. Eventually, they would reach the zone where electronics fizzled out, but Xander didn't think he could keep ahead of them for that long. Even if he could, it would still be three or four men to his one.

He glanced back again. Why hadn't they shot at him?

A strange thought crossed his mind. Quince said they were after him in particular. Maybe they needed him alive, and in one piece. It would explain why they hadn't tried to take him out.

If so, that gave him some leverage.

He tried to remember what lay ahead, casting his memory back to the last time he and Alix had come out here. They had done some wild shit together out here on their cycles. Xander had a slight advantage because of his wings—they allowed him to manage maneuvers that Alix was unable to match, and they might just save him now. If he remembered correctly, there was a bluff ahead that might work.

Xander tapped his forehead, starting to query Ravi again about how far ahead that part of the terrain was, but nothing happened. He sighed. It was *maddening*. He would just have to wing it.

He grinned.

"Xander Kinnson. Pull over, or we'll bring you down," a loud voice boomed down from the hoversport, just over his head.

He looked up. A pulse laser turret was pointed directly at him.

Time to roll the dice.

He held up a hand and extended his middle finger. Then he pushed the bike forward even faster.

He braced himself for death, but no shot came. The ship continued to tail him.

He grinned victoriously—he'd been right. They must have been ordered not to hurt him.

At last, the place he was looking for was just ahead. The road cut through the edge of a hillside, curving in the process. If he timed it just right….

Hoversports were made for air-to-ground combat. They were shielded underneath and all around, but they were vulnerable from above.

It was perfect.

He pulled off the road just a little, angling toward the bluff at a ninety-degree angle, glancing back to be sure the hoversport was still behind him. As the bike flew up the steep incline, he wrenched at the handlebars with his arms, his wings guiding him in a circle up into the air.

In seconds, he had flipped himself around and was heading straight at the oncoming hoversport.

His wings lifted him up above it and he passed neatly over the top. He tried to imagine the confusion inside the vehicle. In one smooth motion he pointed the pulse pistol down at the ship and fired into it, and then he was past it, flying through the air and descending toward the road, heading back in the direction he'd come.

He got his bike down to the ground and pulled to a halt.

He looked back.

The hoversport was wreathed in fire and light as it slammed into the bluff, striking the ground hard and exploding into a million pieces.

Xander blew imaginary smoke off the end of his pistol and tucked it back into his belt. It'd been a near thing, but now he was free.

He looked back the way he'd come, considering going to help Quince. Then he thought better of it.

She could take care of herself. Going back would only put him in more danger.

Better to follow the original plan and strike out toward their meeting point.

CHAPTER 6
WEREVEREN

IT WAS late afternoon by the time they reached the edge of the forest, the true beginning of the Outland—or so Quince had told him. It still felt like midday. He had to remember that the days were shorter here.

Far overhead, a shuttle arched down toward Oberon City in the distance, leaving a contrail across the green sky. There seemed to be more traffic lately between Titan Station and Oberon City. Something had stirred up the hornet's nest.

She guided the bike underneath the trees, leaving the last of the boxcorn fields behind.

Jameson hoped Xander had come out all right against his own hoversport, but there was no way to know until he showed up at the rendezvous point.

Not that Jameson really cared, but the man *had* risked himself to draw off one of the hoversports. For now, he just wanted a safe place for them to make camp, and to wash up. He still had a foul taste in his mouth from his nausea.

Jameson looked around. Strange, thin trees topped by tufts of silver foliage loomed over them, inhabited by some kind of cooing animals. The air here smelled alien—sharp but sweet, perhaps scented by unknown blossoms, and untainted by the industrial wastes of Oberon City.

It reminded him a little of the forests back home. Beta Tau had been fully terraformed from a lifeless ball of rock with Earth-normal flora and fauna.

Yet this was also nothing at all like the forests he remembered. The shapes of the trees, the sounds of this alien forest, and the smells—they were all wrong.

The late afternoon sunlight slanted down through the branches of the trees like it did at home, but it was a canopy filled with leaves of blue and silver. Strange things called out in the semidarkness, things that twittered and screeched and grumbled.

They continued on through the woods for maybe half an hour, the cycle humming along over the forest floor. The shadows lengthened, and eventually Quince brought the bike to a halt beside a copse of the strange trees. They had skinny trunks, and their bark was silver like their leaves. They swayed back and forth in the slight breeze, their leaves making a sound like running water.

Quince pulled off her helmet. "We'll make camp here. We've got about an hour to set up before the wereveren find us."

Jameson dismounted from the bike, and Quince followed him.

"Wereveren? That doesn't sound good."

"They're not bad, if you take precautions. If you don't"—she steered the bike in-between the trees—"they'll rip out your throat."

Jameson shivered. "So what do we need to do?"

"I hope Xander has a deterrent field with him." She pulled out a long rope she'd had tucked into her saddlebag. She handed one end to him. He held it up and looked at it in the sunlight. It consisted of three cables—red, blue, and green—wrapped in a translucent casing. Every three inches or so, the wires protruded from the casing to form a small loop. It reminded him of a strand of DNA, the way the wires wrapped around one another.

Quince surveyed the clearing they were in. "We need to run this from tree to tree around this space." She tied one end of the rope around a tall, thin trunk. "This one's a silverbark. See the dark line on this side? That's always the north-facing side."

Jameson looked up. The tree was impossibly thin and tall, and its first leaves were at least a hundred feet above the ground. "Silverbark. Got it." He played out the rope as Quince ran it in a rough circle around them, encasing their sleeping space, wrapping it around the trunk of each tree. "So these... wherevers?"

"Wereveren?"

"Right, Wereveren. What are they?"

"Little birds, about as big as your hand. But don't let that fool you. They're deadly."

He snorted. *Killer birds? Seriously?* "So what do we do when we reach the distortion zone, where little electronic gadgets like this don't work to keep these... *birds*... out anymore?"

She laughed. "Good question. We'll figure that out when we get there."

Privately, Jameson wondered if this whole thing wasn't simply a ruse to keep him in line. Maybe this rope was more a *Jameson* barrier than a wereveren one.

Quince finished the circle, wrapping the excess rope around the original tree and snapping the ends of it together to complete the circuit. Jameson waited for a force field to spring up. Or maybe an electric sizzle of power.

Nothing happened.

"Is that it?" he asked, trying to keep the skepticism out of his voice.

"Yup. Once the sun sets, stay within this circle, and you'll be safe." He could tell she'd heard his skepticism.

His back was itching again. He rubbed his shoulder blades, but couldn't seem to get at the spot.

"You all right?" Quince asked, glancing over at him as he squirmed to reach it.

"Yeah. Just an itch." He looked around. "What now?"

"It's going to get chilly tonight. We'll need fire to keep us warm, at least until we go to bed."

"We're *sleeping* here?"

"Of course. You don't see a nice hotel anywhere nearby, do you?"

He looked around at the dirty campsite and scowled. This was *not* how he'd thought this mission would go.

Something howled off in the distance, sounding like a cross between a feral cat and a grizzly bear.

"What the hell was that?"

"We call them swamp bears. They're harmless, though they can give you a nasty infection if one of them scratches you."

He sighed. "I had to ask."

"We've got another hour before sunset. Why don't you go find some fuel for the fire? There's a fungus that grows around the base of the trees here called croyol. It's white, and usually about a hand's width wide, like this...." She made the shape of a heart with her hands. "It burns without any smoke."

He nodded. "Got it. Heart fungus." He stepped under the wire, looking around. Nothing happened.

"Stay close enough to see the campsite," Quince warned him. "I don't want to have to come after you."

He nodded. The forest was beautiful for all its alien strangeness—the light slanted through the trees to make dappled silver-green patches on the fallen leaves. The sound of the wind through the leaves was calming, and it was comfortable enough here in the late afternoon shade. Maybe this wasn't so bad, after all.

He started to look for the fungus, checking the closest trees first, then moving farther off, every minute or so looking back at the camp.

As he searched, a flock of pretty red birds alighted on a tree branch above him. At least, he *thought* they were birds. They were about the size of a crow, with wingspans about as wide as his forearm. Instead of feathers, they were covered in a fine red fur. They did have birdlike beaks, though, but instead of being yellow, they were black. Their feet clung to the branch like bird feet, and they sang a cheerful song as they watched him go by.

If those were wereveren, he figured he could handle them.

See? Not so bad. Then another strange growl sounded in the distance, and he shot a glance back at the campsite to make sure it was still there.

He did *not* want to get lost and end up eaten by a swamp bear.

Quince watched Jameson go. The boy was far too confident in himself for his own good, especially out here in an alien environment.

Then again, princes often were.

She snorted. Soon she'd need to tell him the truth, but for now, she intended to let him get his ground legs. One thing at a time.

She went back to preparing the campsite, taking out a small spade and clearing a place in the center of the camp for a fire pit and lining it with rocks she found nearby. She looked up in the midst of her labor. Jameson had wandered about thirty meters from the camp. "Any luck?" she called.

"Got a few. These ones, right?" He held up a small white heart.

"Yup. Circle around a bit. You'll probably find more over there where the trees are denser."

Quince was worried at the ease with which OberCorp had found them. Granted, they had still been close to Oberon City, but she'd been sure Rogan would do everything he could to keep their departure a secret. After all, the man had a hell of a lot to gain by keeping up his part of the deal.

If he hadn't given them up, then who?

Would the company enforcers be able to track them down again?

She spent the rest of the remaining daylight going over each of the items in her saddlebags, one by one, looking for some sign of a bug or tracker.

Jameson returned with an armload of the fungus. She had him stack them up inside the perimeter and sent him out for more.

Then she checked the bike.

At last she found it. There was a dark patch on the underside of the headlight. She took out her knife and pried it off carefully. She held it up to the light. It was a trackpatch. She could see the circuitry inside the black metal cylinder. "Gotcha."

"What's that?" Jameson said, returning with a second load of croyol.

"This is how they tracked us." She handed it to him.

"That little thing?"

She nodded. She wondered when they had affixed it to the hoverbike. Had it been attached during the initial fight over the city? That seemed unlikely.

That left the warehouse. Had one of Rogan's men done it, working for OberCorp?

The thing sprouted wings and tried to jump out of his grasp. He closed his palm around it.

"We should destroy it." Jameson dropped it on the ground and lifted his heel.

"Wait!" The boy was far too hasty.

"What?"

"Think about it. They already know where we are. What's the first thing you would do if your tracking device suddenly stopped functioning?"

"Send someone to find out why…." His face went pale. "Oh."

"Yes. Oh. So we'll leave it for now and let them think we're not onto them. Then in the morning, we can dispose of it before we leave. Let's hope they don't come tonight."

Jameson nodded. "That makes sense. We should find something moving to attach it to. Throw them off the trail."

"Good idea." *The boy was no fool, at least.*

He handed it back to her carefully, and she broke off the wings. "In the meantime, we take turns mounting a guard. Just in case they make a move tonight." She was relieved to have found the tracker, but something still bothered her.

Why was OberCorp going to all this trouble to find them? Was it related to Robyn's news of the invasion?

No sense worrying about it now, she supposed. In a few days, they would be beyond the reach of OberCorp and the Syndicate. In the meantime, she'd keep her guard up.

The sun had set an hour or so before, and the strange wood had only grown more disquieting to Jameson. The swamp bears had apparently gone to sleep, but now the forest was filled with more vicious cries—a kind of high-pitched howling—and gut-wrenching screams that sounded like something was getting its guts ripped out.

Jameson huddled on a rock by the fire, sipping a warm mug of cafflite, this world's sorry excuse for coffee. Was that small bit of human comfort really too much to ask?

An MRE was cooking on the fire for him, and another for Quince. He'd chosen beef stew, though he hadn't seen any cows here since he'd arrived. He suspected it was synth-meat, but hungry was hungry.

He was still trying to figure out how, in the course of just twelve hours, his life had been turned entirely upside down—how he'd found himself camping in an alien forest in a broken world with an angel.

As a child, he'd dreamed of flight. Everyone did—it was a classic subconscious symbol of the yearning for freedom. Psych 101.

Xander, though.... Something about the man's casual disdain combined with the dark beauty of his black wings.... Jameson wondered what it would feel like to have his own, to be able to soar up and away, above everything. Away from everyone.

Quince glanced up at him, giving him a knowing smile. "I imagine you have some questions."

"You could say that." *Nothing but questions, in fact.*

"Shoot. I'll answer what I can." She picked up another heart fungus and threw it on the fire. It caught fire with a blaze of light, then settled down to a nice golden glow.

The little hearts were smoke-free, as advertised, but they put up a terrible stink at first, like the stench of the swamplands back home that abutted his parents' estate. Jameson wrinkled his nose. "Okay. I came here to investigate a pith shortage. At least, I thought that's why I was here. I'd assumed I'd be meeting with someone from OberCorp. They run the planet, right?"

Quince frowned. "Yes and no. They run the mining operations, yes, and probably most of the government of Oberon City and the other cities along the coast. They do *not* 'run the planet.'"

"So who does?"

"That's a complicated question." She took a sip of her own cafflite, staring into the fire.

Though she was a fair amount older than he was—how much he wasn't really sure—she was beautiful. Ageless.

"Maybe I should start by telling you a story," she said at last. "I've been on

Oberon for twenty-five years now. But a long time ago, I lived in a different place. Not too far from here, but far enough...."

Quince looked around the House of the Stars one last time. She and Robyn had spent so much time here, the royal summer house, before she had been banished to Errian, the city along the Argent Sea.

She held little redheaded Lyrin in her arms. The babe was fast asleep. His mother had been dead now almost a week, and he had finally stopped crying constantly.

These were unusual times, and such times required difficult choices.

Quince stared at the doorway before her. Soon, she'd go through it, and everything would change. As the nimfeach had promised her that day in the woods outside her village.

She felt, rather than heard, the arrival of the other woman behind her.

She turned slowly to face Robyn, who held Davyn in her arms. Robyn's black wings drooped, and her eyes were wet. "This child is more precious to me than gold. You must promise to look after him. In this world and the next." She laid a hand on Quince's shoulder. "Promise me."

"I promise," Quince said softly as she reached for the child. It had all the weight of a ritual.

"I can't do it...." Robyn pulled the child back, her voice ragged with grief. The sound tore Quince's heart in two.

Quince put her hand on Robyn's shoulder. "You have to. This is what we agreed to. It's the only way they will be safe."

Davyn squealed, and Robyn laughed in spite of herself. "I suppose we must." She held out the boy once again, and Quince took him, tucking the child into one of the slings strung over her shoulders.

Then Robyn embraced her, their children between them. Robyn kissed her, their lips sealing this agreement between them. Quince savored the moment. She was leaving behind more than just her home and her Kingdom, and she didn't know if they would ever see each other again.... "It's for the best, Daughter of the Moon." Lyrin squirmed between them. How am I ever going to take care of two children?

"He must not come to harm," Robyn said when they separated. Her dark wings were still wrapped around Quince and the children protectively.

"I will care for him like my own."

"If there were another way...." Robyn's voice trailed off.

"If wishes were rainbows," Quince said sadly.

"Be strong, little one," Robyn whispered. She gave Quince one of the round amalite keys to the waygate.

Quince stared at it. She had never seen one before. It was smooth and matte black, with no defining features. She held it up to the gateway, and it opened before her, revealing a room on the other side very much like this one, but in disrepair.

Robyn gave her one last wan smile and turned away, as if she didn't want to see the act of departure.

Quince knew how much that must have cost her. In her arms, the two little boys began to cry.

She shushed them gently and stepped through the waygate.

Jameson blinked. For a moment, he'd become so entranced by the story that he'd forgotten he wasn't witnessing it firsthand. Then the fog in his head dissipated.

Quince was staring at him intently. "What?"

"You felt it, didn't you?"

"Felt what?"

"Like you were there with me."

He frowned. This whole thing made no sense. "I just got caught up in the story, that's all," he said defensively.

Quince looked at him, really *looked* at him, as if she were seeing through his soul. "You were *there* with me."

He absorbed that for a minute. "What, like some kind of time travel?"

She shook her head. "You were there with me at the time." She put a hand on his cheek, searching his face. "I know it's a lot to swallow, but one of those babies was you."

"It couldn't be." It was nonsense, surely. How could he have been? "I was born on Beta Tau. My parents are Joseph and Angela Havercamp. I've never even been to Oberon before." What was this crazy angel trying to pull over on him?

Her hand still rested against his cheek. It was warm and comforting.

"I brought you to Oberon, along with Davyn, who is now called Xander, almost twenty-five years ago. You were both children then, Xander a little older than you." Her eyes had a distant look about them. "I carried you across the threshold, and then I found you both homes. Xander here, and you on another world."

He jerked away from her touch as if he'd been burned. This wasn't happening. She couldn't be right. He was a Havercamp, born and bred. "Look, I don't know what your angle is here, but I'm not who you think I am. I just came here to investigate the pith shortage, and now I've gotten mixed up in this crazy scheme of yours—"

"Your back itches, doesn't it?"

"What?" he asked, struck by the sudden change of subject.

Quince stared at him, fully present in the moment. *"Does your back itch?"* Her tone was deadly serious.

"Well, yes, but I don't see what that has to do with anything." This was getting stranger and stranger, and he had nowhere to run. She'd made sure of that.

Quince got up and rummaged through her saddlebags, pulling out a mirror. "Take off your shirt."

"Why? Are you going to hurt me?" He backed up toward the rope that surrounded the clearing.

Quince snorted. "With a mirror? Hardly. I just want to show you something. Then if you don't want to believe me, I'll let it go."

Fair enough. He shucked his shirt, though it seemed tight coming off.

"Now turn around."

He complied, and she held the mirror up so he could see his back. "What do you think those are?"

He looked and his face went cold. Protruding from his shoulder blades were two strange lumps, the skin over them looking red and bruised.

He reached around frantically to touch one of them. It was tender and warm. "Jesus, Mary, and Joseph...." He spun around, trying to reach them. "What are they? What did you *do to me*?"

"Your wings are coming in. It's something that happens to every one of us from the first-wave settlers of Oberon—we usually induce it at puberty with a special hormone. Yours were delayed, but you drank some of the ethilium in that water I gave you—"

Jameson's breathing quickened, and he felt trapped in the small clearing beneath the alien trees. Everything was *wrong.* "I don't know... I can't...," he rasped, unable to get enough air. *What the hell is happening to me?* He looked wildly back and forth, his heart racing and his mind struggling to follow.

She reached out to him, but he stumbled away from her touch. He didn't want her to touch him again. He didn't want to be *here.*

He turned and ran blindly away, ducking under the rope and into the open forest. His panic carried him off into the darkness, ignoring Quince's frantic calls to come back. He was blind to everything but the need to flee, to escape this strange trap that he could feel slowly closing its jaws around him.

Branches slapped at his face, stinging him. He stumbled and fell, but picked himself up again to keep running.

When he finally slowed down, breathing harshly, the campfire was a distant glow, and he was all alone in the darkness.

Jameson stopped then, his hands on his knees and his head down, and let his breathing slowly return to normal. He had to get a grip on himself. He was here, for good or ill. He was stuck with this woman, and something strange was happening to him. That much was clear.

There were two options—he could run from it, or he could turn around and face it. His career had been built on helping people deal with things they didn't want to acknowledge. Now it was his turn.

He'd been stupid to run.

Jameson had just turned to start back toward the distant campfire when there was a rustling in the branches above. *Just one of those stupid birds.* He'd be back in the warm circle of firelight in a moment anyhow.

There was a loud flutter right behind him, and then he felt a sharp prick in his neck.

"Owww!" He put his hand up. It came down wet.

Around him there was a sound like a thousand little fans, and then he was surrounded by things flapping past him in the darkness. There was another peck on his arm and one on his leg, and he suddenly realized the danger he was in.

"Quince," he shouted, and started to run, but the flock of wereveren followed him like an angry cloud, diving in to harass him and then flying away again, one after the other. He tried covering his face to protect his eyes, but then he couldn't see. He stumbled forward, now bleeding in half a dozen places, hoping he was headed back toward the campfire.

He had no way to know without opening his eyes.

The attacks came faster. He was going to die out here, all alone, in an alien wood, fallen prey to a beast no bigger than his outstretched hand. All because he'd been a thick-headed idiot.

He fell down and curled up on the ground, trying to protect as much of himself as possible from the attacks. He felt weird—groggy, like he'd just awoken in the middle of the night.

A roar and a couple loud thumps startled him back to awareness. His assailants scattered momentarily, and a pulse rifle went off, twice. Then he was dragged up onto a seat.

Someone shouted "Hold on!" and he did as he was told, hugging her waist. *Quince,* he thought.

The cycle swung around and raced back toward the protection of the enclosure.

The wereveren returned, but in less force, and before they could take many more swipes at him, his savior had reached the firelit clearing. Quince guided the cycle under the deterrent rope, parked it, and eased him off the seat.

Jameson opened his eyes, but he couldn't quite focus on her face. He was tired beyond imagining, and the campsite around him swam in and out of focus. The last thing he was aware of was being laid down to rest on a sleep sack. Warm hands touched his cheek, and he thought someone kissed his forehead.

Then he fell into a deep sleep and was aware of nothing else.

CHAPTER 7
MORGAN

XANDER DECIDED he was better off getting away from the road. Sure, travel would be slower, but he'd also be much harder to track.

He checked the map on his bike's navigation system. Although he'd disconnected it from the grid, it still kept a rough track on his position. He was a bit east and north of the rendezvous point—a wide bend in the Theseus that was easy to spot on the map.

Xander clocked another hour heading east down the road first, taking advantage of the fact that it would take time for OberCorp to scramble another team to come after him. Then he dropped off the road into the forest and started looking for a suitable place to spend the night.

He'd meant it when he'd warned Jameson about the predatory wildlife out here in the forest. He had a deterrent field with him, but he preferred to find something more secure for the night, if possible.

Xander rode under the silver canopy of the forest, weaving across the landscape to find the smoothest path that would take him on a southbound course toward the rendezvous point.

The last time he'd been in the Outland, it had been with Alix on a three-day camping trip. Alix had loved it out here. He'd always said he felt at home under the feather trees and silverbarks. Xander, for his part, was much more of a city boy, though he did like getting away from the scheming and politics that were a regular part of Oberon life.

He rode out from under the tree cover into a large clearing. From the even rows of earth, the square shape of the field, and the few trees that dotted the expanse, he guessed this had been an old homestead farm. A hundred years before, seeking to bleed off some of the excess population before the arcos had been built, OberCorp had offered citizens of Oberon City a deal—come out and homestead a patch of property, and you could make it your own.

The program had been successful until the homesteaders had realized how difficult life was out here, especially with the swarms of wereveren that infested these woods.

The homesteading program had finally collapsed, and more arcos had been built instead.

Sure enough, an old, abandoned farmhouse sat at the back of the field. It had once been a grand structure, two stories tall, with a wide porch and a peaked roof above the second floor.

Now it was in shambles. The front door was half off its hinges, and the roof had seen better days, having collapsed entirely on one end.

Xander pulled up his cycle alongside the dilapidated structure. He glanced at the sky; he probably had another two hours before the sun set. He slipped off the bike and climbed the stairs to the porch. Despite the way it looked, it was firm underfoot, solid enough to take his weight.

He stepped through the open front door.

It was dusty inside, but other than some weeds that had poked up through the floorboards, there was no sign of anyone or anything living there.

"Hello?" he said anyhow, just in case. His voice echoed through the house.

He searched each of the rooms on the ground floor—all were empty, the furniture and appliances likely having been stripped out when it was abandoned. There was a rope embedded in the walls all the way around. It looked like the place was wereveren-proof. That decided him.

He eyed the staircase, but it looked even less safe than the rotting front porch. He'd stay downstairs for the night.

Xander went back outside and pulled his cycle around the back, hiding it in the tall weeds and shadows so it would not be seen by casual inspection. Just to be safe, he took out his hunting knife and chopped down a few feather tree branches to cover it so that it wouldn't be visible from the air. Then he grabbed his saddlebags and went back inside the old house, preparing himself a place to sleep for the night.

The kitchen was the most intact room in the house. It had just one window, looking out across the field in front of the home, which was miraculously still in one piece.

He found an old broom that had been left behind in the pantry and managed to sweep clean a patch of floor. He laid down his sleep sack there, and then placed and activated his own deterrent rope to keep the wereveren out, just in case.

Satisfied with his preparations, he sat down with his back against the old clapboard wall and pulled out an MRE.

He'd have to find some water soon—he'd brought enough for a couple days, certain that they would run across a freshwater stream on their journey, although pretty much any water source would do. He'd brought a purifier that should render even the most brackish water drinkable.

As he ate, he wondered how Quince and Jameson had fared, and if they were all going to make it to the rendezvous point in one piece. Jameson was a pain in the ass, but still… there was something about him.

He also wondered why OberCorp had suddenly developed such a keen interest in him.

The sun was falling behind the trees in the distance. Xander finished his meal, feeling exhausted as the events of the day caught up with him.

He closed his eyes, and in a moment he was fast asleep.

Xander dreamed of a world with a red sun, where the air was redolent with the smell of sugar blossoms and the land was full of life.

He ran through a field covered in blood flowers, chasing a butterfly. She soared on ahead of him, leading him on a merry chase. Then she flew up into the air and he leapt after her, his arm extended, but he was too slow.

He crashed to the ground and started to cry.

"There, there," his mother called to him. In an instant she was at his side, soothing him with a soft cooing. "You can't fly yet, my little angel," she whispered, picking him up in her arms. "Poor little sparrow."

She kissed him gently on the forehead, and he felt better, forgetting the pain in his scraped knee.

Then she hugged him fiercely, and when she held him out at arm's length, there were tears in her eyes. "Remember always, my little sparrow, that I love you with all my heart."

With that, she launched herself into the air with her son held tightly in her arms.

Xander awoke, and the dream melted away into the ether. Something had jarred him awake.

He picked up his hunting knife, and rose into a crouch quietly, wings pulled in tight behind him. He looked around the dark room. Hermia's pink moonlight slanted in through the window, making a crosshatch pattern on the floor.

Xander stood, his wings spreading out behind him instinctively. He pulled them back and walked silently to the window. Something had awoken him, but he couldn't quite figure out what. There were no wereveren about. He would have heard their bloodcurdling screeches.

The field outside was bathed in blue moonlight, but nothing moved. He held himself perfectly still and silent, waiting for whatever it had been to make itself known once again.

Seconds stretched into half a minute, then a minute. A light breeze blew through the overgrown clearing outside, tossing the lonely trees back and forth. Nothing else moved in his field of vision.

He was about to give it up and go back to sleep when there was the slightest of sounds, somewhere above him. A creak. Maybe it was just the old house, settling?

Then it happened again, on the second floor.

He turned and crept into the hall, trying to make as little noise as possible. He waited again, staring up the stairs.

He had to wait for a long time before it repeated. Eventually it did, and that decided him. He couldn't stay in this house for the rest of the night without knowing what it was.

He stepped up to the base of the staircase. "I know you're up there," he said in his calmest, most authoritarian voice. "It'll be easier if you just come down."

He waited, but there was only silence.

Sighing, he started up the stairs.

The wood underfoot creaked, and he placed his steps carefully, all the while shooting glances above. He didn't want to be caught unawares.

On the ninth step, his foot went through the rotted wood. He grabbed for the rail, but it crumbled under his grasp as the whole bottom half of the staircase separated from the wall, falling to pieces under his feet.

As he fell, he extended his wings and swept them down powerfully, pulling himself up to the landing halfway up the staircase. He grasped the edge of it and pulled himself onto its flat surface as the bottom half of the staircase collapsed into splinters and dust. His breathing gradually slowed back to normal.

The landing seemed to be connected more firmly to the structure of the house, and it bore his weight easily. He looked down at the mess of debris below. Maybe he should give up this little quest and move on to someplace less… creepy.

Xander wasn't one to run from a challenge. Besides, traveling in these woods at night, full of wereveren, seemed like a bad idea.

He stood cautiously and resumed his climb up what remained of the staircase, which seemed to be in better shape. He made it to the second floor without further incident.

The hallway at the top of the stairs had three doors. Xander pushed open the first one, wary as the floorboards squeaked beneath his feet.

The room was empty save for a thick carpet of dust.

He eased his way to the second door and threw it open.

There were tarps covering several objects in the room—perhaps old furniture the owners had left behind when they departed.

He tested the flooring inside the door with a toe. It seemed sturdy enough.

Xander stepped into the room, looking around.

The moonlight showed him four distinct *things*. It was impossible to tell what they were under the tarps.

One way to find out. Xander took the edge of one of the tarps and whipped it off.

The air of the room instantly filled with dust, and Xander cursed himself for being an idiot, coughing and waving the cloud away from his face.

Another of the covered bundles exploded, showering him with more dust just as the air had started to clear.

Xander stepped backward out of the room, desperately seeking the cleaner air of the hallway, and something ran past him toward freedom. He reached out instinctively and caught an arm, hauling its owner backward. "The stair's broken," he said as he hauled… a boy? In front of himself.

The boy was almost naked, save for a pair of old, worn pants that might once have been white but now were so dirt-stained that it was almost impossible to determine their true color. He was also really scrawny. Poor thing looked like he hadn't eaten in weeks. His dark hair was wild and unkempt, and he had freckles across the bridge of his nose, though they were hard to make out under the grime that covered his face. He stared up at Xander, a surly, defiant look on his face.

He couldn't have been more than twelve years old.

Xander stared back. What in the Split was a kid like this doing out here in the middle of nowhere? Had his parents abandoned him?

By the looks of it, the house hadn't been lived in for close to a hundred years, so it was highly unlikely he was the child of the old owners. "What's your name, son?" Xander asked, kneeling before the boy.

The boy stared at him and shook his head.

"Don't you speak?"

Another shake.

"Okay," he said, trying to figure out what to do next. "Do you understand what I am saying?"

The boy nodded.

Well *that* was something. "Do you remember your name?"

The boy shook his head. Poor little thing stank. He probably hadn't had a bath in ages. Who knew how he had managed to survive out here? He needed a name. Xander thought about it. "I'm going to call you Morgan. That was my foster father's name."

The boy looked up at him, wide-eyed.

"I'm going to let go of your arm. Do you promise not to run?"

The boy he'd named Morgan nodded.

Xander released his arm, and Morgan stood there, looking back and forth, as if not sure if he should stay or go.

"Are you hungry?"

That got Morgan's attention. He nodded vigorously.

"I kind of destroyed the staircase—sorry about that." Xander glanced back at the stairwell. "You have to know this place needed a lot of work."

Morgan gave him a blank look.

"So I'll have to fly us down. I'm going to pick you up." When Morgan didn't object, he took the boy around his waist and led him back down the surviving part of the staircase, wrinkling his nose at Morgan's smell. They reached the landing safely.

"Here we go." Before the boy could object, Xander jumped.

His wings brought them both down safely to the ground floor.

Xander set Morgan down, breathing in the fresh air gratefully. He had to get the boy a bath—he thought he'd seen a well outside. Maybe they could attend to that in the morning.

He led Morgan into the kitchen. The boy seemed unmoved by Xander's actions—for all that he had hidden away from Xander before, he seemed curiously passive now.

Xander shrugged. He rummaged through his bags for something the boy would eat. He chose an MRE that had lots of calories, and found an old glass that had survived in one of the cupboards.

He put them before the boy on the floor. "Sorry there's no, um, table. We'll just have to make do...." Before he had finished, the meal was gone. Morgan looked up at him expectantly.

Xander snorted. "Hungry little thing, aren't you? Want another?"

Morgan nodded.

Xander sighed. This boy was going to eat him out of house and home. Which, given the state of this place, wouldn't take long.

CHAPTER 8
INTERLUDE

QUINCE SAT with her back against one of the great blueoaks that mingled with the silverbarks in their little protected clearing. Though she was supposed to be keeping watch, her eyes were half-closed. It had been a long night, and the sun was just beginning to peek through the trees.

Jameson might be a psych, but the poor man had absolutely no wood smarts.

She supposed it was at least partly her fault. She had placed him with the first family that had come up—an off-world couple who had arrived on Oberon looking to adopt a child. She'd felt that it was better to have the boys separated. Anyone searching for the two of them would have a much harder time identifying them, and it would be more difficult for them to find the child of the House of the Sun if he were worlds away. It had been so hard to send him away.

The life he'd lived on Beta Tau had spoiled him.

He'd taken a beating for that last night. The wereveren saliva carried a poison that acted as an anesthetic—and he had sustained six bites, one on his back, three on his arms, and two on his left leg. She could see the sharp teeth marks, eerily like small human bites.

After Quince had dragged him back to the safety of the clearing, she'd laid him out on his sleep sack. She'd used boiled water to clean out his wounds, and then bandaged him up as best she could. The poison would work its own way out of his system.

Throughout the process, he had slept like the dead—thankfully, for it would not have been pleasant for him otherwise. It wasn't that pleasant for her either.

Afterward, she wrapped him in her own sleep sack. His was covered in blood and no longer usable. He'd likely sleep until midday, if not longer. She didn't think they'd be going any farther until the next day.

In the meantime, she would do what she could. She'd wrapped the tracker in an airtight sack and would drop it in a stream later that morning.

She had sat next to Jameson all night, keeping an eye on him. He looked so young and innocent in sleep, and his blood loss made his skin pale and translucent. It wasn't his fault he was like this, or that he didn't yet trust her. That would have to change.

She remembered holding him in her arms as a tiny baby, how he had looked up at her with those big brown eyes.

Things were going to get harder for him now. For them all. At least he'd had the chance to live a normal life, to grow up like any other child.

She yawned. It was clear she wasn't going to get any more sleep this morning. She might as well get up and get some work done.

She picked up the bloody sleep sack and carried it outside the clearing, ducking under the rope to carry it somewhere away from Jameson. He didn't need to see it. She went a ways off, finding a place on the far side of a hill to leave it. Maybe it would keep the wereveren busy the next night.

With luck, Jameson would be strong enough to move tomorrow. They had a rendezvous to make, and time was running short for the end game.

On her way back, she found a stream to drop the tracker into. She watched the bag float down the watercourse until it was out of sight.

She stopped back in to check on Jameson once more. He was sleeping soundly.

Then she set off to see what she could find in the way of more fuel for the fire and something fresh to eat to stretch their MRE rations.

Jameson woke up. His body was on fire. He lay still as a stone, not trusting himself to move. *What happened to me?*

He'd been with Quince in the forest. She'd told him something about a baby, and wings. It was all a bit fuzzy in his head.

Then he'd run, and there'd been a lot of pain. Searing pain, and then nothing.

He opened his eyes.

The sky above him was green.

Jameson lifted his arm up to his temple. He tapped his cirq to ask his PA where he was.

There was no response.

Then he remembered. They'd disabled their bioware the day before, in the mad flight out of Oberon City.

He suddenly felt very alone out here in the middle of nowhere on this godforsaken planet.

He sat up slowly, and parts of his body from his head to his feet protested.

"I'd imagine you're a little sore," Quince said from behind him. "Wereveren venom does that—it tires out your muscles. Not to mention all the bites I had to clean out and bandage."

Jameson turned his head to see Quince sitting there, regarding him with a look close to pity.

"I shouldn't have run." He was starting to remember some of the things she had told him. Something about princes. And wings? "I'm sorry. I wasn't sure I could trust you—"

"Don't be. We put you in a difficult situation, and I figure you've suffered enough for it."

"You… you saved me, didn't you?"

She nodded, holding up her finger and thumb. "You were this close to being a meal for those little bloodsuckers. You were a torn-up mess by the time I hauled your ass back here. Are you thirsty?"

"Yes." He *felt* torn up. He couldn't remember a day, in fact, when he'd felt worse. His head throbbed. His arms and legs throbbed, and it was like he'd been beaten by a Tander's World miner.

She handed him a canteen.

He took it gratefully and swallowed a few gulps of lukewarm water. "Hungry too. What time is it?"

"Midafternoon. Your body needed the sleep." She handed him a strange, stippled red fruit and an MRE. "I did some foraging this morning."

He accepted those too, and bit into the fruit. It was a little tart but full of sweet flavor, kind of like a lemony apple. "We're supposed to be meeting Xander somewhere, right?" He tried not to let his keen interest in the answer show.

"Yes, but you need another night's rest before I'll feel safe taking you anywhere."

"I'm really sorry—"

"I said leave it be." Quince glared at him.

"Okay, okay," Jameson said, laughing. He finished his meal and felt a little better. He checked over his body—he had bandages on one leg and both arms, and one on his back. "I must look like a mummy."

"Close enough."

He tried to get up, but he was woozy.

"Your body's not ready for walking just yet."

"Um, I have to pee."

Quince laughed, and it was a rich and welcome sound. "All right. Let me help you." She got him up on his feet, and they started toward the forest. "This wasn't how I pictured my day."

He snorted. "You and me both. I'm not sure I want to go out there again."

"It's okay. I'll be with you, and we're safe from the wereveren until nightfall."

"Okay, but if I so much as hear a bird call, I'm running back to the camp."

She shook her head and gave him a sly grin. "I'd like to see you try."

WHEN HE opened his eyes again sometime later after a dreamless sleep, it was fully dark out. Not the dark of his parents' estate, or the dark of the mining camp on Tander's World, but a pitch blackness only partially relieved by the little fire, like ink held back only by the flickering of the flames.

Quince had kept the fire going, and Jameson sat up gingerly to edge closer to the warmth.

His dreams had been full of wings. Birds fluttering all around him. Angels singing a strange, mournful song. His own body transformed, carrying him through the air, as free as he had ever been.

That *had* been a dream, right?

He'd always dreamt about flying. His psych training taught him that flight dreams were all about seeking freedom or release from an underlying or subconscious problem.

What had Quince told him about wings?

He reached over his shoulder to scratch absently at one of his shoulder blades, and stopped.

There was something on his back.

He twisted around and saw something golden. He ran his hand along it—it was soft and damp. It was about a foot long.

"They'll get bigger soon." Quince stepped into the firelight. She must have been standing there the whole time, watching him. It was creepy, but not as creepy as what was growing out of his shoulder blades. "You're gonna be awfully hungry for a bit."

It was as if her words had triggered his stomach. He was so hungry that he found it hard to think. "I am." He stared back at the little wing. As if in response, it stretched out, and he could see the individual feathers, brown at the base shading into brilliant golden hues at the tips. "What the hell is happening to me?"

Quince sat on a rock next to him and passed him some more of the red fruit and a couple MREs. "It's quite natural for a skythane. You just have to accept it."

"*Skythane*." He rolled the word around on his tongue. It was strange, but somehow right. "What does it mean?" His back itched where the wings sprouted from his shoulder blades.

"That you're one of us. Like Xander and me."

"Am I…. Is anything else different?" He looked down at his waist.

Quince chuckled. "Not down there, no. And no, you won't grow bird feet, if that's what you're asking. But your heart's a little bigger than the landers', and your shoulders and rib cage a little more robust."

He nodded. "The doctors thought it was a birth defect." He took some fruit and downed one of them almost whole. "What are these?" he said, holding another one. Red juice dribbled down his cheek, but he didn't care. "They're good."

"They're called obieberries. They're native to Oberon. I found a tree of them not too far from here this morning."

He nodded, trying to reach the itchy spot, but he couldn't quite get to it. "Are you sure we have enough food? I don't want to eat it all."

She laughed. "I brought extra. I figured you were going to need it." She picked up a knife and a block of wood that were resting on another rock by the fire and started whittling away at it.

"Wait…. You knew this would happen?" He kept eating as he was talking, downing a box of pasta and another with some kind of meat and gravy.

"Yes. People like us, here on Oberon, usually grow our wings when we reach adolescence. There's a hormone we take, when the time is right. I told you this last night, but I'm not surprised you forgot. You had a pretty rough time of it."

He ate another obieberry. "I'm sorry. I'm having a hard time processing this." His hands were shaking. "Two days ago, I was just Jameson Havercamp, a young psych from Beta Tau, sent here on what I was told was a midlevel mission to track down the source of a Class X psychoamoratic. Now I'm in the middle of a hostile forest on a backwater planet, eating god-knows-what kind of fruit and *I have fucking wings coming out of my back?*"

"Well, when you put it that way—"

"What the hell is happening to me?" Jameson was breathing too quickly; he could feel the air *wheezing* in and out of his lungs, and the damned itching on his back was driving him *crazy*. He was having a panic attack, like he used to when he was a child and everything felt *wrong*. He started shaking all over. He was no longer hungry; he just wanted to be back home, his childhood home on Beta Tau, safe in his bed with his mother's arms wrapped around him.

Quince put her carving off to the side and pulled him into her arms, her own white wings closing over them both in a warm embrace. "There, there, little robin, it will all make sense soon," she whispered, rubbing his back gently.

He let himself melt into her arms. They were safe, even familiar somehow. The forest around him melted away, and all he felt was warmth and love. His heartbeat gradually slowed, and his stomach settled. Eventually the shaking stopped too.

Quince seemed to sense the change. She squeezed him one last time, and after a long moment, they separated. "I'm taking you and Xander to a place where everything will be explained. You just have to be patient."

"I'm not good at patience."

Quince laughed. "We have that in common." She looked at him appraisingly. "Your old clothes are going to need some modifications. Turn around."

He obeyed, displaying his back for her inspection.

"Those are going to be a handsome set of wings," she said approvingly. "Golden, like an eagle."

Jameson felt an unexpected rush of pleasure at the compliment, and his new wings extended themselves and shook off their moisture. "Oooh, that was weird." He wasn't quite sure how he'd done it. He tried to reach the itch with a stick.

She nodded. "I remember when my wings first came in. It does take a bit of getting used to." She traced her fingers around his shoulder blades. "We'll adjust some of your current shirts to fit around these. Those wings won't fit underneath for much longer."

He nodded. "Okay."

"Other than being a freak of nature, though, how are you feeling?"

He laughed, releasing some of the tension he'd been holding inside. "Better, I think." He glanced at his bandages. "I'll be sore for a few days where the wereveren bit me, but my muscles don't ache as much anymore."

"Good. Hand me one of your shirts."

Jameson pulled one out of his carry sack and handed it to her. He only had a couple, and one of those had been halfway torn to shreds the night before.

"Quince," Jameson said, shyly. It was weird to ask a stranger for help, but there was something familiar about her that put him at ease.

"What?"

"Could you scratch my back, between my… wings?"

"Sure. Turn around." She ran her nails gently up and down along his spine and around his shoulder blades, easing the itching that had been bedeviling him.

It was one of the best things Jameson had ever felt.

QUINCE SAT with her back against the blueoak tree once again, watching Jameson sleep. He'd insisted on taking a watch, since he'd slept all the previous night and most of the day. She'd been reluctant to agree, as she wasn't sure he'd be able to stay awake.

It was good for him to have something under his own control right now, she decided eventually, and she had needed some sleep herself if she was going to be able to stay awake on the cycle tomorrow. She hoped to make up some ground toward the rendezvous point.

So she'd allowed herself a brief nap.

Sure enough, he'd been sound asleep sitting up against this very tree when she'd woken up.

She had picked him up and tucked him into their only sleep sack like a child, and he hadn't awoken.

No harm done. There was a chance they'd already been tracked to their current location, but there was little more she could do about it now, anyhow. They'd be on the move in the morning.

She looked at her charge, still sleeping soundly in the wee hours of the morning. She had only told him a small piece of it, so far. He would have to shoulder a great weight, but there was no need to burden him with it just yet.

She had carried the knowledge herself for more than two decades. What was a few days more?

She kissed his forehead. "I love you, Lyrin," she whispered.

Her little boy had finally come home.

CHAPTER 9
MORNING

XANDER LAY *on the simple mattress Rogan allowed him, a kindness that kept him up off the hard concrete floor of the cell he called a room. Rogan took pride in keeping his property in usable shape, and in Xander's case, that meant external perfection.*

Xander had no way to tell time, but he had a pretty good internal clock. In another half an hour, give or take, one of the guards would come for him to take him to "exercise"—his daily time working his body on Rogan's machines to keep him fit and athletic.

Rogan hadn't used him in a few days, apparently having found a new favorite—a younger blond boy off one of the farms outside Oberon City. Xander was seventeen now, as near as he could figure.

He had learned to treasure those times when he wasn't needed by the Syndicate boss. It was the closest he ever got to a vacation from the hell that was his life.

Something jangled in the lock, and the metal door to his room opened with a heavy groan. Xander looked up, surprised, at the bright light that flooded his room.

This was new.

A man stepped inside and looked at his naked form.

"Is that the one?" Dax, one of Rogan's enforcers, asked.

The man nodded. He looked familiar somehow. Red hair, brown eyes, wearing nice clothing.

Xander started to shiver. Had he done something wrong? Had he somehow offended Rogan?

Were they going to sell him now? Or worse, kill him?

He imagined the bomb ticking inside his head.

"That's him. 50k?"

The guard nodded. "That's what Rogan is asking."

The blood left Xander's face. He was being sold. Life with Rogan had been bad enough. By now he knew what to expect from the old Syndicate boss, but this new man…. He shivered.

"I'll take him." He held up his wrist, and the guard nodded. He put his own wrist next to the stranger's and the man slitted him the funds. "Are we good?"

Dax queried his PA. "All accounted for. You want him shipped to you?"

The man shook his head. "I'll take him now. And I want Rogan's little head bomb disarmed before I take him anywhere."

The enforcer laughed. "Can't have him messing up your transport."

"Something like that."

The guard took a tool and grabbed Xander roughly by the head, sticking it against his temple. Xander felt a piercing pain and howled. "Shut up," the guard said, smacking him upside the head. "Don't want to put off your new owner." Dax let Xander go to collapse back on the mattress, a trickle of blood running from the side of his head. "All done."

The man backhanded the guard, hard. "Don't you ever mistreat my property like that again."

Dax glared at him, but nodded. "Sorry, Mr. Preston."

The man ignored him, instead kneeling down next to Xander. "I'm going to take you away from here," he said softly. "Can you walk?"

Xander looked up into the man's eyes and remembered why he seemed familiar. It was the kind man from the street. He nodded.

"What's your name?"

"Xander."

"I'm Alix." The man helped him up.

Maybe things were going to be okay after all.

Xander woke. That day when Alix had taken him out of the Slander seemed like forever ago, though it had only been ten years.

He and Morgan were tucked away in a rock hollow he'd found above a stream bed that carried cold runoff from the Pyramus mountain range in the distance down to the Gildensea. It was well after midnight.

Xander had managed to sleep for a few hours, but something had awoken him from his dream. Now he sat with his back against the smooth veined granite, staring out at the forest below.

He looked over at the boy, sleeping peacefully, as if he didn't have a care in the world. Xander felt an unfamiliar sense of responsibility toward him. The boy needed him, and that pulled on a certain part of Xander's heart that he had thought long dead. He wasn't used to being needed.

Xander and Morgan had left the old farmhouse early the morning before, as Xander had wanted to get a good start on the day. He'd hoped to find a game trail through the forest to ease their passage.

He'd decided he couldn't just leave the kid behind. Sure, maybe Morgan had figured out how to get by, but if something happened to him, Xander would never be able to forgive himself.

Morgan was still strangely passive. When Xander had asked the boy if he had any possessions he wanted to bring with him, he'd shaken his head. Xander had shrugged. Maybe anything the poor child owned brought him painful memories.

He'd tried to get Morgan to talk, but to no avail. The boy either couldn't or wouldn't speak.

He did still have his tongue. Xander had been able to ascertain that much when he'd devoured his meals the night before and first thing in the morning.

Their progress through the forest had been achingly slow. He'd had to thread his way through thick stands of silverbarks, and several times they had been forced to double back when he came to a cliff that was impassable with the cycle.

Without the bike and Morgan, he could have flown, but then he'd be leaving most of his supplies behind too, and he couldn't abandon Morgan.

The boy reminded him of himself at that age. Life seemed to have hollowed him out, and Xander could relate to that.

The stream trickled along its course, playing a water-filled music that served to calm him. It sparkled red and gold under the twin lights of Hermia and Lysander, Oberon's two moons that chased one another around the half planet in an erratic course.

He glanced at the boy, puzzling again over his presence out here. After Morgan's initial reluctance, he had taken to Xander like an older brother, keeping close to him when they stopped several times during the day to eat, to take a piss, and just to stretch their legs.

His small hand was always reaching for Xander's, and once, late in the afternoon, Morgan had actually smiled up at him.

He had no idea what he was going to do with the boy.

Quince and Jameson were somewhere out there. The woman who had been like a godmother to him for most of his life, and the infuriating and intriguing psych. Xander found his thoughts going back again and again to the man.

Maybe it was his resemblance to Alix. Maybe it was just that he had an annoying way of getting under Xander's skin.

A flash out of the corner of his eye caught his attention. It was a shooting star, skipping across the atmosphere before disappearing over the rim of the world.

It was followed by another, and another, and then a whole swarm of them.

He watched in awe as the whole sky came alive with silver-white streaks, looking for all the world like Oberon was shifting into hyperdrive.

Through the middle of it, a shuttle rocket flared as it made its way up to Titan Station from Oberon City.

Things had been weird lately, from strange meteor falls to huge storms to the sun changing color.

There was that old Earth curse. *May you live in interesting times.*

He was afraid things on Oberon were about to become *very interesting.*

MORNING DAWNED clear and cold. Oberon was edging toward winter, but at least it wasn't raining today. The sun was still that strange rose-tinted color. Xander glanced at it frequently, willing it to change back to its normal yellow, but it continued to defy him.

He woke Morgan, and they managed a quick meal together. They were almost halfway through his rations already, so he'd have to look for something else for them to eat on the way. Alix had shown him which plants were edible out here. He'd look for a bit of water cane or maybe a few tubers to supplement their supplies.

Xander had been pleased to find some edible fungus called pocans. They were about as long as his forearm, a pale white color, shaped like a fat string of pearls. Alix had shown him these on the last trip. You could break one off and scoop out the center, which was sweet, a little like a musky chocolate, and the outside shell tasted something like yeasty bread.

He handed one of these to Morgan, who took it and stared at it as if it were the most alien thing he had ever seen.

Xander cracked one open, demonstrating how to eat it.

Morgan followed his example, and soon he had eaten four of them, the sweet centers smeared across his face.

"You're a glutton," Xander said teasingly.

"Glutton," Morgan repeated, as if he was tasting the word in his mouth.

Xander's mouth dropped open. "So you can talk." The boy had been silent for so long that hearing his voice was a shock.

"Can talk," Morgan agreed, a shy smile on his face. "Forg...." He frowned. "Forg...."

"Forgot?"

The boy nodded, grinning. "Forgot how."

Xander wondered how long it took, being all alone, to forget how to speak.

"I can help you remember, if you want."

Morgan nodded. "Help remember."

Xander stared at his charge with new respect.

They spent an hour or so over breakfast going over the words for common things. Morgan was a fast learner, or at least a fast rememberer. Soon he knew Xander's name, his own, and how to ask for basic things.

Xander found himself trying to recall some of the basic rules of English grammar; how verbs worked, why you put things in certain places.

The physical stuff was easy. Rock, tree, hand, even cycle were recognizable, tangible things. The intangible stuff, on the other hand....

For instance, it took him fifteen minutes to explain the word "feelings." He balked at trying to get the concept of "time" across to the boy. Finding out how long he'd been all alone in the little house and how he'd managed to survive at all would have to wait.

He put away the small amount of packaging left over from the meal. He pointed to the stream below, and then at Morgan. "You stink."

"Stink?" the boy repeated, wrinkling his forehead.

"Yes, stink." He squeezed his nose shut and made a face. "Time for a bath." Probably the kid's first in a long time.

"Don't like bath."

Damn, he'd learned that one quickly. "Sorry, Morgan. No bath, no more food."

The boy considered for a minute, then nodded. "Okay, bath."

Xander sorely missed his ionic shower, but he supposed he was probably getting rank too. He pulled out a bar of soap and led the boy down to the stream, finding a quiet eddy where they could clean themselves off. A stand of red colifir trees marched like sentries along the stream banks here, trailing vines from one side to the other. The morning was warming gradually, but the water was ice cold.

He pulled off his clothing and splashed water on himself, lathering up with the soap, showing Morgan how it was done.

The kid took the soap and ran headfirst into the stream, laughing and splashing cold water everywhere.

Xander shook his head. *Kids.*

It took Morgan three washings to get all the dirt and gunk out of his hair and off his skin. He splashed about the whole while, looking like a normal child for the first time since Xander had discovered him. Without the grime, he looked even younger and more innocent.

Xander felt more like a father than a big brother. He didn't hate it. Not entirely.

Soon they were both as clean as they were going to get. It was a marked improvement on the state the boy had been in, and would make the day pass more easily and less fragrantly.

They climbed the slope back up to their little campsite in companionable silence.

An empty MRE tin came rattling down the hillside.

Xander held Morgan back. There was something rummaging around in his pack. He crept up quietly, hoping to catch whatever it was unawares.

He grabbed the pack, pulling it up off the ground, and a small river cat fell out hissing, its rubbery tail flicking back and forth in agitation.

"Scat," Xander said hotly. He looked through the pack. The damned thing had eaten most of their remaining food.

Morgan walked calmly past him.

"Hey, stay away from that thing. It might bite you!" River cat bites weren't fatal, but they hurt like hell.

Morgan ignored him, picking up the animal, which immediately stopped hissing and settled into his arms and began to purr, a *huffa-huffa* sound that Xander had never heard one of them make before. The boy carried the cat back down to the stream, where he set it down. It hastily swam away. "Like cat."

Xander snorted. "Damned cat ate our food." He held up the pack.

"Find food."

"We're going to have to." He'd been banking on having enough to keep them eating until they found Quince and Jameson again, but now they'd have to slow down and look for more on the way. There was nothing to be done for it, he supposed.

His plan was to continue south toward the Theseus River. Once he reached it, they could follow it to the rendezvous point.

He checked the bike's map to make sure they were still going in the right direction. Then he packed away the last of the camp, tucking everything securely into his saddlebags. "Ready to go, little man?" he called to Morgan, climbing onto the cycle. The boy nodded and smiled shyly, climbing up behind him and wrapping his arms around Xander's waist. Xander wondered if this was what it was like to be a father.

He and Alix had never wanted to be parents. Oberon City was no place to raise a child—Xander himself was proof of that. But if things had been different....

He shook his head. The world was what it was, and wishes wouldn't change that.

They set off toward the stream below. He found them a safe place to cross where the water was shallow, and they reentered the forest beyond.

The country here was flatter as they approached the Theseus. It made for easier riding, and around lunchtime, he happened upon a game trail that pierced the forest. According to his map, they'd reach the Theseus by nightfall.

THAT SAME morning, a fair distance west, Quince and Jameson were also breaking camp. Jameson pulled on the modified shirt Quince had prepared for him, with holes for his nascent wings. He still wasn't anywhere near comfortable with the idea, but he'd filed it under the can't-do-anything-about-it-now part of his brain.

When he returned home, he could always have the damned things surgically removed. Though he'd have a hell of a time explaining them to his parents. Or to Jessa. *What, honey? Oh, yeah, those. They just sprouted there one day....*

He wondered if she was worried about him. Now that his cirq was burned out, he had no way to get a message back to her to tell her that he was okay. Maybe she'd get worried and would send in the cavalry after him.

Jameson drew on his psych training to put himself into a calmer space. Getting anxious about this whole thing would do him no good. He needed to deal with it serenely and objectively.

His muscles felt better, but his punctures still pulsed and ached. He did his best to ignore them.

He helped Quince gather a few more of the obieberries to supplement their food. He used the time to clear his head, and to think about his next course of action. Which at the moment was basically to wait and do nothing. He was out here in the wilderness with a relative stranger. She seemed nice enough, but he had no way of knowing if she was telling him the truth, or if she was really on his side. In the heat of the fight with the hoversport, he'd thrown himself into her arms, almost literally, but what did he really know about her motives?

On the other hand, there were no suitable alternatives to sticking with her, at least for the time being. He had no clue where he was or how to get back to civilization from here. He'd have to bide his time, and then take his chance if and when it came.

In the meantime, he could gather more information.

Jameson wondered where Xander was. If he had survived the last attack. If he was even then on his way to rejoin them.

He carried a shirt full of berries back to the campsite, handing them over to Quince. She had refilled their canteens from a nearby stream.

Quince put the berries into a small, airtight container, sealing the lid. "I found a few tubers too," she said without looking up. "They're really good cooked over an open flame."

"I'll bet." He rubbed his temple where his cirq had been. He felt strangely alone without it. "Quince, where does pith actually come from?"

"Somewhere in the Outland." She still wouldn't look at him.

Jameson knew when someone was lying to him. He tried again. "You promised Rogan you'd set him up with a regular supply. Come on, tell me. It's why I came here. You owe me at least that much."

This time she did look at him, as if she was assessing his request. Finally, she nodded. "It comes from the other side of the waygate."

"The waygate?" He searched his memory of all the materials he'd read about Oberon. He didn't remember anything about a "waygate." "Do you mean the Split?"

She shook her head "You wouldn't believe me if I told you. You'll have to wait and see. Let's go. We have a lot of ground to make up today."

He frowned. He didn't like being shut down like that, but if his experience to date with Quince was any guide, that was all he was going to get for now.

She mounted the cycle and gestured for him to do the same. He climbed up behind her and put his hands around her waist.

The bike lifted into the air, and they left the little copse of trees to continue on through the forest.

All the while, he thought about home, wishing he were there instead of this awful, godforsaken place.

CHAPTER 10
FLARE

MIDAFTERNOON BROUGHT Quince and Jameson down into the Theseus River valley. Quince knew the land here like the back of her hand. She'd spent a lot of time out here over the years, first on her own, and later keeping an eye on Xander and Alix, Xander's boyfriend. She'd even camped with them a couple times.

She still didn't know what had become of Alix. The man had gone out on another camping trip with some friends and had never come back.

For his part, Jameson had been strangely silent for most of the day.

Quince sighed. She supposed she would have been too, in his position—all alone on a strange, alien world, and forced to face his own heritage in such a physical, personal manner. It couldn't be easy on him.

She glided to a halt on an empty, rocky hillside, overlooking the river far below. The sun was dropping lower in the sky, still that worrying red color—a sign of what was coming.

The fog that shrouded the valley in the early morning had long since burned off, and the blue and silver trees and silver fields filled the valley from where they had stopped down to the river's edge. On the other side, the Red Sands stretched off into the distance. "Need a bathroom break?"

"Yes, please." Jameson's hands slid back from her waist and he dismounted, almost running to the privacy of a nearby tree.

Quince smirked. "Don't go too far."

"I don't plan to. I'm still hurting from the last time."

She got off the bike herself and stretched her arms. Riding for such a long time was starting to take its toll on her body. She wasn't as young as she used to be.

The sky was clear and greenish blue above, just like a normal day.

Jameson rejoined her, looking relieved. He squinted off into the distance. "So that's the river?"

"The Theseus, yes."

"What's the red beyond it?"

The far side of the river was bounded by rust-colored dirt for as far as they could see. "That's the Red Sands. It's the desert here on Oberon, and it stretches for hundreds of kilometers south, east, and west."

"Where are we going to meet Xander?"

"Upriver a bit." She pointed to the east, where the Pyramus range loomed in the distance, the edge of the world. "I plan to take us down to the Theseus and cross over to the far side. The journey will go a lot faster over the desert sands, following the river."

Jameson was silent for a moment, looking back and forth across the panorama revealed below. "It looks empty out here. Where are all the people?" He looked tense and tired.

"Along the coast, mostly. There are three other cities besides Oberon—Egeus and Philo in the south, and Hippolyta in the north. There have been a couple attempts to settle the Outland, but they've all failed." She didn't mention the reasons, which were varied, but mostly came back to the same thing, in her mind. Oberon didn't *want* them here.

She glanced back over at her traveling companion. "How are your wings?"

Jameson flexed them experimentally. "Really strange. I haven't gotten used to them. How they move. How they feel. They still itch."

"I can help with that." She pulled a bottle out of her pack and opened it, pressing it against her palm.

Jameson wrinkled his nose. "That smells nasty. What is it?"

"It's an oil extracted from wetreeds. I know it smells pretty bad, but when I was growing out my wings, it was the best thing." She dipped her fingers into the unguent and turned him around, rubbing it gently into the skin of the new wings.

"Oh my God, that feels good," Jameson said, moaning softly.

Quince smiled. "Told you so."

"You just happened to have that with you, huh?" He looked at her over his shoulder, his eyes narrowed.

"No, I knew you'd need it. Not that you deserve it." She snorted. "Running off like that into a nest of wereveren. You're probably hungry again, yes?" He seemed to be loosening up. The Outland had a way of doing that to you, in the same way that the city tensed people up like tightly wound springs.

"A little." His stomach grumbled. "Okay, a lot."

She finished covering his wings with the soothing ointment and put away the bottle. They were already twice as wide as they had been the day before.

Taking out her knife, she peeled one of the tubers she had unearthed earlier in the day. "These are really good cooked, but not too bad raw. Something like an apple, but not as sweet." She handed him the peeled root.

He took an experimental bite and nodded. "Yeah, not too bad. Kind of a hint of cinnamon." He finished the tuber in short order. "Can I have another?"

She peeled him another, and one for herself.

Jameson took it and frowned. "How long am I going to be hungry like this? I feel like there's a hole in my stomach."

"Until your wings are grown out. Probably another week or two, and even then, you'll probably need more calories than you used to." She handed him some obieberries, which he also downed quickly. "Your body is changing inside too. Your muscles are growing, and your bones are getting harder and lighter to accommodate flight."

He'd wished for wings, and it seemed like his wish had come true. Why did it feel like more of a curse? "It's weird. I can feel things changing. It's like having a phantom limb. Or, I guess, like a phantom limb that became real."

She nodded. "You'll get used to it soon enough." She remembered the wonder of her own first flight, on that other world so long ago. "You ready?"

"I guess so. I could probably eat another five of those." He looked hungrily at her saddlebags, but no more food was forthcoming.

"Come on." She climbed back on the bike. "I want to make it to the river before it gets dark."

He climbed on behind her, and they set off down the hillside, back into the forest.

XANDER RODE his cycle over yet another empty field. As they got closer to the river, they were passing more and more abandoned farms, many of them mostly overgrown by silver creeper vines or large patches of yellow hachmoss.

He glanced back at Morgan each time to see if there was a flicker of recognition for any of the farmhouses they passed, but the boy remained silent. He wished he could reach inside the kid's head and pull him back firmly into reality.

Xander glanced up at the sun above. It had taken on almost a reddish tone, something that alarmed him. He didn't know much about astronomy, but he did know that Oberon's sun was supposed to be yellow. The countryside around them seemed bathed in blood tones, and Xander wished for the hundredth time that he could connect to the grid to find out what was going on.

The boy didn't seem to notice.

The shuttle traffic passing overhead had increased. Every fifteen minutes or so, another one flew up from Oberon City spaceport in the distance, or came down from Titan Station. There was definitely something afoot.

He guessed they'd be at the Theseus in another hour. They were making good time now that the forest had receded. The river valley had many open meadows, the silver grasses tipped with blue blossoms, looking like nothing so much as a waving sea in the distance as the winds blew up from the Gildensea.

"You okay?" he called back to Morgan.

"Yes. Is hungry."

"You *are* hungry… oh never mind." The boy's body was still catching up from who knew how long a period of neglect, and he was constantly starving. Xander had spotted some obieberry bushes a ways back, and hoped to find them some river apples once they reached the Theseus. "We'll stop to eat once we—"

The sky exploded in light—radiating lines of color across the spectrum that raced through the atmosphere. His cycle's dashboard went wild, the display flashing and showing garbled images and lights before ultimately going dark. "Hold on!" he shouted, extending his wings to slow their forward motion and guide the bike to a halt. It dipped and bounced along the ground, skidding over the silver grasses of the meadow below. Pieces of vegetation, dirt, and rocks rained over them as the bike ground to a sudden halt.

Xander took a deep breath and opened his eyes. They were down, and the bike hadn't flipped. That was something. He dusted off his jacket and shook off his wings and looked back at his little charge. "You okay, Morgan?"

Morgan was silent, his eyes wide. He pointed up at the sky ahead of them.

Xander looked up and gasped. One of the shuttles was careening out of control in the distance, plummeting rapidly toward the ground. It must have lost power like the bike had when the… whatever it was had happened, but those Oberon-to-Titan Station shuttles were built to glide for a bit without power—they had to enter Oberon's atmosphere over the Split, after all. So whatever had happened must have caused some serious electrical damage.

He watched, helpless, as the shuttle plunged to the ground on the other side of the Theseus, crashing in the desert almost directly south of their current position and sending up a huge fireball.

He turned away, his eyes closed. *All those people.*

He dismounted, checking to see how Morgan was taking it. "Are you okay?"

The boy seemed to have lost interest in the shuttle. He was looking down at his hands as if they were new to him, flexing them open and closed. There was something wrong with him, Xander was sure of it.

"Morgan!"

The boy looked up at him, shrinking away from Xander's loud voice. Then he started to cry.

"Hey, I'm sorry." He was an ass. It was foolish to expect Morgan to act like a normal child. Something had clearly happened to him that had traumatized him deeply.

Xander scooped Morgan up and held him tightly. "It's okay. It's all going to be okay." He patted the boy on the back, feeling Morgan's cheek warm against his own. They stood together like that for a long time, and eventually Morgan's sobs became muffled and then finally stopped altogether.

Xander set him down gently in the tall grass. He pulled out an MRE—one of their last ones—and handed it to Morgan to eat. "I'm sorry," he said. "I shouldn't have shouted at you."

Morgan took the meal, his big serious eyes looking up at Xander.

"Eat that. It will make you feel better." Inside Xander cringed. *I'd make a terrible parent.*

He turned away, looking over the bike that was now covered in dirt and debris. "I have to check out the cycle and see how bad the damage is." *And try to figure out what the hell just happened.*

He looked up. The strange colors were still dancing in the sky, though they were less intense than they had been. They reminded him of the Northern Lights. He and Alix had seen them once on a trip to camp out in the Rim Forest, not far from the Northern Glacier.

Some kind of solar flare, then?

Whatever it was, it wasn't good. They were lucky to have come to ground without serious injury.

While Morgan ate his meal contentedly, Xander set about checking the condition of the bike.

•   •   •

Quince glided her hoverbike to a halt on a small rise directly overlooking the waters of the Theseus. They'd made good time—shortly after stopping on the hillside, they had broken out of the forest into the more open lowlands that bounded the river on its northern side.

Below them, the river curved in a wide loop. The rendezvous spot. "That's where we'll meet Xander," she told Jameson.

"If he makes it."

She glared at him and started down the hillside toward the river.

Another twenty minutes brought them down close to the shore. She searched for a good place to set up camp and settled on a spot above a small inlet that was shaded with tartanga trees, their broad, tripartite silver leaves shading the campsite nicely from the sun.

Jameson was looking up nervously at the trees above. "Are there… wereveren here?"

Quince laughed in spite of herself. "You're safe. They don't come down this close to the water—they're only in the forest in the higher elevations. We might see a swamp bear or two, but they won't bother you if you don't bother them." She tucked the cycle under the cover of the trees. Satisfied that it could not be easily seen from above, she dismounted.

She found a shaded spot with level ground.

Jameson followed.

"Can you set up the camp? We don't need the deterrent field this time."

He nodded. "Where are you going?"

"To see if I can find us a treat for dinner."

She waved and set off toward the Theseus. It was about a hundred meters away, an easy walk, and it felt good to be up on her feet again. She stretched her wings out behind her and her arms to her sides.

On her way down toward the water, she glanced up at the sun again. It had definitely turned a pale red. Jameson hadn't noticed, but he *was* still essentially an off-worlder. Well, he was and he wasn't, but he didn't know the way the sun was *supposed* to look here.

She guessed they had another week, at most. They should probably push on overnight, but Xander wasn't here yet, and she needed a rest after the last two nearly sleepless nights.

It would do no good if she crashed the cycle and got them both killed.

The river spread out across the valley here, filling in little inlets and eddies along the shore where big patches of wetreeds grew, their thick, green and silver-striped stems full of the soft pulp she'd used to make the gel that eased poor Jameson's itching. She might need to harvest a few more before they moved on.

As she approached the inlet, she smiled. She could also see the lily pads from here that heralded the fruit she was searching for.

She waded into the cool water and pulled up one of the plants, exposing the trailing roots. Nestled within the roots were three river apples, small red fruits about the size of her closed fist. She pulled the knife from her belt and cut them free, repeating the process a dozen more times. When she was done, she had a shirt-full of the sweet fruits.

She trudged out of the water and was climbing the hill toward the camp when the sky lit up in angry rainbow colors, undulating ribbons that were as beautiful as they were dangerous.

She looked up at the camp. Jameson had seen it too, and was staring up at the sky in awe.

A great roar half deafened her, and a shuttle spun past overhead, end over end, coming in from Oberon to the west trailing a long line of black smoke.

It continued on toward the east, dropping out of sight after a minute somewhere across the river.

The explosion when it hit sent up a cloud of debris and smoke and fire, close enough to shake the ground beneath her feet.

She covered her mouth with her hand, stifling a gasp. It was starting already.

She hurried up the hill to the camp to reassure poor Jameson—this was well outside the man's realm of experience. She was worried herself—she'd known what to expect on an intellectual level. This was real and immediate.

If her mission failed, a whole lot more people were going to die.

IN THE end, the damage to the cycle wasn't as severe as Xander had feared. The front bumper had taken a beating, but the vehicle was still functional. After about fifteen minutes, Xander finally got the cycle's systems to reboot, and he heaved a sigh of relief.

He left Morgan sitting by himself in the open field for a few minutes and tested out the bike, taking it for a quick spin. Everything was in working order.

He still hoped to reach the rendezvous point by the river before the day ended. The angry red sun was setting, so he scooped Morgan up and they started off again. This time, he decided to ride more slowly and closer to the ground, wary of a repeat performance, at least until the sun set. Once it started to get dark, however, he figured they'd be safe until morning.

They climbed back to their previous cruising altitude, about four meters, and made better progress toward the waters of the Theseus.

The twin moons rose above the horizon, one chasing the other up into the sky.

Xander found himself wondering about the last few moments of the people in that doomed shuttle as it fell to the ground, the terror they must have felt in their guts. He had known true fear in his life, but never like that. Never with the knowledge that there was absolutely no way out. Even having a bomb in his head hadn't been quite like that.

He wondered about Morgan. What had happened to the boy to make him so dead to the tragedy? Did he simply not understand what he'd seen? Or was he broken inside, somehow?

Xander hoped it was the former. Ignorance could be overcome, but a fundamental flaw in one's soul? He didn't know how to fix that.

As he approached the rendezvous point, he saw a small flickering light. A campfire? If they were lucky, it would be Quince and Jameson.

He set the bike down out of range of the firelight and motioned for Morgan to stay still and be quiet. The boy nodded.

Xander crept up toward the flickering light, and at last saw Jameson sitting there, looking miserable.

He stood and walked into the firelight.

Jameson looked up and broke into a smile.

Quince appeared on the other side of the circle with an armful of dry branches. When she saw him, she dropped her load, sticks clattering to the ground, and ran forward to throw her arms around him. "Damn, I'm glad to see you here!"

"Likewise." He stiffened under her embrace. It was strange to see Quince lose her composure.

She stepped back to look at him. "What's wrong? Are you hurt?" She looked him over, searching for some sign of injury.

"Nope, all in one piece."

Jameson gave him a hug too, surprising him. "Glad you're back," he said, holding on a couple seconds too long.

At that moment, Morgan stepped out of the shadows next to him and smiled up at Quince.

Quince stumbled back as if she had been struck. "Xander, Jameson, get back." She pushed Xander out of her way and pulled out her hunting knife.

"What the hell are you doing?" Xander asked, stepping back between her and Morgan.

"Move away, Xander," she warned. "We have to kill it before it causes any harm."

"He's a little boy, not an it," Xander said, puzzled.

She shook her head, keeping her gaze fixed on the waif. "That's not a child. It's a sneach. They're wood demons—they take the forms of children to fool you, then they stab you in the back in the middle of the night. Or worse."

Wood demon? What the hell had gotten into her? He exchanged a troubled look with Jameson.

Jameson put a hand on Quince's shoulder. "Quince, he's right. It's just a child."

She ignored him, staring at Morgan. "Look at its eyes. They glow."

Jameson and Xander turned to look at Morgan. The boy looked up at the three of them innocently, but his eyes didn't glimmer at all. Xander swept the boy up in his arms, glaring at Quince. "See?" he said. "He's just a normal kid. He's been with me all day. I found him alone at one of the abandoned homesteads. He hasn't tried to kill me. Look, I'm not dead. So put the knife away, Quince. Nobody's killing anyone today."

Quince still looked troubled, but she put the knife back in her belt reluctantly and turned away.

"Are we good?" Xander asked.

"I don't trust him," she said, glancing back at the boy. "But I won't hurt him. For now."

Xander stared at Quince's back, trying to read what was going on in that head of hers. He'd never seen her behave so irrationally. Morgan was a little boy. A strange one, to be sure, but who wouldn't be, after what he had gone through? Abandoned out in the middle of nowhere, left to fend for himself, and half-starved…. "Fair enough."

Xander brought his bike in, taking Morgan with him just in case. He parked it next to Quince's in the darkness under the trees, where it would likely go unnoticed by any casual inspection. Then they joined Jameson and Quince by the fire.

"Hey, what happened to you?" he asked Jameson. He'd just noticed the multiple bandages wrapped around the psych's extremities.

Jameson grimaced. "I didn't listen to Quince when she said I needed to watch out for wereveren. And this happened." He turned his back toward Xander.

"Holy hell!" Xander saw Jameson's wings for the first time in the flickering light.

Jameson chuckled ruefully. "Yeah. It's been quite a few days."

"So you're…?"

"Seems so. Our mutual friend Quince here has been keeping quite a few secrets."

"Sometimes secrets need to be kept," Quince said, still glaring at Morgan. "Let's eat something. Then we have a lot to talk about."

"We found some food on the way. The kid's been ravenous." He glanced at Quince nervously, afraid she'd try to go after Morgan again, but she seemed content to keep a stern eye on the boy, for now.

It was so strange. She'd never struck him as a superstitious or paranoid person before. At least, not when it wasn't warranted. He'd seen her more than hold her own in a fight, but against a *child*? He shook his head. "Here's what's left of our food supplies. We were hit by a river cat and lost most of what we had. I did find these…." He held up a yellow fruit he'd found on the way down to the river.

Quince nodded. "Citrones," she said approvingly. "Those are quite good, and nutritious to boot." She pulled out the food she and Jameson had brought, and they all settled cross-legged on the ground around the fire. She poured them some juice she'd made from obieberries.

They parceled out the remaining food among themselves and soon they were all munching contentedly on the rations. "I hope you have a plan to get us more to eat, Quince." Xander looked worriedly at the small pile of MREs, fruit, and vegetables.

"We can go a few days without, if needed," she said. "But I don't think we'll have to."

Xander sipped the juice. It was sweet and cool. "How did you outrun the hoversport?"

"Turns out Jameson here is a hell of a shot."

Xander grinned. "Who'd have guessed our little psych was a gunslinger?" He flashed Jameson a smile.

Jameson blushed. "Just lucky, I guess."

"It was his first kill." Quince took one of the tubers and brushed the dirt off it before taking a bite.

"Did you two see the shuttle that went down this afternoon?"

Quince nodded. "Tumbled past right overhead."

"Whatever caused it brought down my bike too." He glanced over at Morgan, who was finishing off one of Quince's MREs with relish. "Damn near cost us our lives." Quince didn't look surprised. "You've known about this all along, haven't you?"

Quince looked at him appraisingly and nodded. "I have," she said softly.

Xander wasn't surprised. "Do you want to tell us about it?"

Quince took her time answering, finishing the tuber she held in her hands. When she finally answered, she didn't tackle his question directly. "Before OberCorp, there was an earlier, first wave of human colonization on Oberon. You both know that, right?"

"The skythane." Jameson stared at Quince intently.

She nodded.

Xander glanced at Morgan, wondering what the boy made of all this. He was staring blankly into the fire, seemingly oblivious. The kid worried him sometimes.

"The first wavers were adept at genetic manipulation. Once they discovered Oberon's inherent limitations—the zones where no electronics worked—they adapted themselves to fly. It allowed them to move across the planet more easily," she continued. "All three of us are descendants of those first-wave colonists."

"I'm still not sure I believe it—this tale about coming from some magical other place. I know where I'm from. I'm not one of your... your first wavers...." Jameson trailed off. His wings were twitching with irritation. He glared at them and fell silent.

Xander found the whole thing adorable. Which was odd. The man was a psych, he was an off-worlder, and he was obviously in denial. There was no reason Xander should be attracted to him, and yet....

"Titania's not magical. Not in the sense you mean, anyhow." Quince stared at Jameson silently for a minute. She sipped her own juice, as if considering what tact to take.

"Titania?" Xander asked. He'd never heard of such a place. Not on Oberon.

"We'll come back to that later." Quince set down her cup and sat back, her hands on her knees. "You have a birthmark in the shape of a small cross on the inside of your left thigh," she said to Jameson.

"What, were you checking me out while I slept?" Jameson asked indignantly, but he sounded less certain than before.

"When you were eighteen standard, you decided to search for your real parents, because you were convinced you had been adopted."

"How could you know that?"

Quince smiled, looking for all the world like a wolf that had cornered her prey. "You told your psych advisor that sometimes at night, while you sleep, you dream of flying in a pink sky under a red sun."

Jameson sputtered, and then fell silent.

"She's got you there." Xander grinned. "But that still doesn't answer the question."

"Be patient. I'm getting to it." Quince stood, stretching, and turned away from the fire, her hands behind her back. "Something lived here before either wave, before humankind ever set foot on Oberon. No one knows who or what they were, but they weren't human."

"What, like aliens?" Xander asked, smirking.

Quince laughed. "Kind of, yes. Though technically, we're the aliens here."

Touché. Xander smiled.

"So the flare that brought down that shuttle wasn't an isolated incident?" Jameson asked.

"The one that crashed my cycle?" Xander was still indignant and worried about that.

She nodded. "Oberon's sun goes through a dangerous cycle. Every seven hundred and fifty years, give or take, it flares up and shoots a furnace-blast of radiation throughout the system. It's going to happen again soon."

The blood ran from his face. "How soon?"

Jameson looked stunned as well. Morgan was still in his own little world, eating a handful of obieberries.

Quince shook her head. "I don't know. Based on the signs... maybe a week?"

They were all silent. The murmur of the river was the only sound.

"How bad will it be?" Jameson asked at last, looking up at the starry sky as if he could see the sun there.

"For the planet? Bad enough, but the forests will recover in a couple hundred years. For mankind here? It would be an extinction-level event."

Xander thought of all the people in Oberon and the other cities along the coast. Of the corporate types and the Syndicate bosses and hustlers and whores, the worker bees and wing men. None of them aware of what was about to rain down on them from the hostile sky. "How do you know all of this?" he asked, staring at Quince intently.

"There's an old legend...."

"Are you serious?" Jameson looked incredulous. "We're on some kind of wild-goose chase because of an old *legend*?"

"It's a lot more than that. But yes, there's a legend. And I have reasons to believe it."

Xander could see she was still holding something back. Because she didn't want them to know it yet? Or because she knew they wouldn't accept it?

Jameson had a point, though. They seemed to be ending up on the same side of things more and more often.

"So why bring us out here? Nicer place to die?" He couldn't help letting the sarcasm slip into his voice. This whole thing was fucked-up.

"No," she said. "To try to prevent it."

It was Jameson's turn to laugh, a brittle, anguished sound. "What are we supposed to do? Stop the sun from shining? I'm a good psych, but even I can't talk heavenly bodies out of mass destruction."

"Basically, yes." Quince smiled grimly. "I brought you out here to save the world."

QUINCE SAT back to watch the firestorm her statement would set off.

Xander was the first to blow. "What the hell are you talking about?" His wings twitched with agitation. "I mean, that's *batshit crazy*, right? What can we do about a solar disaster?"

Jameson chimed in too. "I don't even know what the hell I'm doing here. I came here on a mission for the Guild." He shrugged. "Now I have these… these *wings*, have been nearly pecked to death by a bunch of red vampire birds, and I'm supposed to be responsible for saving the world too?"

Quince saw the way Xander looked at Jameson, nodding, and smiled. She put a hand on Jameson's knee. "This has been hard for you to accept, I know. The way I see it, we have a simple choice. We can stand and fight, or we can turn tail and run."

Jameson still looked unconvinced.

"Why did you become a psych?"

He stared at Quince, his eyes narrowing. "To help people. It's all I wanted to do since I was a boy."

Xander snorted, but Quince shushed him. "You have a chance to help more people here, right now, than you would have helped in a lifetime as a psych."

He stared up at the darkening sky. "Maybe…."

She smiled at his continued intransigence. She was so proud of the man he had become, even if he couldn't see it.

"Sleep on it. Day after tomorrow, we'll reach the House of the Sky, or what's left of it. Then I'll be able to show you the answers." She gestured to Jameson. "Time to change the dressings on your wounds."

THEY SETTLED in for the night.

Xander unpacked his sleep sack from his saddlebags and laid it by the fire. He tucked Morgan into it to get some sleep. He had a connection to the boy, a protectiveness, as if he were the child's father, especially in the face of Quince's unexplained hostility toward him.

Xander had watched Quince and Jameson together as she unwrapped the bandages from Jameson's arms and leg. He imagined touching Jameson's skin with such care, perhaps eliciting a little sigh of gratitude from the man.

He shook his head, dismissing the thought. They had enough to worry about without romantic flights of fancy.

Quince took the first watch. He debated staying up with her to talk, but he was dead tired.

Xander found a semicomfortable place to wedge himself next to Morgan's sleeping form. It felt good to take care of him. He silently wished the boy a good night, and then closed his eyes and drifted off to sleep.

Xander huddled in his bed, his covers drawn partially over his head, staring at the door, his eyes wide with fear.

His new stepfather, Rogan, had come into his room the night before and had put his smelly, hairy body over Xander's. The man had done… things to him. Things he didn't want to remember. Things he couldn't make himself forget.

He'd cried out and screamed and pleaded with the man to stop, but Rogan didn't listen. He just cupped a hand over Xander's mouth and kept doing those things.

Xander was a slight boy at eleven years of age, and he had no way to fight back. His parents were gone—shot by one of the Syndicate men. Rogan had taken him in, promising to take care of him, to feed him, to be his new daddy. He had seemed so nice, and Xander had been all alone on the streets, with nowhere else to go.

Now he wished he'd just died. At least he'd be with his parents again.

He shivered, thinking again of what Rogan had done to him, and watched the door in fear that it was about to happen again.

Someone touched his shoulder.

Xander's eyes opened. He was covered in a cold sweat. He hadn't had those kinds of dreams in years, and he thought he'd put it all out of his mind.

And yet, here they were again. It was because of Morgan, he was sure of that. He felt a strange sense of responsibility to the boy, a need to make sure he didn't fall prey to the same misfortunes Xander had at his age.

He looked up at Quince. "My turn?" he whispered.

She nodded. Poor thing looked exhausted. She lay down on the ground on her side near the fire, and he took up the watch.

Somewhere around midnight, he closed his eyes… and woke with a start. He shouldn't have let himself nod off like that. He looked around the campsite, his gaze settling on Morgan's sleep sack.

The boy was gone.

He jumped to his feet in alarm, looking back and forth across the moonlit riverfront. The river glistened in Lysander's gold glow. Hermia had already set for the night.

A small form stood silhouetted there, looking out across the water.

Quince and Jameson were still fast asleep.

Xander jumped up and ran down the hill to Morgan's side to make sure the boy was okay.

Morgan turned to face him, and Xander could see tears on his cheeks in the moonlight.

He scooped the boy up, secretly glad to see him finally reacting to the shuttle crash. "It's okay," he whispered, hugging Morgan tight. "It was fast. I'm sure they didn't feel anything."

"Sorry," Morgan replied softly. "Sorry that man did *that* to you."

Xander stiffened under the boy's embrace. Was he talking about Rogan?

How could he have known?

He hardly noticed the boy was speaking almost perfect English.

CHAPTER 11
ALONG THE THESEUS

QUINCE EASED the bike up into the air, leaving their campsite behind. It was still dark out; the sun had not yet risen over the horizon, and the air was chilly. The last days of summer had passed them by.

Behind her, Xander and the sneach, if that's what it was, followed on Xander's bike. She wasn't as sure now about the gleam she thought she had seen in the little boy's eyes the night before. He acted like a lost human boy, and he certainly had done them no harm.

The skythane told tales of the little tricksters, imps that once appeared in the forests of Oberon. Little creatures that seemed human enough, until they robbed you blind or slit your throat in the middle of the night.

She didn't trust him. It. Morgan.

He was Xander's problem for the moment, though.

She'd managed to get in a few hours of uninterrupted sleep the night before, but she had gotten everyone up early so they could reach the rendezvous site by the afternoon of the next day. They were running out of time.

They had made a short evening of it, eating the water apples and some more of the tubers and MREs they had left. Jameson had eaten the lion's share of them, his new wings demanding a ton of calories to continue their rapid growth. She gauged that they were now about half their ultimate size, and he seemed both pleased and embarrassed about that.

She had started to change the dressings on his wereveren wounds, cleaning them with soapy water, but then Xander had asked to take over the task, surprising her. She watched as he carefully unwrapped one of the bandages, and then used soap and water to rinse it off. His hands lingered just a little longer than necessary.

Jameson's wounds were already better, the skin around them looking pale pink and healthy.

Xander caught her staring at him and scowled, hurrying to wrap the wound back up.

She laughed quietly. The dynamic was starting to shift between the two of them.

She sat down next to them and addressed Jameson. "Are you ready?" she asked, thinking about their planned route along the river.

"Yes. I'm still tired, but as ready as I'm likely to get," Jameson said.

Xander looked tired too, but he nodded. "Now or never."

"Then let's go." Quince urged the cycle forward.

She had initially planned to cross the river to take advantage of the flat, open territory on the far side. The desert would have been far easier to navigate than the forested banks of the Theseus.

But with the downed shuttle somewhere in their path, she was afraid they might draw the wrong kind of attention. There were probably search-and-rescue and investigative teams over there. Moving out into the open risked exposure. So the riverside it was.

The Theseus would lead them up to where it met the Demetrius, which flowed down from the southeast end of the Pyramus Mountains. The confluence of rivers was where they would find the waygate.

It was time for the two princes to come into their own.

"So what *was* that yesterday, exactly?" Jameson asked, breaking her out of her reverie.

"What?"

"The lights in the sky. The shuttle crash."

Quince cocked her head, trying to decide how much to tell him. She had been reluctant to talk about it the night before. "It was a solar flare," she said at last. She steered the bike along the shoreline, looking ahead to judge the best course through the stands of tartanga trees that crowded along the water's edge.

"I've never heard of a solar flare causing that kind of severe and immediate damage," he said. "Not unless it was huge."

"It *was* huge. I've never seen anything like it, and I've lived here for decades. That was just the effect of the solar radiation thrown off by the flare."

She felt him shiver. He went silent, for which she was thankful.

The sky was starting to lighten. She turned inland to detour around the dim form of a rock outcropping along the river, easing past a stand of feather trees, their plumes silhouetted against the rosy sky. Xander followed her, single-file.

The cycles could run over water, but she didn't want to chance a repeat of yesterday's flare—it could drop them into the depths of the river if it happened at an inopportune time, and while they might well survive the dunking, they would lose their supplies and their transportation.

"Do those kinds of things happen often here?" Jameson asked.

"No, but it's going to get worse." She wished they could have had this conversation face-to-face, but time was against them. "There's a reason you're here, Jameson."

"You keep saying that. When are you going to tell me more about how I'm supposed to save the world?" His grip around her waist tightened. "I wish I'd never come."

"Yes, I know." Quince wasn't a sugarcoat-it kind of person. "I'm sorry about that. Truly I am. It sounds like you had a perfectly nice life back on Beta Tau, and I dragged you away from it to help save this world."

"Well, Tander's World, where I was stationed last, wasn't the nicest place...."

Quince snorted. "Listen, I get that you're angry. I understand that you don't know what's going on, and that it's freaking you out. For the moment, the three of us are stuck with each other. Agreed?"

"The four of us."

"What?"

"You, me, Xander, and his pet project back there. The… sneak?"

"Sneach." She sighed. She'd managed to forget the little monster for a moment. "All right, the four of us. We have to stick together."

"I don't see anywhere for me to go at the moment. You didn't leave me with a lot of options."

"I'll make you a deal. After we get to the House of the Sky, I'll tell you everything. What's going on. Where you came from. What I need you to do. If you don't want to go on, I'll take you back to the spaceport myself and put you on a shuttle up to Titan Station."

Jameson laughed, harshly. "Hopefully not like that one yesterday."

Quince shook her head. *Those poor people.* "Hopefully not. So do we have a deal?"

He was quiet again.

Weighing his options. Like he has any. Quince glanced up at the sky. It was clear now, but there were cirrus clouds on the horizon. Likely rain tomorrow, then. The solar instability had been shaking up weather patterns for weeks, and she worried that the next storm might be even bigger than the last.

"Deal," Jameson said after a moment. "My girlfriend back home has probably noticed by now that I'm gone. I wouldn't want her to worry."

Oh honey, Quince thought. Aloud, she said, "I'm sure she's already missing you."

XANDER THREADED the space between a couple tartanga trees so close his elbows almost brushed the silver trunks. It was slow going along the river's edge, but Quince had said that she wanted to keep them out of sight from pursuit for as long as possible. He remembered how she used to come visit him before his parents had died, "Auntie Quince" would take him to the little zoo in one of the arcos, or out to walk along the beach of the Gildensea on a warm summer afternoon.

He didn't think they were blood related, despite the fact that he used to call her his aunt. But there was a bond there, forged when he was very young, and strengthened after Alix had saved him from the Syndicate.

His eyes kept straying to Jameson. It was unsettling, the way the off-worlder drew his gaze. The man held on to Quince's waist as she threaded her way through the trees. Xander wished those arms were around his waist instead.

He shook his head to clear it.

Quince. He was thinking about Quince. She was being cagey about where she was taking them. She'd mentioned the House of the Sky, whatever that was, and she'd talked about a "waygate" once or twice, but he had no idea what she meant by it.

He tried to remember when he had first met Quince. It seemed like she had always been there. Or at least since he'd been little.

He still remembered that dark day when his foster parents had been gunned down on the streets, his mother's hand falling away from his as her lithe, beautiful form had crashed down to the pavement in a crumpled, broken heap. *No, Mommy, no!*

Then the man who had shot them had taken him away.

He had prayed for Auntie Quince to come, that night and for many afterward, as his life had spiraled down into a new kind of hell. He'd finally given up hope.

Did he still trust her?

And how did Jameson fit into her grand plans? Xander was starting to feel some sympathy for the psych. He hadn't come out here through any choice of his own, and somehow he was skythane like Quince and himself. *That* had been unexpected. Quince had known all along that Jameson was skythane—she'd confessed to treating the man with ethilium to start his transition.

Jameson was, truth be told, pretty good-looking too, skythane or no. The man was whip-smart—maybe too smart for his own good. But Xander had always been attracted to brainy guys.

Jameson glanced back at him, and he turned away quickly.

The land ahead of them opened up again, and he caught up to Quince. "Remember last time we were out here? You, me, and Alix?"

"Caught a couple swamp bears, if I remember right." Quince grinned.

"How are you handling this?" Xander asked Jameson.

He flashed Xander a wan smile. "Right now I'm just hanging on. Literally." Jameson's golden wings flapped behind him in the wind.

They were going to be beautiful when they reached their full length. "Me too," he said, trying to keep his voice professional.

That earned him a real smile.

The forest was encroaching on their pathway again, and Xander eased back behind Quince reluctantly. At least it gave him a good view.

THEY STOPPED for the night not far from a stream that fed into the Theseus from the north. Jameson dismounted from Quince's bike, his muscles sore from the long day's ride. He was beginning to see the advantages of flying.

He'd been aware of Xander's eyes on him all day. The man seemed fascinated with him now. It was surprising, considering the disdain with which Xander had treated him when they'd first met.

He wasn't sure which was worse.

He wondered what Jessa would make of him now. His new workman clothes were grimy from travel, and torn where Quince had modified them for his new wings. Those wings!

Every child wanted to fly. He should have been ecstatic at the prospect. Instead, Jameson's new wings were taking him further and further from himself, or at least who he had always known himself to be. He wasn't an offworlder. He was skythane. Connected to this world by blood—his own and that of those who had come before him and had spilled it on his behalf.

He wasn't sure how he felt about that. Who was he, really? Jameson the Psych? Jameson the off-worlder? Or Jameson, the man who could fly?

"Want to refill the canteens?" Quince asked, holding them out to him. "And search out some croyol for a fire? I saw some on the way here."

"Sure." The forest here was pleasant enough, a riparian lowland shaded by tall trees, a cool breeze blowing down along the watercourse.

"I'll help." Xander took two of the canteens. "Quince, will you watch Morgan, and promise not to kill him?"

"Yes." The response sounded unusually curt, even for her. "If I must."

"Come on." Xander led the way.

Jameson felt like a schoolkid off to do something naughty. There was something in Xander's attitude, his absolute surety about himself, that was frighteningly attractive.

As they walked side by side, he felt Xander looking at him again. "What?" Jameson refused to glance at the man.

"Can't a guy look?"

Jameson shook his head. "I'm not like that."

"I didn't say you were." Xander laughed, a light, happy sound Jameson hadn't heard him make before. It made him seem more human. "You've had a lot thrown at you, all at once. I just wanted to see how you were doing."

They reached the stream, the cold water trickling through the forest over a bed of rounded pebbles. Jameson found a deep pocket where he could dip a canteen in and filled the first one, trying to keep out of the mud at the water's edge as much as possible. "I don't see how I have much of a choice." It came out sounding more bitter than he'd intended.

Xander knelt next to him. Jameson was acutely aware of his masculine scent. "We all have choices. Not always good ones, but choices nonetheless."

Jameson could feel the heat from Xander's arm next to his, radiating like a furnace. He imagined those arms around him, being lifted into the air by those black wings.

Without thinking, he set down the canteen and reached over to kiss Xander. It lasted a brief, intense moment, and then he pulled away, stumbling backward and falling into the mud. "I shouldn't have done that." His face flushed hot. "I'm sorry. Forget it happened."

He grabbed the half-filled canteen and ran back to the campsite without looking back.

· · ·

Xander lay by the campfire, staring at Jameson, fast asleep in his sleep sack across the other side of the firelight.

His mouth still burned where the man had kissed him. He'd had a steadily growing interest in the young psych over the last several days, but that kiss had ignited it like a forest fire, and now all he could do was think about it. About him.

Luckily it was his turn to keep watch. He doubted he could have managed a wink of sleep in the fevered state he was in.

Xander decided he needed to do something about that, or he'd be a mess all the next day. He stood quietly, intending to retreat into the forest to do his business. He took two steps—and came face-to-face with a man in black.

"We're being attacked!" he shouted. The man was as surprised as he was, and Xander elbowed him and dropped to the ground to reach for one of his pulse pistols. Thank the gods he'd gotten them both fully charged. He swung the gun up and took out the first of their attackers, the man in enforcer black who had slipped from the trees as soon as he'd called out. The man had his own pistol out, but Xander took him down first, sending the man's pulse wide. There was a crack, and a large branch fell off a tartanga tree a few feet away.

Quince was up on her feet, and a knife flew from her hands with deadly accuracy into the throat of another attacker.

Xander watched as she swept Jameson up in her arms, depositing him on a tree branch high above.

Then she came down like an avenging angel on top of another man, knocking him backward into a tree with a sickening crunch.

"Quince," Xander said as she turned toward another attacker.

"A little busy at the moment—"

"Quince!"

She turned to see where he was pointing.

Morgan was standing by the fire, his little face twisted in anger. He was *glowing*.

"Get down!" she yelled, and dove for the forest floor.

Xander followed her example as five more men ran into the firelight.

Morgan put his hands in the air and clasped them, and the glow around him brightened.

Xander turned away, covering his eyes.

There was a sound like a thunderclap, and the air whipped around him as if in a hurricane, hot and wet. He squeezed his eyes shut, willing the terrible heat to go away.

All at once, everything was silent.

He opened his eyes and sat up, checking himself over. He seemed to still be in one piece.

The enforcers weren't so lucky.

They were all burnt beyond recognition, as if they'd been in the path of a laser blast. Or a firestorm.

Morgan lay collapsed by the fire.

"Holy shit," Jameson called from above. "What the hell was that?"

Quince flew up to get him, while Xander ran to check on the boy who had likely just saved them all. He picked Morgan up in his arms, cradling him gently.

Quince and Jameson came up behind him, looking down on Morgan.

"Is he alive?" Jameson asked.

Xander nodded. "He's still breathing. Shallowly, but he's alive."

Quince looked grim. "Still think he's a normal boy?"

"Maybe not. Maybe he is a sneach." He smiled grimly. "But if so, he's apparently our sneach."

Quince found the second tracker on Xander's bike. "I should have checked for it when you found us last night." She shook her head. "I could have gotten us all captured. Or killed." After all this trouble, their little world-saving quest had almost ended in a heartbeat because of her.

Xander put a hand on her shoulder. "Don't beat yourself up over it. I didn't think about it either. We've all been through a hell of a lot."

Morgan was resting on one of the sleep sacks.

"So what do we do with him?" Quince asked. "He's dangerous."

Xander looked at her in disbelief. "He just saved your life, and mine. He comes with us."

"What if he does that to us?"

"He comes, or I don't." He crossed his arms and stared her down.

Quince didn't want to argue. He was right, dammit. The boy had saved them all, but trust wasn't something that came easily to her, at least not anymore. "All right. We need to move. They might send reinforcements when these ones don't report back. Do you think he can travel?"

Xander nodded. "He seems better now. I can rig up a harness to carry him on my back."

"I can help," Jameson said softly. "I was a Wood Scout once."

Xander smiled. "You don't seem very woods-wise to me."

"It was a long time ago, and the woods on Beta Tau were less… deathy. But still, I'm good with knots."

"Fair enough," Quince said. "I'll pack things up while you get the boy settled."

In fifteen minutes, they were on their way again in the darkness.

Quince despaired of ever being able to get a full night's sleep again.

CHAPTER 12
STORM

THEY CRUISED THROUGH THE DARKNESS, broken only by the light of one of Oberon's two moons. Xander could feel Morgan's warmth against his back in the makeshift harness they'd rigged up. His wings settled over the boy—or whatever he was.

Xander felt no malice in Morgan's demeanor, but he was clearly something more than just human. Nevertheless, Xander still felt the need to protect him. No one had been around to protect Xander when he had been a child. He didn't hold that against Quince—done was done—but he wouldn't allow the same thing to happen to someone else. To Morgan.

He stayed close to Quince and Jameson, not wanting to lose them in the shadowed blackness. Shapes loomed up above him as they progressed, trees and boulders sometimes three times taller than the forest canopy. They spoke of a history of violence and destruction on this mostly peaceful world.

Every now and then, Xander would look over his shoulder for pursuit. It was stupid, because anyone coming after them would be well hidden by the darkness, and would take great care after the loss of three hoversports' worth of enforcers.

Still, he looked.

They had considered finding and taking the hidden hoversport, but it would be too easy for OberCorp to track them.

Slowly the sky turned from black to gray, the stars winking out one by one. The stone monoliths grew more numerous, and he could see that some of them were covered by what seemed to be geometric carvings.

Maybe evidence of Quince's "alien race"? They looked to be at least several millennia old.

Citrone vines climbed up the sides, covered in the bulging yellow fruits. They stopped to harvest a few before continuing eastward.

Jameson glanced back at him over his shoulder from time to time, with a look on his face that might have been fear. Or need. Or maybe longing. It was hard to tell in the darkness. That kiss….

They would have to explore it later, together, what it all meant.

Although daylight finally came, it wasn't much brighter than the early morning. Overnight, a heavy ceiling of gray clouds had encroached upon the Theseus river valley, promising rain. If it was anything like the storm that had blown through a few days before, they'd want to find shelter before the worst of it hit.

Thunder sounded ominously overhead, and lightning lit up a sky full of heavy clouds.

He hoped Quince had a plan, because things had just gone from bad to seriously weird, and he wasn't equipped to deal with it.

THE GATES of hell had opened above them, pelting them with hard rain.

Jameson held tightly to Quince's waist, trying to unsee what he had just witnessed back at the camp.

He was a psych. It was his job to deal with individuals, couples, and triads when they were in emotional free-fall, often at one of the darkest points in their lives. He had seen death, or at least its aftermath, and he had seen the many effects it had on people.

He had helped others through it too; often a long, painstaking process of honoring the dead, of remembering them and learning to let them go. He had helped those who had lost their spouses, and parents who had lost their children. He had even counseled miners on Tander's World who had lost a workmate or close friend in an unexpected incident in one of the mines.

None of that had prepared him for what he'd just seen. Death in its raw, primal form, delivered at the hands of other human beings. And by whatever Morgan was. By people he knew and was starting to trust. It was brutal, and primal.

He closed his eyes, his stomach roiling.

He couldn't do it. There was no way to un-see it—Quince's knife entering a man's throat, the blood spurting out, red and violent. Xander throwing another man bodily against a tree trunk, his bones crunching audibly. Quince's knife through another man's throat. And Morgan....

Intellectually, he knew these men bore him and his companions ill will, that they were here to capture or kill him. Xander and Quince had done the right thing, but his empathetic side, the part of him that had always wanted to help everyone else, that had been honed to a fine edge by his training, cut him the most.

He couldn't help but think of those poor men and women's families. Did they have partners at home? Children?

In the background, before the violence… the kiss.

Why had he done it? He hadn't meant to kiss Xander. It had just happened. He'd wracked his brain for a suitable explanation from his psych studies. Maybe he was falling in love with his captor. It happened sometimes, in extreme situations like kidnapping or hostage taking.

Or maybe it was the events themselves that were to blame. Shared near-death experiences and all that. He'd been reaching out for simple human contact.

He shoved it all aside. At the moment, they had bigger worries.

The powerful storm was all around them now, lashing them with pouring rain that was blowing sideways in the heavy winds. Cold rain that ran down his face and his back, soaking his clothes and chilling him to the bone.

Quince continued on doggedly, following a path apparently only she could see. The bike's headlight was shot through with rain falling in twisting, crazy, contradictory patterns.

Vast forks of lightning lit up the sky on a regular basis, and one of them had split open a tree trunk not thirty yards off to their left just minutes before.

"We have to stop!" he yelled in Quince's ear over the thunder and whipping rain. "You're going to get us killed!"

She shook her head. "We're almost there. There's no safe place for us to stop, anyway."

He glanced back. Xander's bike was following them, being rocked back and forth by the storm.

A strong gust of wind buffeted the cycle, almost throwing them into one of the big rock towers. Quince jerked them away just in time. "Let me be," Quince shouted. "I can't steer and talk."

Jameson subsided into his own thoughts, hoping this whole thing would soon be over. He wondered what Xander was thinking, with the boy—well, it looked like a boy—strapped to his back. He'd seen what Morgan was capable of, and hoped he was truly on their side.

He wondered, too, when he had started thinking of the three of them as a team.

Quince made a hard right turn, and they emerged over the Theseus. Or at least he assumed it was the Theseus. The river was swollen, massive, overrunning its banks. The churning water rushed toward the sea, carrying branches and sometimes entire trees along with it, sloshing over the shore as if its course had been upset by the footsteps of a giant.

If they fell into that maelstrom of water, they were dead.

Quince poured on the speed, and they raced across the waters. Xander followed them, and the two bikes fought their way through the wind and rain.

Out in the open, the force of the gale threw huge raindrops against his face like pebbles. The lightning had gone from intermittent to constant, lighting up the river and the far banks in a silver light that reduced all color to black-and-white.

At one point, he glanced down to see some kind of gray, furry animal, big as a man, clinging to a tree trunk. Its eyes glinted as it looked up at them forlornly. He wondered if it was a swamp bear.

The crossing seemed to last an eternity. The thunder grew louder, and he started to wonder if he would go deaf from the noise.

Then they were above solid ground once more. He slowly stopped shaking.

Quince urged the bike up the hillside, away from the raging floodwaters and into a thicket of blueoak trees. The rain slacked off here, blocked by the massive trunks, and after a bit the ground leveled out.

Soon the rain seemed to stop altogether, and the thunder receded, becoming a distant growling. He looked up, and to his amazement, there was green sky and sunshine. The storm was gone.

That was when he first noticed the building. It was a tall, dark rock structure, stark against the bright sky. It was made from hand-cut stone, as far as he could tell. It looked like a small castle. A very old castle.

One of the walls had collapsed, and the stone was worn down by time and weather. It was strangely familiar, though he couldn't imagine he had ever been here before. "What is this place?" he said wonderingly.

"Its real name is lost to time, but we call it the House of the Sky. This is where you'll find the answers to some of the questions you asked me."

THE HOUSE of the Sky looked ancient to Xander. It had been built mostly of some black stone, maybe volcanic in origin, and seemed to have been slowly collapsing to the ground over a period of centuries. Creeper vines snaked through the ruins, and there were trees growing inside the courtyard.

The road they followed had been paved at one time, but that too was crumbling away, split by silver moss and the roots of small bushes and trees. It was strange that he'd never heard of this place before. Archaeologists would have had a field day with it.

Stranger still, the storm that had been bearing down out of the mountains seemed to have all but dissipated. When he looked up, there was only a clear green afternoon sky, with streaks of white cirrus clouds high above in the upper atmosphere.

Morgan had awoken at some point during the storm. He seemed entirely unimpressed by the whole thing. Xander chuckled softly. That was *so Morgan*.

Xander set the bike down next to Quince and the outer walls of the House of the Sky. It was maybe fifty meters wide, but only three or four stories tall. It had a center "keep" and an outer wall that was basically square, with rounded turrets at each corner, except in one place where the wall had collapsed outward, leaving a scattering of stones.

There was a wide entrance on this side of the wall, complete with rusted hinges on either side. He supposed there must have been a large door or gateway here at one time.

"This place is amazing," he said to Quince. He undid the harness and lowered Morgan to the ground.

"It's older than even the skythane culture here on Oberon." She looked around at the ruins.

"The House of the Sky," Jameson said softly, looking up as if imagining the night sky.

Quince nodded. "It's hidden from view from above. Something obscures it, making it hard to find unless you know where it is."

Jameson frowned. "Like a cloaking device?"

Quince shrugged.

"Should we go up and take a look from above?" Xander offered.

"Um… sure… up in the castle? Is it safe?"

"Like this." He picked Jameson up in his arms and beat his powerful wings, lifting them into the sky.

Jameson gasped.

It was thrilling to feel Jameson in his arms, to share the skies with him. Plus, he had to admit he enjoyed startling the other man a bit, jolting him out of his safe little world. Xander's wings pulled the two of them upward with powerful strokes. It felt so good. He hadn't flown in days.

Sometimes Jameson's guard slipped, and Xander got a look at the man underneath. He was smart and surprisingly warm when he wasn't clinging to his psych persona.

Looking at the fear and wonder in the man's face, Xander knew this was one of those times.

When he was high enough, he found an updraft and rode it up into the sky in lazy circles, surveying the area below.

The House of the Sky stood in the midst of a dense stretch of forest, an area around it cleared of all but small brush and grass. There were indications of other structures here and there, and maybe an outer wall that was missing in many places.

"Xander, look."

He followed Jameson's gaze.

The storm was still there. The walls of it veered around the House of the Sky as if they had hit an invisible barrier. It was like being in the eye of a hurricane.

From here, they could see the confluence of the two rivers under the walls of the storm. The Theseus flowed down from the Pyramus Mountains in the northeast, collecting the waters of about a quarter of the lowlands basin.

The Demetrius was a smaller tributary flowing up from the southeast, bringing into the Theseus water from the southern part of the Pyramus chain, which stretched from pole to pole along the eastern edge of the world. Beyond that, the world was hidden.

He shared a glance with Jameson and shrugged, giving him an *I have no idea what the hell it means* look.

They went a little higher, and the ruins shimmered and vanished as if they had been just a mirage, replaced by thick forest.

"Quince was right," Xander said, surprised. Jameson was shaking in his arms. "You okay?"

"Not really. Down, please?"

He hadn't meant to scare Jameson. Not really. "Your wish," he said, and brought them gently back toward the ground. The castle reappeared below them, and in a moment they were back on solid earth.

Jameson took a little longer than Xander thought was necessary to disengage himself.

Quince was unloading their gear. "We'll camp here and rest before going on tomorrow, when the waygate opens. We should be safe here."

Xander nodded. He looked around—if the rain stayed away, it would make a decent enough campsite. "Where's Morgan?"

Quince looked at him blankly. "He was right here...."

There was no answer.

"Dammit," he swore. Where had the boy gone to this time?

CHAPTER 13
WAYGATE

"MORGAN'S MISSING." Xander looked around for any sign of where the boy had gone. A neat set of bare footprints led into the House of the Sky. How had the boy managed that? Xander had been staring at the place practically the entire time.

"He won't have gone far," Quince said.

Xander nodded and pulled out a glow sphere, following the boy's footsteps into the maw of the House of the Sky.

They searched the courtyard first. It was roughly fifty meters wide and half that deep. It was paved with stone, but the surface had been covered over the centuries with muck and dirt. A few of the paving stones showed through here and there, the same black rock as the walls.

Three blueoaks had grown up through cracks in the pavement and now dominated the space. Hanging from them were some of the citrone vines, weighed down with their bright yellow fruit.

"Morgan, where are you?" he called, holding up the glow sphere to light up the darker recesses of the courtyard. "This isn't funny." He shared a worried glance with Quince.

"Maybe… maybe it's better if he's gone?" she suggested.

He glared at her, and she turned away.

"Morgan!"

There was no response other than the whistling of the wind.

There was nothing else to do but to search the House of the Sky itself.

He climbed over a fallen tree, pulling back the vines and branches that almost covered the doorway. He shone the glow sphere inside. It was hard to make out much detail through the small opening, but the hall looked empty. "He must have gone inside. Is it dangerous?"

"Only because it's so old," Quince said.

Xander pushed his way through the entangling vegetation, getting some leaves and twigs stuck in his hair for the trouble. He brushed them off, starting to get annoyed. "Morgan, are you in here?"

He was in a large open space. He rubbed the glow sphere to brighten it, and threw it up in the air. It floated up to about three meters above his head and stopped, lighting up the entire room.

It must have been a grand hall at one time. The floor beneath his feet was tiled in a checkered black-and-white, placed in a spiral pattern that started on the edges and ended at the center of the room. A spiral staircase hugged the edge of the room, doing a half circle and ending somewhere up above.

Windows let in the diminishing daylight from outside.

Quince gasped behind him. "The waygate is open."

"Waygate?" Xander's eyes adjusted slowly to the dim light. He called the glow sphere down and closed his hand around it. It went out, extinguishing the light. He shoved it into his pocket.

She pointed. "We can open them once a day, at noon, when the sun is directly overhead. It shouldn't be open now…."

Xander looked across the room. Set into the back wall of the grand chamber was a stone archway. He'd thought it was just a doorway, but there was something strange about it. It glowed with a pink light, and the space under the arch seemed to *shimmer*.

"There's no time to explain. We have to go back and get our things. This wasn't supposed to happen, but we have to turn this to our advantage."

"I'm not leaving Morgan behind."

She looked ready to argue, but instead she nodded. "Wait here. Jameson and I can go back to gather our belongings. Just don't go through the gate until I get back."

She hustled Jameson out with her before he could ask what she meant. What gate? The only gate he'd seen was the one they had come through into the courtyard.

The light leaking in through the windows seemed to be slowly getting brighter.

Xander took one more look around the room. There was nowhere down here for Morgan to hide.

If something had happened to the boy, he'd never forgive himself.

Xander ran up the stone staircase, marveling at the beauty of its construction. The stones seemed to have been fitted together without mortar, and the black-and-white motif continued up the staircase, the colors tinged with pink from the light outside.

The staircase was maybe two meters wide, and the steps were taller than the stairs he was used to back in Oberon City. Curious.

He reached the landing, and a pair of old doors confronted him, standing slightly ajar. He squeezed through the doorway. He found himself in a circular room, right above the center of the hall three stories below. There was another door, this one metal, old and rusted, also ajar.

Xander peered through it. It led out on a wide terrace overlooking the clearing where the House of the Sky sat, the walls of storm in the distance.

It was starting to get dark outside. He looked down. Quince and Jameson were collecting their supplies.

Xander hurried back downstairs. There was one more place to check.

He stood before the shimmering patch on the wall for a moment, debating whether to cross through it or wait for Quince and Jameson.

Morgan might be in trouble over there. Wherever *there* was. That decided him.

He stepped through and found Morgan on the other side, standing there and looking up.

Xander grabbed the boy and twirled him around in his arms. "I was so worried about you, little man." Then he looked up too.

He was standing in a mirror of the room on the other side of the portal, but this one looked almost new. Pink light streamed in through the windows outside, not the normal yellow-green of Oberon's skies.

Far above, a glass ceiling showed him a pink daytime sky in all its glory, fleecy clouds slipping by, and a giant silver moon.

He wasn't on Oberon anymore.

JAMESON FOLLOWED Quince back into the House of the Sky, carrying one of the saddlebags. The wide hall was empty, but it must have been impressive in its day. The gloom outside gave it a decadent majesty where beams of light from the setting sun struck metal sconces that might once have held torches embedded into the walls. The details were hard to see in silhouette. He looked up—the remnants of a grand candelabra hung there at an awkward angle, rusted almost into oblivion.

Xander was nowhere to be seen.

"Xander?" Quince called. Her voice echoed in the huge space. No one answered. "Dammit, he must have gone on ahead of us. I told him to wait."

Jameson was trying to ignore his growing attraction to the Oberon man.

There was something about his arrogance, his penchant for taking control.

It was likely just a byproduct of the stressful situations they had gone through, his psych side reassured him once again. Being kept under intense pressure with someone else for long periods of time often fostered feelings of connection and intimacy.

His training was silent on the fact that he felt no physical attraction whatsoever to Quince.

"Looking for me?" Xander appeared through an archway at the back of the room, carrying Morgan in his arms. A strange pink light shone through it behind him.

"What the hell is wrong with you?" Quince shook her head. "What if the waygate had closed while you were over there?"

"I was worried about Morgan. We would have figured it out."

She grunted. "Well, you both are safe, at least." She reached into her pocket and pulled out two chains. The first one she held out was a silver chain with a thick argent pendant; it was in the shape of a quarter moon. "I was planning on sharing this with you tonight, but events have outrun me. Through that doorway is another world, as you've probably already guessed. The other half of Oberon. We call it Titania."

Xander nodded. "It's certainly not Oberon."

Jameson wondered what Xander had seen through that doorway.

"Xander, it's time that you knew your birthright. Your true name is Davyn Sléite, and you're a Prince of the House of Gaelan—House of the Moon," she said to Xander. "This is your sigil." She lifted up the chain.

Xander stared at her. "Are you kidding me?"

She shook her head. "Your mother is Robyn Sléite, and your father was Theron Sléite. I knew them both before I brought you here."

He frowned, but bowed to allow her to put it over his shoulders. Then he stood up straight and brushed his hands across the metal. It glimmered silver at his touch.

Quince turned to Jameson. "You were just a babe when I carried you through that doorway to this world. Your true name is Lyrin Madainn, and you are a Prince of Errian—the House of the Sun. This is your sigil." She held up a golden sunburst on a gold chain.

Jameson started to open his mouth, but Quince put her finger over his lips, silencing him. "I promised to show you everything, and I will. If you still don't believe me once we step through that door, you are free to leave and find your way back home. I'm asking you to trust me."

He felt like he was dissolving, the last little pieces of the Jameson he had been blowing away in the wind. A prince. How did you even process something like that?

He was no prince. He was nothing special, a cog in the machine. A low-level psych who was never meant for anything greater than midlevel success.

What was left? If the persona he'd built up around himself over these past twenty-five years was a lie, then who the hell was he?

And yet, Quince had proven time and time again that she had his back. He was learning, step by painful step, that the world was not what he had imagined. He bent his head and let Quince put the chain around his neck.

He touched the sigil. The metal was warm, and glimmered with a golden glow. *A prince.* And Xander was one too.

Jameson had one more question. "Why can't anyone go through that door? Surely they must have discovered it."

Quince shook her head. "This place is well hidden, and the waygate will only open once a day at noon, with a key." She pulled out a small black sphere. "It's made of amalite. That's all I know."

"But it's not noon."

She nodded. "I know. Something has opened the gate for us early, saving us more than half a day's wait. We must cross over now. I don't know why the waygate is open—maybe your friend Morgan had something to do with it. In any case, we should go before that changes."

Jameson looked at Xander, who shrugged, giving him a *how should I know* look. Two princes. And to think, when the day had begun, he'd been just a scared-shitless off-world psych. Who said things weren't getting better?

"Let's go," Quince said, and they followed her through the door in single file, passing over to Titania.

PART TWO
TITANIA

TITANIA

Mora
Mountains
RiamhWood
Argent Sea
Gaelan
The
Mountain
Ballifor
House of
the Stars
Bolcà Isle
Orn River
Errian
Taycrob
Torr
Talam
BANDIA

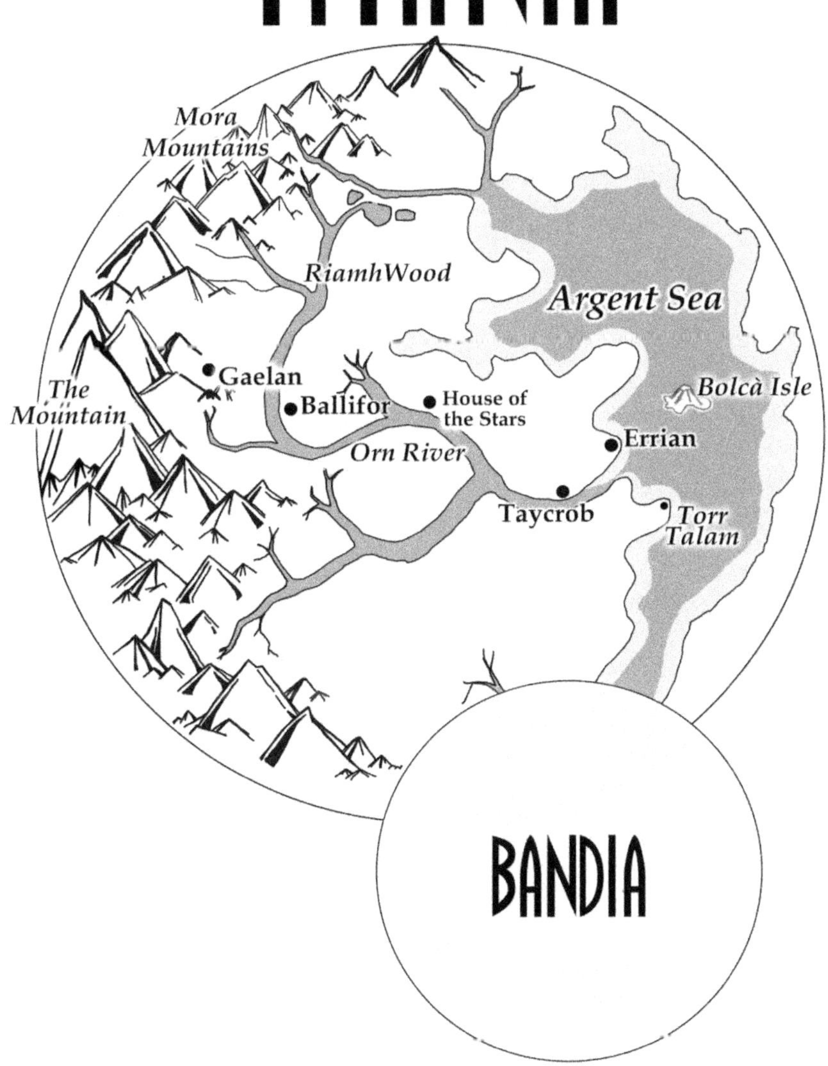

CHAPTER 14

NIGHT WATCH

XANDER LOOKED around the great hall. Unlike the room they'd just left on Oberon, this one was mostly clean. There was no caked dirt on the floor, only a light coating of dust. It was filled with white tarps covering bits of what he suspected were furniture, reminding him of the room in the deserted farmhouse where he had found Morgan, but the walls of this room were white stone, not black, and they looked to be in much better repair. He filed it away with all the mysteries that were piling up in his head.

Xander looked back in time to see the doorway behind them shimmer out of existence, to be replaced with a wall of white stone. Quince was right. He could have been trapped here.

He looked up to take in the view that had captivated him before. The sky was a light pink, so different from Oberon's green-tinted blue. Cirrus clouds streaked the sky above. The silver moon had moved, and now was framed in the center of the glass ceiling.

"It's called Bandia," Quince said. "Come on. There's more to see." She led them to the doors of the great hall and flung them open to let in the fresh air.

Jameson gasped, and Xander followed the man's gaze down.

It looked to be late afternoon.

The place was deserted, but what a *glorious* desertion. They stood at the top of a wide stair. The courtyard below them and the wall behind them were made from the same bright white stone—in sharp contrast to the black stone of the House of the Sky that they had just left behind.

Capping the gate were two wide silver bowls that looked like they had once held flames—bits of soot around the edges and a metallic pipe in the middle of each betrayed them.

Beyond the gate was an elaborate garden that would have put the Governor's mansions on Oberon to shame. White marble paths wound through faerie gardens, and though they were now somewhat overgrown, he could see that they had been created with a beauty to rival or surpass anything he'd ever seen on Oberon. The plants were predominantly purple and red and gold, unlike the silvery blue hue of the vegetation on Oberon.

There in the middle of it all stood a statue. "It's Gael, the moon god," he said with certainty. The statue was as silver as Bandia's moonlight, twice as tall as a man, one hand outstretched toward the sky, the other cradling a flawless sphere. His wings were extended behind him as though he were in flight. "I've been here before."

Jameson looked at him strangely.

Quince nodded. "Yes, you were. This is the House of the Stars. To the East lies Jameson's Kingdom—Errian and the Hundred Villages. To the West, Gaelan and the villages of Xander's people. Both of our peoples used to come here to meet for the summer and winter solstice, before the division. This is the dividing line between the Kingdoms. You were probably too young to remember...."

Xander shook his head. "There's another statue. On the other side. The sun god, right?"

"That's right."

He sank back against the stone rail. "I... I do remember. Damn, I remember."

Quince shook her head. "That's impossible. You were just a baby."

Xander shrugged. "Nevertheless." This couldn't be real. There was no way they'd just stepped from one world to another, through a stone archway. That kind of thing didn't happen, not in real life, and yet... the air smelled different here. Like... he couldn't place it exactly. It was something like honeysuckle. Sweet, but not cloying, something that triggered deep associations in the back of his head.

He took a deep breath. A little like chocolate too?

Then something Quince had said a minute before registered. "What division?" he asked.

"It was the reason your mother sent you away. She feared for your life, and I was worried for Jameson as well. Now you've returned. It's time to set things right." She looked around at this new place. It was a homecoming for Quince. "The fate of this world, and your adopted one, depends on it."

"Where is this place, Quince?" Xander asked.

"It's Titania. I told you—"

"No. Where are we? Where is this world? We came through that waygate to a different place."

"Ah." She picked up one of their citrones and raised her knife. She split it in half with one blow and held up the two pieces. "This is Oberon," she said, lifting her right hand. "And this is Titania."

"How do you know which is which?" Jameson smirked. He seemed to be feeling better, after all.

"Clever boy. So one time, long ago, they were together, like this. We think the ones who lived here before devised a plan to spin the world into an alternate universe. Maybe to escape a solar flare like the one that's coming. Maybe the shift created it."

Xander tried to picture it, but it was too grand an undertaking to comprehend.

"In any case, from what we can tell, it failed, splitting the world in two, one half in our universe, and the other here."

"Holy shit," Jameson said.

"We're in a whole different universe," Xander said softly.

Morgan watched the whole exchange silently, soaking it in.

"That's why Oberon doesn't collapse?"

Quince nodded. "The two sides are still connected, across the Shift. Our job is to complete the transition, and pull Oberon over to this side. At least until the flare ends. Then we can restore the status quo. And we don't have much more time."

Xander spat. "We should just let Oberon burn. It's mostly a rat's nest anyhow."

She shook her head. "There's something else I didn't tell you."

That was an understatement. "I'm guessing there are a lot of things you didn't tell us, Quince."

She managed a rueful smile. "True enough. See the sun?"

He nodded.

"It's changing. It's hard to tell, but it used to be more red. The two realities are connected. They're like reverse images of each other. Not exactly, but there's a bond. As the sun there moves closer to its flare stage, this one becomes more yellow."

He stared at Titania's primary. "Okay. I get that, but still...."

"No you don't. It's not just the stars that are connected." She held up the two halves of the citrone. "This world, Titania—or this half a world, counterbalances Oberon. They're still connected too. That's why Oberon hasn't crum-pled up into a ball of broken stone."

"So what?"

She split the two halves apart and dropped them to the ground, where they smashed into pieces, scattering seeds across the stones of the courtyard.

Xander went pale. "Oh crap."

She nodded. "If the flare is bad enough, it could break the connection between the two sides…."

"… sending both careening off into the void like the broken halves of a citrone, with their insides leaking out."

She nodded. "Not to mention the danger if one of the three moons were to collide with Titania or Oberon."

"Holy shit," Jameson said again.

"Holy shit indeed."

QUINCE DECIDED they would spend the night in the courtyard of the House of the Stars before setting out the next day. She was anxious to get going, but they needed to teach Jameson to fly, and she didn't want to attempt that in darkness.

Morgan was walking around the courtyard, taking everything in with his wide eyes. She still didn't trust the little creature. Maybe he *was* a boy, but he was also much more. After all, what were the odds that he would have turned up in a house in the middle of nowhere, just when Xander had arrived?

Too many mysteries.

Quince left her charges setting up a rudimentary camp and headed off to the old orchards to look for something for them to eat.

She found enough redfruit and some protein-rich mushrooms to make a meal, if not a very satisfying one. She didn't dare light a fire here, lest the smoke give them away.

It was strange to be back home after all these years. She breathed in the fresh air deeply—she had nearly forgotten that scent, but now it all came rushing back to her.

She had been far too young for the responsibility she had taken on, but there had been no other choice. Already banished from Gaelan because of Robyn's fears of discovery, they'd only seen each other once in a while in secret, in places such as this.

How much had she missed over these last twenty-five years? How much had changed?

Did Robyn still love her? She itched to be on her way, for the world's sake as well as her own.

She sighed. For better or worse, her long exile was finally over, and soon she would have done what she could.

A part of her hadn't wanted to return. She had made peace with her decision, and had adapted herself to Oberon's high-tech, fast-forward culture. Now things were coming to a head, and she had little choice but to face the consequences of her decisions so long before.

She returned to the House of the Stars with a sack full of fruit and mushrooms.

Xander and Jameson were sitting on opposite sides of the courtyard, ignoring one another. Jameson was in shock over the events of the last few days, especially the violence and death. She understood it, but he needed to be shaken out of his shell.

And Xander? Well, Xander was being Xander.

"Xander, want to wash this fruit? It's not much, but this and the mushrooms I found will keep our stomachs from rumbling too much."

"Of course. Hand them over."

"Jameson, there's a well out in the gardens. Want to bring me some more water? I can make a cold soup with the last of the MREs to stretch them out a bit."

"Sounds delightful." He grimaced.

She handed him a canteen. "You know how to work a well?"

He nodded. "We had one on Tander's World. Pretty low-tech."

She waited until both of them were busy with their preparations, and then emptied the last two meals, both chunky soups, into a pot. She slipped in a few drops of pith, stirring them into the mixture, and hid away the phial by the time Jameson returned. She was careful with the dosage; too much, and she might end up with a couple pith-addled addicts on her hands.

"Here you go." He handed her the canteen and returned to his end of the courtyard.

Xander watched him go, surreptitiously, but said nothing.

Quince smiled. *Bit by bit.*

In a few more minutes, everything was ready, and the motley group sat down to the meal. She poured each of the boys a helping of the stew.

"Don't you want some?" Jameson asked, sniffing it. "It's cold, but it doesn't seem too bad." He took a cautious sip.

"You two will need your strength for the next few days. Morgan and I will manage on mushrooms and fruit."

Xander nodded appreciatively at her use of the boy's name. Morgan himself didn't seem to mind what he ate, devouring whatever she put in front of him.

Jameson flexed his golden brown wings unconsciously. They were growing quickly now, almost two thirds the expanse of Xander's black ones. He seemed to be getting used to them too, little by little.

"Have to test those out tomorrow." Quince pointed at his wings.

"Test them out?" His face was blank. "Oh, you mean try to fly? Oh no. I'm nowhere near ready to try that. Thanks, but no thanks."

"You'd rather walk a thousand kilometers?"

"To where?" Xander's eyes were intent on her.

"To Gaelan, your family's ancestral home," she told Xander. "It's time for the two of you to make an appearance."

"I guess I can try it," Jameson conceded, flexing his wings. "But nothing too high."

"Once you know how to use them, we have to be on our way. We've wasted enough time already."

"Are things really that dire?" Jameson asked.

"You saw the shuttle crash in the Red Sands. You tell me."

"Point taken."

"So what happens when a Prince of the Sun House, or whatever, shows up in this Moon place—Gaelan?" Xander shot a look at Jameson.

"That's a great question." Jameson squinted at her. "I'm not going to get a pulse shot to the head, am I?"

Quince shrugged. "Cross through that waygate when we come to it."

Neither man seemed satisfied with her answer.

THEY'D SET up camp in one corner of the House of the Stars' courtyard. Darkness had fallen, and the chance to rest and eat a little should have cheered Jameson up.

Instead he felt even worse than before. He hadn't figured out how to move past his feelings of guilt and shame for the deaths of those men and women back on Oberon. Those he had killed, and whom he had seen killed by others.

Back on Oberon. It sounded so strange to say that. He had followed Quince through the waygate, leaving behind everything he knew and loved.

Quince came to sit next to him as he stared into the fire.

Morgan was asleep in one of the sleep sacks.

He looked up at her, not seeing her for a moment, seeing instead the sudden, painful deaths of all those people.

"Are you all right?" she said softly, putting a hand upon his knee.

"I'm not sure. Nothing feels the same." He flexed his wings behind him. "I thought I knew who and what I was. Now…."

Quince nodded.

His view of her had gradually shifted. She'd seemed cold when they first met. Now he saw past her façade. It hid a lot of pain, really old pain.

"I owe you a full explanation," she said, looking into his eyes.

He noticed for the first time the fine network of lines that radiated from the corners of her eyes. She looked beaten down and tired.

"You're my mother, aren't you?" He'd been thinking it through, and it made sense. Why she called him Lyrin, and why they had been together when he was a babe.

"What?" Her eyes went wide. "Oh goodness no." She laughed, but she must have seen him narrow his eyes. "Not that I wouldn't be happy to be. I'm not your mother, but I did know her. She was a beautiful, wise woman, but she died before her time." Her eyes lost their focus. "That was a dark and evil night…."

Quince awoke. Something had disturbed her rest. She opened her eyes and looked around the room.

The baby was quiet in his bassinet, but something was wrong. She wasn't sure how she knew, but she could feel it.

She slipped out of her bed and onto the cool stone floor, and crept across the small room to check on Lyrin, not wanting to wake his mother, Andra. The Queen was fast asleep in her own bed.

Lyrin was awake, staring quietly at the ceiling.

She reached in and picked him up, cradling him in her arms. Rocking him gently back and forth.

She opened the door to her small terrace, stepping out into the warm night. It was somewhere past midnight. In the distance, she could hear the waves of the Argent Sea crashing against the shore. The town below the House of the Sun was quiet, save for an occasional drunken outburst as the door to one of the taverns flew open.

"What are you doing in here?" Andra's voice, harsh against the silent summer night, brought her around.

Quince was about to reply when she heard a man's voice.

"We've come for the child. He is an abomination, and must be put to death."

"He's just a child."

"He's a child of the nimfeach. He'll bring death down upon us all."

Quince peered through the darkness to see a man holding a lantern in one hand and a sword in the other. Two others stood behind him.

"He's off with his governess. How dare you invade the Queen's chambers like this—"

"Search the place," the man said, and one of his companions started toward Quince's bedroom.

Andra stepped in front of him. "Get out of my room before I call the guard down on you."

Quince considered coming to her mistress's aid. She was handy enough with a sword. Even so, it would still be three to two, and there was Lyrin's well-being to consider.

"Move out of the way, Your Highness." The last was said with a sneer.

"I will not. You have no right to be here. Leave right now and I won't—"

The last words were choked off.

Quince watched in horror as the man's knife slashed through Andra's neck. The Queen clutched at her throat, croaking, trying to stop the bleeding, and fell to her knees.

Quince looked away, her stomach clenching.

The man stepped over her still-twitching body. "Pardon me, Your Highness."

She had to go, now, *or both she and Lyrin would be dead.*

Quince leaped off the balcony, vanishing into the darkness before the men could find her.

She had no idea where to go, only that she had to get away.

She could go home.

She set off toward Ballifor, her old village. She could hide there with her mother and brother while she figured out what to do next.

Jameson stared at her, his mind blank. As before, it was as if he had been there with her watching the scene unfold.

It was just a story. It wasn't true. It couldn't be.

He hadn't just witnessed his own mother die.

But his resistance was crumbling. A floodtide of information and emotion was sweeping away the last of the pillars that underpinned Jameson Havercamp, and he was helpless to stop it. "Who was he?" Jameson asked, grasping at something, anything to anchor himself against the tide.

"His name is Danner Black, and he's one of the men who runs the pith trade to Oberon."

Jameson closed his eyes, still hearing his mother's death scream. It echoed in his head with the screams of the men Morgan had killed.

He pulled his knees in and held them tight, willing them to stop. Willing the whole world to go away, to just *leave him be.*

Quince put a hand on his shoulder. "Are you okay in there, little robin?"

Something about that nickname reached him. Touched him deeply. Jameson looked up, aware his eyes were wet. He shook his head. "I don't know. I'm not sure who I am anymore."

"Oh, baby." She pulled him into her arms. "You're Lyrin Madainn. It's who you've always been." She held him tightly. "You just didn't know it until now."

Xander came to sit next to them. "Is he okay?" he said softly.

"He will be. I just gave him some news about his mother, and he's taking it hard. That and the enforcers we killed earlier."

"His mother?"

"I'll explain later."

Xander nodded. "Listen, Jameson, I know it's hard to deal with all this." He put a warm hand on Jameson's cheek. "*I'm* still struggling with it, but you learn to push past it. Make yourself hard, like a rock."

Jameson looked up at the man hovering over him, concerned. Xander was concerned for *him.* Xander, who'd barely said two kind words to him in all their time together. Sure, he'd defrosted a little, but this—he decided he liked having Xander show an interest in him. He nodded, wonder battling with his inner turmoil.

"You've lived a sheltered life," Quince said. "You haven't seen the things the two of us have. I know that must have been hard for you." She held him at arm's length, looking him right in the eyes. "Xander's right. You have to make yourself hard, and wall out the emotions surging through you right now. You have to put the images out of your head, or they will make you weak." She took him by the chin. "Can you do that?"

Jameson stared into her green eyes, seeing only purpose and compassion there. He looked up at Xander, who nodded.

More than anything, he wanted to make Xander proud of him. "I can try."

"We should get some sleep. We have to train you to fly in the morning, after all, and then we have a long way to go in a short time."

With just two sleep sacks and four people, he and Xander gallantly gave up their beds to Quince and Morgan.

They had agreed to take shifts watching over the camp. Jameson had volunteered for the first one, figuring it would be easier to stay awake in the early evening, rather than trying to keep his eyes open in the middle of the night or the wee hours of the morning.

The moon was about three quarters of the way across the sky. It was larger than either of the twin moons that swung around Oberon. It was full, huge and silver. He could make out several big impact craters on its face.

The whole place was quiet and peaceful.

He felt better, more at ease with things, but he still was split inside between the Jameson he had been and the Lyrin he was becoming.

Jameson closed his eyes and saw his birth mother's face again. She had been beautiful. He touched his own cheek, wondering if he looked like her.

His time on Beta Tau—growing up the privileged son of a founding family, learning how to be a psych, to help others—all seemed less and less real as the days passed.

Even Jessa. He tried to hold on to her face in his mind, but she slipped away from him, laughing and fading into darkness.

He could still feel the warmth of Xander's hand on his cheek. He shivered with the anticipation that touch had engendered in him.

Maybe he didn't have to lose Jameson. Maybe there was a way to still keep ahold of that part of himself as this other part began to assert itself.

In the morning, Quince had promised to train him in the use of his new wings. Tomorrow he was *going to fly*.

It was the dream of every little boy and girl—to be able to soar over the world like a superhero. Or a god.

It was even an achievable dream for most people. With a flight pack or a glider, you could fly above the earth whenever you wanted, but this was different. And the fate of not one, but two worlds was apparently on his winged shoulders.

These wings were a part of him now. He was becoming something new—someone who could fly. Someone with a higher purpose than a psych practice back on Beta Tau.

Jameson scanned the courtyard, looking for any signs of trouble. After all, he *was* the one on watch. Quince and Morgan were fast asleep in their sleep sacks.

Xander was curled up against the courtyard wall, lying on a blanket.

"Lyrin Madainn." He whispered the name Quince had given him, trying to reconcile it with the name he'd known all his conscious life. He was Jameson Havercamp, the psych from Beta Tau, with the conservative parents and the beautiful, rich fiancée, Jessa, waiting for him back home. Yet somehow he was also this other creature.

This "Lyrin," who had wings and a destiny of his own in this strange, distant world.

Maybe he could find a way to be both.

XANDER WOKE, uncurling his body and stretching. It felt inordinately good. He was still tired, but he could cope with that. Besides, sleeping on the hard rock of the courtyard floor without a sleep sack was damned uncomfortable. They only had two between them—Quince had told him she'd had to throw out the third one when Jameson had been attacked by wereveren.

He sat up, glancing around. Everything seemed fine. Quince and Morgan were asleep, and from the looks of things she'd managed not to strangle the boy in the middle of the night. That was progress.

Jameson still sat against the wall of the House of the Stars, but his head lay across his knees. The man was asleep.

Xander frowned. He'd been worried about leaving Jameson to watch over the rest of them, but Quince had overruled him.

Then again, Jameson had gone through a really rough day. Part of him longed to comfort Jameson, to tell him everything would be all right.

Xander stood, stepping quietly past Quince and Morgan. The boy was fast asleep, one arm flung off to the side. Xander knelt and tucked him back into his sleep sack.

Quince's eyes opened, but he nodded silently to her, and she closed them again and fell back into sleep.

Xander sank down next to Jameson, noticing once again how much he resembled Alix. He nudged Jameson with his toe, meaning to give the other man a dressing down for falling asleep on watch.

Jameson stirred and looked up at him. His eyes widened, and he sputtered. "I think I fell asleep. I'm so sorry!" he whispered. "I thought I could stay awake." His skin was silver in the moonlight. Then he yawned, and Xander suppressed a smile. He was *adorable*.

"It's all right," he said quietly. "Nothing bad happened." He swept his arm across the courtyard. "See? Nothing has changed. No harm done."

Jameson shot him a grateful smile, and then stretched his own arms. "So what do *you* think of all this?" He gestured at the world around him, and the back of his hand grazed Xander's arm. A thrill ran up his shoulder.

"It's a lot to take in." Xander touched the moon sigil that hung around his own neck.

"What about him?" Jameson gestured to Morgan.

"I don't know." Xander had been wondering about Morgan since the boy had rescued them with his still-unexplained power. "I'm glad he's on our side. Whatever he is."

Jameson nodded. "Me too."

They sat in silence for a few moments, looking up at the alien sky.

At last, Xander continued. "When I was growing up, I always wanted to believe that I was special. That I was destined for better things. But I never imagined anything like this."

Jameson nodded. "I used to stare out my bedroom window at home at night. There was a wide green pasture outside where we exercised the horses, and beyond that the dark trees of the forest. The moon would rise, even bigger than that one." He pointed into the sky. "I would wish to be somewhere else. My parents were… strict with me."

Xander was intensely aware of Jameson's male form, so close to his. Part of him longed to touch Jameson's cheek. To draw him in and kiss him boldly, passionately.

He hadn't wanted anyone this way since Alix, and it was scrambling his brain. "I know what you mean. I had a horrible childhood. I kept wishing to get away from it all, but nothing ever happened."

"Until now."

"Until now," he agreed. "Do you want to go back home?" He glanced up at the house where they had first entered this world.

Jameson was quiet for a moment, considering. Then he shook his head. "I don't think I can, now. I've come too far. I need to see this through, whatever it is."

Xander nodded. "Me too."

Jameson shivered. "It's getting cold. Do you think… do you think you could warm me up a little?" Their faces were inches apart.

Xander's libido roared back to life. He shut it down ruthlessly. "Are you sure? You're *not like that*, remember?"

Jameson's lip trembled, but he nodded. "For the heat."

"Okay. Just so we're clear."

Jameson turned over on his side, and Xander snuggled up to him, reaching around under his wings to pull him close. He pulled Jameson's blanket over the two of them and breathed in Jameson's scent deeply.

He just hoped Jameson didn't feel his arousal.

. . .

QUINCE WOKE in the early morning. It was time to take her turn at the watch.

It had gotten chilly out, as summer edged into fall. The poor boys hadn't had a sleep sack to keep them warm.

She sat up quietly. Morgan was still asleep next to her. The boy truly looked innocent when he slept. *What secrets do you hold?*

Then she spied Jameson and Xander. They were fast asleep, together, Jameson's wings tucked in between them and Xander's wings wrapped over Jameson protectively.

She smiled. The bond between the two of them was finally forming, and just in time. A few more days....

That's all they had. A few more days.

Part of her wanted to roust them from bed and move on right away, but it would do her no good to arrive in Gaelan with two broken men. Or to lose one on the way.

She took up her watch post, finding a place just outside the courtyard facing the gardens, and settled in to wait for the dawn.

CHAPTER 15
FLIGHT

JAMESON AWOKE SLOWLY. His whole body felt cramped—not surprising since he'd fallen asleep on the hard ground of the courtyard.

His wings were tucked tightly against his back, and he was warm. His eyes flickered open. There was a black line across his vision. He frowned, focusing on it. It was the leading edge of a long black wing.

What the hell? He scrambled out of Xander's embrace, waking the man up in the process. "What do you think you're doing?" He pushed himself away from Xander on his hands and his butt.

Xander sat up, and Jameson couldn't help but admire his beautiful body. *Not going down that road.* "You were cold," Xander said. "Don't you remember?"

It all came flooding back. The fight, the vision, the aching soul-searching. He must have fallen asleep, and then Xander had woken him up. The night air *had* been cold. "Did… did anything happen?"

Xander smiled slyly. "Anything like what?"

"Anything like… you know." Damn Xander for feigning innocence.

"Morning." Quince interrupted them. "How did you two sleep?" she asked with a sideways smile of her own. *Damn you both to hell.*

On the other hand, his natural sense of optimism was clearly reasserting himself. He no longer wanted to remain curled up in a fetal position.

"Relax, Jameson. Nothing happened." Xander stood and stretched in the sunlight.

My God, he's beautiful. Xander's body was nicely muscled, each line and curve standing out in the light of the morning sun. His back was crisscrossed with scars. And his eyes... his green eyes. Jameson could get lost in those eyes.

Jameson shook his head. *One life-changing event at a time.*

Quince was preparing something for breakfast—probably a cold meal again. His stomach longed for something hot, and maybe a little spicy. He was sick of bland.

Morgan sat in a corner of the courtyard, eating a citrone greedily.

Jameson wondered if Jessa had missed him yet. Not that she'd ever be able to find him here, wherever "here" was.

His next thought was how much he needed to piss. "There aren't any... um... dangers here I should know about, are there?"

"Don't look at me." Xander grinned. "I'm as new to this place as you are."

"No, you should be safe enough," Quince said. "No wereveren or any other dangerous local wildlife. Just don't wander too far. We'll have a quick breakfast and then we'll get to work teaching you to use those wings of yours."

They fluttered in response of their own accord, startling him.

He excused himself and strolled out through the open gates into the garden, looking for a good spot to relieve himself. He tried to remember this place, to dredge up some long-lost memory of it.

The pathways that wound through the grounds were marble or some other white stone. The fountains that lined them had long gone silent, but he could imagine the water leaping up into the air over the pathway, the musical sound of it laughing as it splashed back into its basin. They were all made of marble too, carved into the shapes of trees and animals and, occasionally, people, with an attention to detail and realism that amazed him. The carved people were like Xander... like him. With beautiful wings that spread out a couple meters from tip to tip.

Bright flowers lined the path in irregular patches, in golds and pinks and blues and yellows. He could imagine how amazing this place must have been in its heyday, the pruned artistry of a formal garden rather than the decadent, wild beauty that occupied it now.

It was still delightful, nonetheless.

He found a place to pee, under a tall tree that reminded him of one of the weeping willows back at home on Beta Tau. It gave him some privacy. Soon he felt much better.

Jameson decided to walk around the House of the Stars, exploring the gardens before he was called back to work on his wings. He'd had little enough peace and quiet these last six days since arriving on Oberon and having his whole life turned upside down.

A few minutes later, he reached the statue of Erro, the sun god. This, for some reason, he did remember. The god stood on top of a fluted column of white marble, looking down beneficently, a calming smile on his golden face. His wings were spread out above Jameson, blocking out the sky, and his hand was outstretched, as if he were offering to take Jameson's hand and lift him into the air, the way Xander had done the day before.

Erro was the symbol of his own people, the Erriani—those of the skythane who lived west of here, along the shores of the Argent Sea.

He reached out to touch that golden hand.

A shock like electricity ran up his arm, and the world dissolved into nothing.

Jameson remembered. Memory flooded through him like a tsunami tide, rushing into his mind and carrying with it a horde of information. He saw this place as it had been in its prime, a shining example of the skythane culture before the second wave of humanity arrived on Oberon. When the wing men had ruled both parts of the world before being beaten back and subjugated by the corporation.

He stood in the midst of the gardens of the House of the Stars. The structure back on Oberon was the House of the Sky.

Jameson remembered the agony of the Great Retreat, when the landers had come and the Gaelani, Xander's folk, had been forced off Oberon and into Titania, a path of trial and pain and suffering to rival the great resettlements of the Native Americans on Old Earth. That influx had not been without strife or bloodshed, though the Erriani and the Gaelani had eventually made peace.

The Gaelani refugees who had overwhelmed Errian, the House of the Sun on the shores of the Argent Sea, had been relocated to Gaelan, the House of the Moon, in the foothills of the Mora Mountains.

He saw the Seven Weeks' War that had erupted twenty-five years ago after the death of his mother, when the blame for her death had fallen squarely upon the Gaelani.

And so the Great Division of the skythane, which had its seeds in the Gaelani's forced migration, had begun.

His mind was overwhelmed with information, and his head felt like it was about to split open.

Jameson blinked, but everything seemed too bright and out of focus. He let go of the statue's hand and collapsed to the ground.

. . .

"I FOUND him!" Xander called to Quince, kneeling before Jameson's prostrate form.

When Jameson hadn't returned after twenty minutes, they'd gone out to search for him.

Xander looked up at the golden statue of the sun god looming over them, the reddish sunlight glinting off its wings.

Quince hadn't seemed all that worried when Jameson hadn't immediately returned, but Xander didn't know this world and its dangers. He didn't want to see anything happen to Jameson. For purely practical reasons, of course. They were in the same boat.

Fortunately, Jameson hadn't gone far. He lay in a heap in the little semicircular amphitheater that surrounded the sun god's statue, prostrate on the broken pavestones.

Xander turned him gently over onto his back. He was still breathing, if shallowly. That was a good sign, but his skin was deathly pale.

Quince arrived with Morgan right behind her.

"I found him like this." Xander cradled Jameson's head in his lap. "He was lying here by the statue. He doesn't look so good."

Quince put her hand on Jameson's forehead. "He's ice-cold. Morgan, go and grab me one of the sleep sacks."

The boy seemed to understand. He ran off toward the campsite.

Xander raised his eyebrow. It was the first time she had addressed the boy directly. Once again, progress.

The boy had gone silent again of late—Xander wondered what was going on in that little head of his. Once they finished this quest, he could try to get to the bottom of the mystery of Morgan.

"Xander, pick him up, gently, and hold him to your chest. He needs your warmth."

Xander nodded and lifted Jameson as if he were made of glass. He pulled the man close to him, wrapping his wings around them both. "What do you think happened to him?"

She looked up at the statue. "Divine intervention?" The way she said it sounded like a curse.

Xander stared at her blankly. "Surely you're joking." Quince had lived two and a half decades in Oberon. She should have left such ridiculous superstitions behind.

She glared at him. "Bite your tongue. You don't know the rules of this place yet. You have to remember that we're not on Oberon anymore."

Yes, but superstition was superstition.

Morgan arrived with the sleep sack. Quince took it and opened it up all the way, wrapping it around the two of them.

Jameson fit so perfectly in his arms. He looked at the man anew, seeing how handsome he was, and how vulnerable. Totally dependent on Xander at this moment for his well-being.

He held Jameson in his arms for what seemed like an eternity, but at the same time felt like no time at all. The red sun inched up into the pink sky, but otherwise it was as if time stopped its advance.

The last time he had held someone, or just been held like this, before Jameson, had been with Alix. *Long-lost Alix.*

After a while, Jameson stirred. Xander put his hand on Jameson's forehead. It was definitely warmer, and the color was coming back into his face.

The man's brown eyes flickered open. He looked up at Xander, and this time he didn't flinch.

"Welcome back, handsome." Xander leaned down and kissed him.

Jameson accepted the kiss for a brief moment, but then turned away, his face flushing crimson. He pushed himself gently away from Xander, who let him go.

Xander masked his disappointment with a cough.

Jameson stood up on his own, still a little wobbly. "What happened to me?"

"I don't know." He stood and helped Jameson up. "I found you collapsed here, cold as ice. Quince said we needed to warm you up."

Jameson glanced over at Quince and Morgan. "Thanks. I think." He cast an uneasy look at Xander, wiping his mouth with the back of his arm.

Quince looked up at the statue of the god. "He touched you, didn't he?"

Jameson stared at the statue for a moment, and nodded. "I think so. I... remember a lot of things." His brow knitted with concern. "Things I couldn't possibly have seen myself."

Xander wondered what he meant. "You okay now?"

Jameson nodded. "I think so. My head still hurts like a sonofabitch."

"The touch of the gods can do that." Quince gave him a rueful laugh. "Come on, let's eat. Some food will do you good." She led him back toward the camp like a child. "You need to get a flying lesson this morning, and we have to be on our way."

Jameson looked back at him, mouthing, "Gods?"

Xander shrugged and shook his head.

He trailed after them, wondering about this strange world he found himself in, and why it suddenly seemed that he liked Jameson more than Jameson liked him.

. . .

Jameson and Xander stood on the wide balcony of the House of the Stars. Jameson looked over his shoulders at his golden wings. They were still smaller than Xander's, but they were catching up quickly. He stretched them out to their full width and took a deep breath.

"Do they itch?" Xander rubbed some more of Quince's unguent into them.

Jameson nodded. "A little, but not so bad as before. That salve is amazing." His gaze lingered on Xander, but then he ripped it away. He was trying to forget the kiss. The *second* kiss.

Xander, for his part, kept his voice detached, professional. "Okay, let's try a few drills. Stand here and face me, with your legs a little apart."

Jameson complied. Xander walked around him, looking at his outstretched wings. He touched Jameson's back with his hand, his warm palm resting between Jameson's shoulder blades. Jameson's pulse quickened.

"I want you to try to feel your brain's connection with your wings. Feel my touch?"

Jameson nodded, not trusting himself to speak.

"Feel the connection from your muscles here"—he moved his hand across Jameson's back to his shoulder blades and his left wing—"to your wings here."

Jameson shivered, hoping Xander wouldn't notice.

"You've done it before by instinct. Now you need to learn to control them intentionally. Put out your hands like this." He stepped away to stand next to Jameson and swept his hands out and up from his side.

Jameson followed Xander's motion. He had strong arms, tanned from their time in the sun. His own arms were thin by comparison. He imagined Xander's arms laid over his own, warm skin against skin....

"Feel that? How natural it seemed? Now do the same with your wings." He demonstrated, sweeping his black-feathered wings up and out with a swoosh.

Jameson tried, but although his wings quivered, nothing happened.

"Up!" Xander jumped at him, with a short, sharp shout. Jameson stumbled back and his wings went out defensively. Jameson glared at him, and Xander laughed. "There you go—just needed to put a little fear into you. Now do it again."

Jameson shook his head. "I don't know how I did it...." His wings spread out behind him. "Damn."

Xander smiled.

Damn that suggestive smile.

"Now you're getting it. Let's practice."

They spent the next two hours working on his control of his wings and his reflexes. Xander ran him through the basics of control—how to pull his wings tightly to his sides when he wanted to plummet, how to catch an updraft on a warm day.

By the end of it, Jameson could make his wings do what he wanted, at least when he was standing on solid ground, and he had a better idea of wing mechanics. It was all strangely exhilarating.

"It's time for your first flight," Xander said at last, standing at the edge of the balcony. "Normally I wouldn't rush you like this. We should probably train you for a week, or at least a few days, before throwing you into the deep end, but as Quince pointed out, we're short on time. What with the world ending and all."

"I'm not sure I'm ready," Jameson said, grimacing. Theory was one thing, but a man could get himself killed in the air. Or rather, slamming into the ground.

Xander flashed him a wicked grin. "One way to find out." He grabbed Jameson's hand and pulled him off the balcony, and they plunged toward the ground below.

Jameson screamed.

"Spread your wings. Like this!" Xander's black wings flew out on either side of him, and he let go of Jameson's hand as he was lifted up into the sky.

Jameson searched for that place inside like Xander had taught him. The ground raced up toward him. Impact from that height would hurt him badly, if it didn't kill him. "Spread, damn you!" he swore, and they did, yanking him up into the air, pulling back his shoulder muscles as his wings did what wings were supposed to do. *Damn, that hurts.*

Then he was soaring just meters above the ground, and it was just like he had always dreamed. The cool morning air whistled past him, and the ground whisked by below.

He looked up. Xander was above him, circling. "Feel for the thermals like I told you," Xander shouted down at him. "The warm air. You can ride them up into the sky."

Jameson concentrated on his wings, and found he could sense the temperature of the air currents through the membranes. There—a warmer updraft. He veered into it. It took a couple tries, but soon he was riding it up toward Xander, into the clear blue sky.

I'm flying.

He *remembered.*

Flying like this. It was his first time, and yet he remembered doing it before

—the feel of the wind on his wings, how to ride an updraft. As if he had been doing this forever.

Xander grinned at him. "You're going to need some practice, but you've got the basics."

"You could have killed me, you bastard!" He pushed those memories aside, for now.

"You made it. I had faith in you."

Jameson couldn't hold on to his anger for long. The sensation of flight was too glorious.

They soared over the House of the Stars, and Jameson could see the lay of the land for miles around. They were in the middle of a vast forest, the morning mist over a river nearby just starting to burn off. The leaves of the trees had a purple hue, so different from the silvery blue of Oberon's forests.

It was like being in a plane or a shuttle, but so much better and more immediate. Real.

He never wanted to come back down.

Eventually, though, they had to.

They made it back to the balcony safely, although Jameson bungled the landing, slamming into the wall and earning himself a nasty bruise on his left arm. Still, he got up, and they tried it again a few more times until Jameson had a handle on it. *I can do this.*

When they landed together for the last time, Jameson swept Xander up in a big hug, feeling the man's warm chest against his own.

"What's this for?" Xander squirmed.

Jameson grinned. "You taught me how to fly."

QUINCE WATCHED Jameson plunge from the balcony, and her heart almost stopped. "Damn you, Xander...," she whispered as she ran to the edge to watch twenty-five years of hard work and planning crashing toward the ground. He wasn't going to make it....

Then Jameson extended his beautiful golden wings and swept up into the air, missing the ground, and her, by less than two meters. So like his mother.

Her heart started to beat again.

The bond was growing between the two of them. She could see it. It was aided by the pith that she'd put in each of their meals, but it would have grown with or without it, if she'd judged these two right. The pith just hastened the process along.

Although she disapproved of Xander's teaching methods, she was grateful that Jameson was learning so quickly. He was a natural in flight, and it gave her hope that they'd be able to reach the city on time. It was growing short, and they were still three days' flight from Gaelan. They needed to be on their way.

She still didn't know what she would find there. The King was dead—that much Robyn had been able to tell her—but what had happened with his Ober-Corp "allies"? Was Robyn herself in command of the city now? If so, why hadn't she sent Quince another message before they'd departed Oberon City?

She glanced up at the sky, wondering if the gods were watching over them. It was rare for them to intervene in the affairs of mortals, but she recognized their touch when she saw it. Jameson had been chosen. She just didn't know if it would turn out to be for good or ill.

The gods were famously fickle.

CHAPTER 16
BALLIFOR

THEY HAD A BRIEF, cold lunch in the early afternoon in the courtyard of the House of the Stars, the sun warming them as they ate in a companionable silence. Quince had snagged some of the citrones on the far side of the waygate before they'd come through, and she used them to supplement their rations.

Then they took to the sky. Quince led the way, taking them west toward the mountains that Quince called the Mora, the great line of peaks that ran along the western edge of the world. She leapt into the sky, and Jameson followed, straining his wings to keep up.

Xander brought up the rear with Morgan strapped to his chest in the recon-figured harness, leaving his wings free. It felt good to fly again, to soar up into the sky. He wasn't sure where they were going or what would await them there, but for the moment he had no worries.

The day was warm and breezy, a summer straggler as the season moved steadily into the fall. The House of the Stars fell away beneath them, its white walls shining in the afternoon sun, quickly becoming just a dot in the distance.

The terrain below mimicked the part of Oberon they had left behind, save that there was no desert to the south. Just a seemingly unending succession of tree-covered hills, mostly red from this high up, with bits of gold and purple woven in like some grand tapestry.

Just south of the House of the Stars, a river wound from the west out to the east, the reverse image of the Theseus.

Quince kept them fairly low to the ground, hoping to avoid notice, and they followed the course of the waterway.

"What's the river called?" Xander asked Quince.

"It's the Orn," she called back. "It runs from the mountains and Gaelan in the west down to Errian and the Argent Sea in the east."

It was nearly as wide as the Theseus. The waters sparkled in the early afternoon sunlight, giving the river a golden hue.

AFTERNOON WORE on toward evening, but still they continued on. Jameson was looking tired, and Xander hoped Quince would call a halt soon. His wings and the muscles that supported them were still new. He couldn't be used to this kind of exertion yet.

On the north side of the river, the trees pulled back, leaving a long scar in the forest along the water's edge. Although creepers and vines covered a lot of the damage, Xander could see that there must have been a massive fire here at some time in the recent past. "What happened down there? In that big clearing?" he asked Quince.

Her face hardened. She didn't reply.

"Quince, what happened here?" he repeated, puzzled.

"Hundreds died," she said at last. "It was the site of the worst battle of the Seven Weeks' War. Though it wasn't so much a battle as a slaughter."

"The Seven Weeks' War?"

She nodded. "It started when a pith runner named Danner Black killed Lyrin's… Jameson's mother, the Queen of the Erriani."

Xander went pale. "Oh, I'm so sorry. I didn't know."

Quince turned away and swooped down toward the ground. She alighted in what looked like a large, circular plaza in the middle of the vast, decimated part of the forest.

Surprised, Xander followed, with Jameson close behind.

Xander dropped to the ground, surprised to smell a lingering burnt odor. The ground beneath his feet was hard, fused as if there had been a powerful explosion here. Did they have that kind of technology on Titania? There was so much he didn't know about his own people.

He knelt down to touch the ground. It was smooth, like glass.

"What caused this?" He stood and looked at Quince, surprised to find that her eyes were moist with tears.

She drew herself up and looked around the empty space. "This was my home, growing up. It was a village called Ballifor—it means 'forest home.'" She took a few steps, as if trying to gauge her location. "My parents' house was over there, I think."

Xander glanced in that direction. There was nothing but a broken structure that might have once been a chimney hearth.

"I had come back here after the Queen was killed. I was off in the forest with Lyrin, looking for obieberries. There was a loud explosion. Though we were miles from home, I heard it, and saw the fireball that consumed the village. I raced back, keeping low to the forest to avoid detection. When I got home, there was nothing left." That last part came out in a whisper.

"Nothing?"

Quince shook her head. "No people, no village. Just a horrible smell and this gaping sore on the world, and Danner Black."

Both Xander and Jameson reached out to put a hand on her shoulder. "I'm sorry, Quince. I had no idea," Xander said.

Jameson nodded. "We don't need to stay here. I can manage to fly on a little farther."

"No, this is as good a place as any." The poor man was exhausted. They could fly for longer the next day—they had made good progress on this one. She took a deep breath, gathering her resolve. "We can camp over there, under the forest eaves." She pointed across the devastation to where the line of trees began again. "Maybe I can make peace with a few of my ghosts, while we're here."

Xander was having a hard time taking it all in. "Who did this... this atrocity?"

"Neither side ever took responsibility. Each accused my village of working with the other, but I think the horror of what happened here shocked them all.

"Black was behind it, in league with OberCorp, I think. It had to be weaponry from Oberon. There's nothing in Titania that could cause this kind of damage." She looked around, her eyes downcast. "The fighting stopped after seven weeks. There's been an uneasy truce ever since." She knelt and put her palm on the smooth, glassy surface, whispering something that Xander couldn't make out.

Then she stood and led them across the open space, toward the protective red branches of the forest in the distance.

THE THREE of them were starting to fall into a rhythm when they made camp. Xander set up the campsite, while Jameson went out looking for firewood and Quince went in search of food.

Jameson welcomed the little bit of time alone. His mind was in a constant state of flux since he'd touched the statue. He was trying to assimilate all the new memories he'd been given. Sometimes they fled past so quickly that he hardly recognized them. Other times, it was like he was somewhere else for a moment or two, seeing out of the eyes of a stranger.

Sometimes he felt like the old Jameson, the one who had grown up on a different world with a different story—a mother and father, a fiancée, and a stable life as a resident psych on a mining world.

Sometimes now, he was Lyrin, this strange Prince of the House of the Sun. Those memories were strange. They were entirely alien to Jameson, and yet they felt like they belonged to Lyrin. Or maybe to some of his kin. Memories of soaring above the Argent Sea on the first day of spring, when the pink sky was full of puffy clouds. A recollection of standing on a balcony looking out over the purple forest canopy with a babe in his arms—a memory that couldn't be his as either Jameson or Lyrin.

Jameson was tired, too, exhausted from the long flight, and his wounds from the wereveren attack were acting up from the stretching they'd endured during his flight.

He pulled his mind back to the present, concentrating on looking for the wood Quince had sent him in search of. Wrenwood, she'd called it. It was a small bush, with easy-to-break-off dead branches. The wood was a mahogany brown, with small, round, red leaves, and it burned without smoke like the heart-shaped fungi on Oberon.

To help distract himself, he thought about Quince, the woman who had, apparently, been something like a mother to him for the earliest part of his life. Today he had seen her as truly human—a person with wants and needs, vulnerabilities and pain. With her wings and her strength of character, it had been easy for him to view her as an angel. Or maybe a superhero.

There was more to her behind the mask than that.

He followed the forest edge, along the perimeter of the devastated area, not venturing too far from it so he wouldn't get lost. As he thought about the wrenwood bush, he could see an image of it in his mind's eye, as clearly as a memory.

It was. Just not one of his.

The branches were a beautiful deep purplish brown, branching at regular intervals like antlers, tipped with the bright red leaves.

After a few minutes searching, he stumbled upon one of the bushes. It was as tall as he was, and had quite a bit of deadwood. There had been no one here to harvest it in twenty-five years.

Jameson broke off as much as he could carry, arranging it into a compact pile and tying the rope Quince had given him around it. He laughed when he realized it was the protective rope they'd used to keep out the wereveren. They wouldn't need that again anytime soon, God willing.

He threw the bundle of sticks over his back and headed back toward the campsite.

"WHY ARE the skythane separated into Erriani and Gaelani?" Xander asked as they shared a dinner of fish and hoarberries. The little berries were good, leaving a sweet red stain on their tongues.

"They were one people, once, when the first wave of colonists arrived from Earth." Quince finished off her piece of fish and licked her fingers. "With Oberon being a smaller world than Earth with lighter gravity, it made sense to fly. It also eliminated the need for a lot of heavy machinery."

Xander nodded. "I can see that. So what happened?"

"Landers." Jameson looked up, as if surprised to hear his own voice.

"He's right." Xander saw the appraising look she shot Jameson. "Over time, the skythane, as they came to call themselves, spread across Oberon, and discovered the nimfeach, and the waygates."

"Nimfeach?"

"Spirits. The ghosts of the ones who came before. No one knows for sure."

Xander laughed. "Surely that's just rank superstition—"

"I've seen one." Quince looked up at him, her face deadly serious.

"Okay, okay. So there are spirits." He tried to laugh it off, but the look on her face stopped him cold.

"In any case, the nimfeach helped our people access the waygates, and soon we spread across Titania too." She ate a few of the hoarberries, staining her fingers, and handed some to Morgan, who accepted them greedily. "The skythane on Oberon were the Gaelani—the children of the moon. Those on Titania were the Erriani—"

"The sun children." He glanced over at Jameson.

"Then the landers came."

Jameson nodded.

"You know the story?" Quince asked.

"I remember it. Xander's people were pushed off of Oberon when the second wave of human colonists came, though a few remained. The refugees came to Errian, here on Titania."

"Yes. There were… incidents… before the Gaelani were eventually resettled halfway across the world in their own city."

Xander laughed. "We're like Romeo and Juliet."

"Or Romeo and Romeo." Jameson smiled wanly.

Quince snorted. "A couple of clowns, you two are. In any case, things continued in that fashion for a long time… hundreds of years, two nations in competition with one another, but there was no open war until twenty-five years ago…."

"When Danner Black killed my mother." Jameson closed his eyes.

Xander could *feel* his pain. "And now?"

Quince shrugged. "After Ballifor, things cooled off again. Now OberCorp is a part of the game, at least in Gaelan. I don't know much more than that."

"I guess we'll find out soon enough." Xander stared at Jameson across the flames. Were their people enemies still? Or allies with a common cause?

Only time would tell.

They settled in for the night. Quince was numb. She'd known they would pass this place, but she hadn't planned to stop here. And yet, Jameson needed the rest. Besides, it seemed *right*.

She had unfinished business with Ballifor. A quarter century had passed, and she could still remember what had transpired here as clearly as if it were yesterday.

She lay on her side, looking across the firelight at the dark spaces between the trees. Where the village had once lain.

She wasn't sure when she crossed the line from sadness to sleep.

Quince held Lyrin in her arms as she climbed out of the village of Ballifor onto the hillside that looked over the town from the north. She was keeping a low profile. She would have loved to soar with him over the village, but she was wary of Danner Black and his men. The pith runner had a network of spies in both kingdoms. Even here, where she should have been safest, she kept indoors most of the time.

It had been a week without word back from Robyn, and she needed to get some fresh air.

Her brother Dillan had taken her in without question, though his lingering gaze told her he knew who the infant she carried was. Still, despite the danger, he'd pulled her inside when she'd arrived in the wee hours of the morning and found a place for the two of them among his brood.

Her mother had been overjoyed to see her. Both were shocked at the news.

"The Errian Queen?"

Quince had nodded, on the verge of tears as she recounted what she had seen. She hadn't missed the frightened look her mother shot at Dillan before looking back at Lyrin with narrowed eyes.

It was best for them all if she and Lyrin left here as soon as it was feasible.

Robyn still hadn't replied.

Quince had borrowed her mother's old baby harness for the walk, and Lyrin was wrapped in it on her chest, burbling happily. Quince would feed him once they found a quiet spot to rest. She hoped to find some hoarberries—little blue and green and red berries covered in a sweet white "frost"—to sweeten her lunch.

She stopped, frowning.

There was a high-pitched whine in the air. Like the buzzing of a hundred bees, then a thousand. She looked around, but she couldn't see the source of it.

Then she glimpsed something dark shooting across the sky from the east. In half a second the buzzing increased a hundredfold. She covered her ears as the object arched up over the forest and then descended into Ballifor.

There was a flash, and then the ground shook as a blast of heat and wind knocked her on her back, her wings bending awkwardly with the force of the blow.

Then, silence.

She sat up slowly. What in the three hells was that?

Lyrin began to cry.

Nothing seemed to be broken, although her left wing ached. She was likely to have a nasty bruise there.

She stood unsteadily and ran back to the peak of the hill to look back at the village.

It was gone.

Wiped from the face of Titania as if it had never been, along with a swath of the forest. In its place was a smooth black plain, and broken trees smoldered all along the edge.

"Mamma! Dillan!" she screamed, and ran down the hillside, back toward where Ballifor had been.

She reached the edge of the destruction and could go no farther. The ground was hot, and the trees around its edge still burned.

The place she had grown up had been erased in an instant. Ballifor was no more.

She fell to her knees and cried, her tears wrenched out of her, letting go in a way she hadn't done when the Queen had been killed. Great, wracking sobs.

Lyrin wailed with her.

Her family was gone.

She had no idea how long she sat there in the dirt, lost to grief.

Eventually, sanity slowly reasserted itself. Her sobs slowed, then stopped. Her tears no longer fell.

She stood and gazed out at the destruction, feeling numb.

Then she noticed something else in the sky.

Her self-preservation instincts kicked in, and she ducked behind a redoak tree. She shushed Lyrin, holding him gently against her chest, whispering softly in his ear.

Five wing men flew in from the east, hovering above the destruction.

One of them was Danner Black. She didn't recognize the others.

"He's dead for certain, the Queen's bastard," he said to the others. "This will goad Theron and the Gaelani into war against the Erriani. We can take care of the other one then. Accidents often happen in the fog of war."

Quince pulled back behind the tree. She couldn't let them find her now. It had only been by dumb luck that she and Lyrin had survived.

She huddled as close to the tree as she could, hoping they didn't come looking. She could take down two of them easily, unencumbered, but with a babe and five to fight?

The other one.

They must mean Davyn. Robyn's boy.

She had to find the Queen of the Gaelani. She would fly back to the House of the Stars. Robyn would be there waiting for her, if she'd gotten Quince's message.

She had to be.

Quince awoke, her eyes wet with tears. It was still so fresh. This place brought it all back to her, memories she had buried for years. That terrible reckoning, and it had happened because of her. Because she had come back here with the child.

The forest around her was still, and the clearing beyond was lit by the silver light of Bandia. It had to be close to midnight.

Xander had taken the first watch, and she'd managed to get a few hours of much-needed sleep. She sat up and looked around, her eyes adjusting to the light. Xander was sitting against a tree on the edge of the open space. She stood and made her way quietly past the sleeping forms of Jameson and the child, tucked into their other sleep sack together.

Xander looked up at her approach. "Nothing to report," he said softly. He looked back out at the open space beyond the trees. "I've been trying to imagine what it must have been like for you."

She sank down next to him on the soft forest floor. "It was like being confronted by oblivion," she replied. "Like everything I had ever known, that I had grown up with, had never really existed. Other than myself, there was no proof."

Xander nodded. "I guess we all have our own trials and secrets."

She put her hand on his knee. "And our own joys. Always celebrate your joys, your little victories. The bad things are many, but the joys that counterbalance them are so few." She stood again, brushing off the leaves.

"Time to make peace?" He stared up at her, a look of comprehension and compassion on his face.

"Yes. Past time. You don't have to wait."

"I don't mind. I can manage another hour or so. Go."

She smiled, grateful, and leaned down to kiss him on the forehead. "My gallant knight. I'll be back soon, little sparrow."

Xander looked up at her, his head cocked to the side and his brow furrowed.

She took her leave, wondering if, after all this time, he still remembered his mother's childhood nickname for him.

She strode out into the meadow under the silver moon, making for the place where her village had once stood, the place she had left behind to join the service of the Queen. And then had returned to, ever so briefly. They said the middle of the night was the best time to speak to the dead, that their world and the world of the living were closest together then.

When she reached the plain of glass, she took off her shoes and walked barefoot on the smooth surface. It was cool on the soles of her feet, belying the terrible heat that had created it so many years before. She sank down to sit as close to the middle of the blast radius as she could manage, where the ripples in the glass seemed to originate. She crossed her legs and rested her hands on her knees, letting her wings settle against her back. She closed her eyes and took a deep, calming breath, then another, and another.

Then she waited for the dead to announce themselves.

Nothing happened. The glass was cold and hard under her bare ankles, and the night was chilly as well.

She thought about how she must look, sitting out here all alone. Desperate, sad, and forlorn. The moon above stared down at her balefully, mocking her.

She was about to open her eyes and get up to head back to the campsite when she felt something. It was like the touch of a warm hand on her shoulder.

She looked up into her mother's beautiful face.

It was a berry day in the Farrai household. Quince's mother and older brother were taking her into the forest to gather hoarberries for the spring festival that night, when they would all be strung together to make festive decorations for the village square and the maypole.

"Is it time?" She pulled at her mother's arm, vying for her attention. She was, after

all, just five years old. Her mother was hanging some herbs from her garden up to dry from the rafters.

"Give me a minute. Did you and your brother wash up? I won't parade you through town looking like vagabonds."

"Yes, Mother." Dillan trudged to the wash basin. The water from the night before was cold, but still clean enough to use. Quince followed him, and they used some of the reed soap to wash the dirt off their faces and arms.

Quince was excited about the festival. It was one of her favorite times of the year, when even the children were allowed to drink the honey ale that Devrin O'Connell made in his little cottage by the river.

"Ready," she and Dillan said in unison.

Their mother finished her work and looked down at the two of them. "Let's see." She knelt down and licked her thumb, using it to wipe a smudge from Quince's face. Quince wrinkled her nose at the smell. "There, that's better. Okay, grab your coats and we'll be off."

Quince opened her eyes. That had been one of her happiest days at home with her mother, one she hadn't let herself remember in more than twenty-five years.

She looked around at the moonlit clearing. "Thanks, Mamma," she whispered, holding the memory to her chest like a bright star.

She stayed there for a bit longer, basking in the warm memory. Wishing it were more than that.

The night was clear and cold, though. Eventually Quince rousted herself and stood, stretching out her muscles, sore from being in the same position for so long.

It might have just been her imagination, or her senses becoming acclimatized, but she no longer smelled the burnt odor that had been so strong when they had arrived.

She pulled her boots back on and made her way back across the meadow toward their little campsite.

Xander was no longer sitting on watch under the tree at the edge of the forest, where she had left him.

Alarmed, she ran toward the campsite, arriving in a huff. Her eyes adjusted to the darkness. Xander had opened Jameson's sleep sack and curled himself around the other man's body.

They were so *right* together. It was nice to know that there was still beauty in the world.

Morgan had taken up residence in the other sleep sack.

She smiled, and then frowned.

They were going to need to have a serious chat about campsite security in the morning. People were falling asleep during their watches left and right.

Grumbling, she sat down with her back against the tree to keep a lookout for the last part of the night.

CHAPTER 17
FALLING

XANDER FELT sheepish when Quince woke him early the next morning. He'd fully intended to keep watch until she had finished her communion with the dead. He'd sat there for what had to be close to an hour, all the while getting more and more tired. It was one thing to be out at the clubs with Alix until the wee hours, drinking and dancing with his friends, but to sit still in a cold, alien forest with nothing to do but watch an immobile form a hundred meters away? That was close to torture.

In the end, he didn't even remember having dragged himself over to where Jameson slept. One minute, he was sitting watch, and the next, Quince was glaring down at him, the sky light behind her, shaking his shoulder.

Xander sat up gently, trying not to waken Jameson too soon. He was still warm where their bodies had been touching, but his breath came out in clouds. The sun must have been barely up, because it was still dark underneath the trees.

He stood and brushed himself clean of the leaves that were stuck to his clothes and wings. Xander sniffed himself and curled his lips. He reeked. It had been days since he'd been able to get really clean. "Morning," he whispered, not meeting Quince's gaze.

"You fell asleep on watch."

He nodded, looking up. "I'm sorry. I didn't plan to…."

She waved him off. "It doesn't matter so much now, but as we get closer to Gaelan…."

"I know, I know. It won't happen again. Though a little caff would help." He looked around. "Does this place even have cafflite?"

Quince shook her head. "Afraid not. But lucky for you, I brought some along." She poured him a mug of the steaming drink, and he downed it quickly. *Oh my God, that tastes good.*

He glanced back at Jameson. "I guess the whole wings and flight thing is taking it out of him." The psych had fallen asleep almost instantly when he'd hit the sack, and he was still sleeping, right through their conversation.

Quince nodded. "You remember how much *you* ate and how tired you were when your wings came in, and we're pushing him to fly before he's really ready. He hasn't built up his endurance. We'll have to be more careful today. There are a number of inhabited villages between here and Gaelan."

"Can you carry Morgan today?" Xander asked. "I want to keep an eye on Jameson."

She glanced at the boy, a look of distaste on her face, but she nodded. "It's time to wake them. We can eat something. My lines hauled in a couple of fish last night, so we'll have a warm meal. Then we need to fly. Time is short."

"So you keep saying."

She ignored the jibe, and moved to wake Jameson.

"Let me." Xander pushed past her. He knelt down and brushed Jameson's lips with his own.

Jameson mumbled, and he kissed Xander back gently. Then his eyes opened.

"Morning," Xander said, pulling back and smiling.

"Did you just… did I…?"

"I don't know what you're talking about. Though you did miss your turn on watch last night. It's time to get up."

Quince shot him a sly smile.

JAMESON WONDERED how long this day would go on. He had woken up that morning, still tired from the day before, to find Xander staring down at him. He would have sworn the man had just kissed him again, but Xander had denied it.

Why that should make him sad, Jameson wasn't quite sure.

They'd rushed through breakfast—that infernal cafflite, some local fish from the river, and some "whore berries" Quince had found in the forest.

Then they had taken to the sky again, intent on Quince's mad quest.

He was utterly exhausted. The dash out of Oberon City had depleted him, and the attack by the wereveren had sapped some of his strength. This magical, amazing thing—the ability to fly under his own power—had turned from a childhood dream to an unforgiving slog through the endless pink skies.

They stayed close to the river, low to the ground, and twice detoured inland to avoid a populated area.

It also didn't help that the terrain below them was unrelentingly the same. River and trees and meadows. River and trees and more godforsaken meadows. There was little variation, and he was starting to feel as though he was flying over the same patch of land over and over again, even if the leaves were various shades of purple instead of the usual greens and golds.

Quince, by contrast, seemed like a different person, light as the air through which they flew. They'd taken a brief rest for lunch, and through his fatigue, he had seen a new sense of humor and willingness to engage with them that had been muted or absent before.

He wanted to say something. To tell them he couldn't keep this up. He really couldn't. He felt like he was about to fall out of the sky.

Xander and Quince showed no signs of fatigue, and Jameson didn't want to be the one who seemed weak and unable to keep up.

So he kept flying, his mouth set in a grim, determined line. Morning stretched into afternoon, and a deep fatigue set into his wings and shoulders. He started seeing things—little flickers at the edge of his vision, and sometimes whole flashes of someone else's memories.

Still, he kept going as the sun crossed the sky into late afternoon.

Until he just couldn't.

"Xander, I can't...," he rasped, but he found his voice was gone. "I can't...." And his wings stopped flapping.

He started to plummet from the sky, but he was so damned tired he just didn't care.

Xander was worried about Jameson. This extended flight was hard on them all. He hadn't had to fly for this long at a stretch in years. City living had domesticated him.

He didn't want to show it. Better to set a strong example for Jameson. So he hid his own fatigue and tried to keep Jameson's spirits up.

Quince thought they'd be able to reach Gaelan in another day or so, but Xander wasn't sure they'd be able to keep up this pace.

Time was not on their side, either way.

It was strange how quickly he'd come to care for Jameson. Just a few days before, they'd been complete strangers. He'd thought the off-worlder was weak and spineless, but being forced together into rough circumstances had a way of bonding people, and besides, Jameson was clearly his type. There were times that it scared him how much he resembled Alix.

Xander was talking with Quince about the lands they were passing over when he saw Jameson start to plunge toward the ground.

He dove after Jameson, letting himself go into freefall with his wings tucked. There was no time to think. He had one shot to catch Jameson before he hit the trees below.

The wind whistled by as he plummeted toward Jameson's falling form. Damn it, they'd pushed him too hard. Why hadn't Jameson said something?

Stupid male ego. He didn't have a patent on that.

Xander slipped below Jameson, perilously close to the tree tops, and swept upward with his powerful black wings to intercept his falling body.

Jameson dropped into his arms, almost knocking him off balance, but Xander fought to keep his upward trajectory. His wings pushed hard against air, straining all his muscles, and he pulled himself up and away from the danger.

Quince had followed him, and now hovered just above.

"We have to stop." He was unable to keep the anger out of his voice. "He could have died, Quince."

She nodded, her face white. "There's a place we can rest, just ahead. Can you manage his weight?"

"I think so, for a little ways."

"Come on."

Jameson's body was cradled in his arms. "You okay?" he asked.

Jameson nodded. "I'm sooooo tired...."

"You can rest now." He kissed Jameson's forehead, but the man was already asleep.

Quince led them upriver for another fifteen minutes, throwing caution to the wind. Jameson was slight enough, but the extra weight was starting to pull Xander down. He forged on—what else could he do?

Finally, Quince signaled to him. Just ahead, there was an island in the middle of the stream, maybe twenty meters wide and three times that long. It was a rocky outcropping, surrounded by a stand of golden-leaved trees. On one side, a rough terrace had been carved into the rock.

He followed her lead, and they alighted on the terrace.

"It's a way station," she said in response to Xander's inquiry. "I wanted to avoid them if possible, because they may still be in occasional use by Gaelani forces. However, given the circumstances...."

He nodded, looking around. The stone terrace was obviously manmade—it was too smooth and even to be anything else. Hidden under an overhang was an old wooden door, bound with iron hinges, that hadn't been apparent from the air.

She opened it with a loud creak and gestured for him to follow her inside.

There was a room on the other side, maybe five meters square, cut directly into the rock, and thank the skies, there were beds. They were wooden cots, actually, and the thin mattresses were nothing like what he had at home, but to Xander it was like he'd just stumbled across a five-star branch of the Galaxion Hotel.

He laid Jameson down gently on one of the cots and put a hand on his forehead. It was warm, but probably just from overexertion. Hopefully. "Rest now," he whispered, running his fingers gently through Jameson's hair.

He stood and looked around, now that his eyes had adjusted to the dim light of the room.

The walls had been smoothed out, but the angles of the room were rough, suggesting that it had been an existing cavern enlarged for human use. The floor was paved with flat stones and some type of mortar, and there was a wooden cabinet with four doors in one corner.

Quince was outside with Morgan. Xander rejoined her, taking in the view of the forest across the river.

She had unstrapped the boy, and he was sitting on the ledge at the edge of the terrace, looking out over the river below.

Xander knelt next to Morgan. "You okay, buddy? That was kind of scary."

Morgan nodded. "Is he okay?"

"I think so. He just needs some sleep." He patted the boy on the back. "Why don't you carry our packs inside." He sent the boy scurrying off.

Quince was staring at the sun.

"He almost died," Xander said again. Nothing could be worth pushing themselves this hard.

"I know," she said quietly. Her brow was knitted and her mouth was set in a tight line.

He followed her gaze. Was it his imagination, or was the sun above less red and a little more orange this afternoon? "We have to slow down, whether you like it or not. He can't take much more."

"If we don't get there in time, his health won't matter. Nothing will."

Xander shuddered. "Okay, we need speed. I get it. But we can't go on until the morning. Jameson needs at least a little rest. Do we have that much time?"

"I don't know." All her senses told her no, that they needed to keep going *now*, but that wasn't an option. So much of this journey had spun out of her control. She looked back at the way station. "It's not that we have much choice…." She sighed, looking as if the weight of the world were on her shoulders. She turned back to him. "There is good news, though."

He frowned. In the face of such danger, what good news could there be?

"We have food to eat, and a shower."

QUINCE LED Xander down to the outdoor shower. It was under another rock overhang, and used a hand pump to bring water up from the river. She showed him how to prime the pump and then fill up the holding basin.

The water was cold, but nevertheless he looked delighted. She handed him one of their last bars of reed soap and left him to clean himself up.

She had no desire to see his naked body. He wasn't at all her type. Hers was waiting for her in Gaelan, she hoped.

She was nervous about their impending arrival. There was so much she didn't know, so many years she had missed.

She climbed the path back up to the way station. They wouldn't have gotten much more flight time in this day, in any case. It was only another hour or so until dark.

She entered the cave and found Morgan standing over Jameson, his little hands on the man's body. They were glowing.

I knew it. "Get away from him!" She grabbed his shoulders and pulled Morgan back forcefully. He was no normal boy—the last time she'd seen him glow like that, he'd slaughtered a whole squad of enforcers.

She knelt down and shook him by his shoulders. "What were you doing to him? Tell me!"

He stared up at her, trembling. "I was just making him feel better."

She looked over at Jameson, and couldn't believe what she saw. She let go of the boy and went to take a closer look.

His wereveren wounds were completely healed, leaving clean scars. His face was slack and peaceful, and he smelled… clean. Fresh.

She turned back to stare at Morgan. "What are you?" she asked.

"I don't know." He started to cry.

· · ·

Jameson's eyes flickered open. He was lying on something soft. His body felt amazing. The aching of his muscles was gone, replaced by a vibrant energy. His assorted wereveren wounds no longer hurt. He ran his fingers over one. It was smooth and healed.

Just how long had he been asleep?

It was dark wherever he lay, but there were voices arguing.

"We can't leave him behind. He didn't do anything wrong."

That was Xander. He smiled when he thought of the beautiful, dark angel.

"Maybe not, but we have no idea what he's capable of. He survived on his own long enough."

That was Quince. She seemed unsettled. Were they talking about him?

For his part, Jameson was *starving*. He sat up and took in the place where he found himself. It was a dark, roughly square room, sparsely furnished, with four cots and a wooden cabinet in one corner.

The voices were coming from outside. "Nevertheless, we're not leaving a defenseless little child here alone."

Ah, so it was about Morgan.

The last thing Jameson remembered was falling from the sky. He had been so worn out that he had just given up. His muscles had stopped working. How had he gone from there to here?

He stood and made his way outside into the evening light.

Xander and Quince were still going at it. Morgan was crouched against the rock wall, looking up at them, frightened and unnoticed.

Jameson leaned down to pick the boy up, pulling Morgan's skinny form up to his chest. "Hey, that's enough." He hugged the boy to his chest.

Both voices fell silent, and Xander and Quince pivoted to look at him in synch, surprised.

"You should be in bed," Xander said.

Quince nodded. "You need to get your strength back up."

"I feel much better, but you two should be ashamed of yourselves. You've scared this poor boy half to death. Especially you, Xander. He looks up to you!" He turned to Morgan. "You okay, little guy?"

Morgan nodded. "She doesn't like me." He pointed at Quince.

"Why don't you run inside and lie down for a bit?"

The boy followed his instruction, shooting back a brief smile before disappearing into the darkness of the room.

"Now what's this all about?"

Xander and Quince exchanged looks.

"Quince said she came in and Morgan had his hands on you. They were glowing, and then you were healed."

"I told you he was no normal boy." Quince sounded a little too smug about it.

"Whatever he did, I'm no worse for wear. In fact, I feel better than I have in a week." He held up his arms to show off his body. "So my vote's with Xander. The boy goes with us."

Quince held his gaze for a moment, searching his eyes. He thought he saw the hint of a smile on her lips. She nodded.

Jameson had the feeling that she didn't lose very often.

His stomach growled. "Now can I get something to eat?"

CHAPTER 18
TWIST

"WE'LL LEAVE AT FIRST light. We should reach Gaelan tomorrow," Quince said, pausing between bites. The way station was stocked with an assortment of dried meats and fruits, making this the best meal they'd had in days. "Things have been calm between the Gaelani and the Erriani for some time, but there's a force from OberCorp in the city—"

"Seriously? We've come all this way to get away from them, and they're there before us?" Xander almost spat it out.

Jameson passed a handful of nuts to Morgan. "How do you know?"

"They've been there for a while. Robyn… your mother, Xander, sent me a message just before we left. I hope she can help us. Something has changed. The pith shortage has me worried."

Jameson perked up at this information. The quest that had brought him to Oberon seemed almost lost to the past, but it *was* what he had come here to find out…. "Where does pith come from?" he asked. It was strange that he didn't know even this basic piece of information about the drug he'd been tasked to bring back home.

"It's the sap of the púca tree. It grows in the mountains, not far from here." Quince chewed on a piece of dried meat. "It's mostly used here for rituals and during fertility rites."

Jameson laughed. "That's crazy…. Wait, you're not kidding."

Quince shook her head. "Titania is a different place from Oberon. When the second-wave colonists arrived, our people were driven out of their homes. We had already lost much of the remaining technology that we'd brought with us from Earth, and what little was left was lost in the Great Retreat, when most of us fled to Titania."

"So it's a primitive culture—"

"Technologically, yes. But you have to remember, it's a culture that grew up over eight hundred years. It has its own complexities and subtleties."

He'd offended her. "I'm sorry—I didn't mean—"

"Technological advances aren't always better than cultural ones," Xander said. "What has high tech brought to Oberon's cities, other than pollution and squalor?"

Jameson thought about it. Certainly tech had made his life more comfortable at home, but he'd lived an above-average life, financially. Clearly that wasn't the case for many. He'd seen how people lived in the Slander, and the miners on Tander's World. "So how did they get here? The way we came?"

She nodded. "Some did, but there are several other places where the worlds still touch. They can only be opened with a key, in the middle of the day." She took a sip of water.

She gave him some of the dried fruit, which he devoured quickly. He was still unreasonably hungry most of the time, though his wings were approaching their mature size, if Xander's wingspan was anything to judge by.

"So what happens when we get there?" Xander asked. "To Gaelan?"

"We have to sneak in and convince someone to give us the rocthane."

"The *what*?" Xander asked.

Jameson couldn't help stealing looks at the handsome wing man.

"The rocthane. The key. Well, it's not really a key, per se, not like the others. This one can remove the wall that divides Titania and Oberon. We'll need it if you two are going to bring the worlds back together."

"Wait… what?" Jameson almost spit out his fruit. "We're going to do *what*?" A memory surfaced in his head, something that must have been much older than he was.

He stood in a circular chamber hollowed out of stone, across from a beautiful, regal woman. She was magnificent, more than six feet tall, her black wings swept out behind her. She was dressed in a warrior's armor.

There was an archway next to them. Their hands together held a round stone, about as big as a crystal ball and as black as night. It seemed to suck all the light out of the room.

Their eyes met, and she nodded. Their eyes locked on one another, he stepped through the archway, and the world shifted….

. . .

Jameson blinked, and he was back in another cavern, this one lit by a lantern.

Quince was staring at him intently. "Where did you go?"

He shook his head. "I don't know. There was a room… a cave, kind of like this one, and a woman—"

"Did she have black hair, and dark wings, like Xander?"

He nodded dumbly.

"That was Elyra." She sat back, staring at him. "You *were* touched by the gods."

Touched by something. "Is she real?"

Quince nodded. "She *was* the Queen of the House of the Moon, and together with Daedus, King of the House of the Sun, she shifted Oberon, the last time the two worlds were threatened."

"Was? How long ago was that?" Having these old memories suddenly popping into his head was unnerving, to say the least.

Quince considered. "About 750 years ago, give or take, before the arrival of the second wave." She handed him a cup of water. It had a strange taste, but he was thirsty…. It was probably just what "natural" water tasted like.

He shook his head. The whole thing was crazy. You couldn't just go around shifting worlds at a whim. *Maybe I'm the one who's crazy.* He decided that he didn't want to explore that possibility too deeply.

Xander jumped in to save him. "Who made the keys, Quince? From what you've told us, the skythane didn't have the ability to create something that shifts worlds. I'm not sure anyone in the Common Worlds even does, today. So who did?"

"I don't know. No one does. Maybe the gods."

Xander snorted. "Now we're back to rank superstition."

Jameson jumped in. "Assuming we believe you"—he shot a look at Xander—"what would you need us to do?"

"It's simple. Find out who's in power now. Then convince them to give you the key, and to let the son of his foremost enemy walk out the door with you to save the world."

Xander snorted. "Simple as that."

"I never promised it would be easy."

AFTER THEIR meal, Jameson offered to take the first watch again. After what

Morgan had done to him, and with a full stomach, he felt better than he had in days. He also felt a little… randy. It had been a long time.

He took up a place in the shadow of the outcrop, just outside the way station, and sat back to pass his shift.

Quince had stressed how important this duty was, especially as they approached Gaelan, and he had promised to stay awake.

His mind was still catching up to what had happened to his body these last few days—the wings, the strange memories that weren't his, and Morgan's intervention.

His unexpected attraction to Xander.

If he was honest with himself, he'd had these urges before. His parents'—his foster parents, actually, and he was still getting used to *that* idea—religion had frowned upon homosexuality, though his psych training had brought him to a much more neutral understanding of it. He'd long ago decided that it wasn't for him, that he could be whatever he wanted to be. That he wouldn't let his sexual desires rule his life.

He had experienced "feelings" for one of the miners once, a young Tharsisian named Mikelos. Feelings that he was fairly sure had been reciprocated, if never acted upon. That would have been unethical, in any case.

Plus he was still engaged to Jessa. He was supposed to "wait" for her.

So he'd pushed those feelings aside, sure he could just wish the whole thing away. Somehow.

But now….

Xander was so close, and so unimaginably beautiful. Jameson closed his eyes and pictured the man standing in front of him, his black wings catching the moonlight.

He shivered, though it wasn't that cold out yet, and settled in to watch for intruders.

Xander lay down on the cot and closed his eyes, willing the oblivion of sleep to carry him away from all the madness. The day had become a nightmare—almost losing Jameson, and having to pull Quince away from Morgan once again.

Now he lay on a strange bed in a strange world, and all he could think about was Jameson.

The man was so wrong for him. Brainy and stuffy where Xander was forthright and practical. Prideful to the point of distraction, and from a rival family to boot.

Xander had no business thinking about Jameson in that way, and yet....

He turned on his side, counting shooting stars in his head. Usually when he reached fifty he was out like a light, but not this time. *Four-hundred-and-seventy-nine, four-hundred-and-eighty, four-hundred-and-eighty-one.* Still no solace.

Alix had receded in his memory, the man's beautiful face and bright smile little more than a spark.

Instead, when he closed his eyes, he saw the off-worlder. When the shadow of memory had come over his face, Xander had wanted nothing more than to take Jameson in his arms to keep him safe.

He'd gone to bed alone.

Fuck it.

He got up silently, pulling on his pants, and checked to make sure Quince and Morgan were still sleeping. The boy was snoring softly.

Xander smiled and pulled the blanket up to his neck. Then he padded outside to find Jameson.

Jameson looked up, surprised, when he arrived. "Is it time to trade shifts already? It felt like just an hour...."

"Not yet." Xander leaned in and kissed him softly on the lips, their third kiss. This time, he held the kiss for a moment, savoring the taste of the man. Then he pulled back to judge if his advances were welcome, or if he'd missed the mark.

Jameson looked shocked, but then his mouth stretched into a lazy smile, and his brown eyes almost sparkled. This time, he leaned forward to kiss Xander.

Xander's libido surged.

They separated again, and Xander whispered, "Do you want to...?"

"More than anything."

Xander laughed. "Come on. I know a place." He led Jameson down the path to the shower, and laid him down gently on the ground. His wings spread, he knelt down over Jameson and ran his hand over the other man's chest.

Jameson looked up at him expectantly, his breathing short and shallow.

Xander undid his own shirt, exposing his chest and back to the cool air.

Jameson's hands went around his back, and the man hissed when he felt the scars there. "Can I see?"

Xander hesitated. They were part of a dark time in his life, and made him feel marred. Damaged. Finally he nodded. He turned so Jameson could see them, touch them.

Jameson's warm hand passed over his back, tracing the lines left there by Rogan's whip.

"Do you think they're ugly?" he asked anxiously.

Jameson turned him around gently. "Not to me. They're part of who you are, and that makes them beautiful." He pulled Xander down into another kiss, this one longer and deeper.

In response, Xander kissed him, hard. His hand reached down to undo Jameson's pants, finding Jameson aroused and ready for him.

Jameson was slenderer than Xander, his light skin shining in the silver moonlight.

He circled around Jameson's nipples with his tongue, one at a time, eliciting a moan from the man as he arched his chest into the air, reaching for more.

Xander flashed Jameson an evil smile and pulled Jameson's pants down.

The cool river air played over his own bare back.

He nibbled on Jameson's ear, whispering, "I've been waiting for this."

Jameson shivered, but he nodded.

Then Xander did a whole lot more.

QUINCE ALIGHTED *in the garden of the House of the Stars, the moonlight silvering her wings. Lyrin was fast asleep in her arms, held close to her chest.*

She trod softly up the path to the small castle, nodding to the golden statue of Erro as she passed under his extended wings.

The House of the Stars' courtyard doors were flung open, and she entered quietly, looking around the abandoned space. The last time she'd been here, the place had been bustling with members of the Gaelani and Erriani courts for the Midsummer Festival. Now it was deserted, the merriment of that night long past.

She reached forward and pulled open the door to the House of the Stars. Twice as tall as she was, it nevertheless opened smoothly.

There was a small fire in the Grand Hall, smokeless, she was sure. Someone stood before the fire.

"Robyn?"

The figure turned, and then they were running toward one another across the empty space. "Quince!" Robyn kissed her hard. "I was so worried. I sent word. Did you get it?"

Quince shook her head. "I waited. Then something terrible happened to Ballifor.... They...." She couldn't get it out.

"What happened?" Robyn held her at arm's length, looking into her eyes.

Gods, she had missed those arms.

"Tell me what happened."

Quince sat down next to the fire and told Robyn everything.

Next to them, little Davyn was fast asleep on a pile of furs.

When she got to the part about her village, she froze up again. "Ballifor… it's… it's gone," she managed at last.

"What do you mean, gone?"

"Destroyed. By some lander weapon. I was lucky to escape. If I hadn't taken Lyrin for a walk…."

"At least they don't know you're still alive. And they haven't found Davyn and me."

"They'll find us eventually." Quince's voice came out in a whimper. She wasn't brave. She'd only survived so far due to dumb luck and flight instinct. "They'll kill us all. They blamed the Gaelani for what happened to the Erriani Queen."

"There's been fighting. I hadn't heard about Ballifor. I'm so sorry, Quince."

"It makes no sense. Why do they want us to fight?"

"They don't want Davyn and Lyrin to fulfill their destiny. Any change to the world order might threaten their illicit pith trade. Quince, you have to be brave. I need you to be brave. You're the only one who can save us all."

"How?" She wiped the tears from her eyes. Gods, she hated being vulnerable like this. She should be angry at Robyn for having sent her away in the first place. But her anger was long gone.

"You have to take the boys and run. To Oberon. Lose yourself. Lose them, so no one can find you."

Quince shook her head. "I can't. I just found you again. I can't leave—don't ask me to leave."

Robyn laid a hand on the side of her face. "We'll be together again, love. I promise. We'll figure it out. When the boys are most needed, we'll be ready." She kissed Quince softly, gently. Then she looked at her again, her eyes wet, belying the strength in her voice. "You can do this."

At last, Quince nodded. "I wish I could take you with me."

"I have to stay here, to grieve the loss of my son." She looked at Davyn's sleeping form. She did not cry. Quince was heartened by her strength.

"When do I have to go?"

"Tomorrow morning is soon enough, my love." She drew Quince with her to another pile of blankets and furs before the fire. "Tonight I want you next to me."

Quince nodded. "I'd like that. It's been too long."

They settled in together, Lyrin tucked in front of Quince's chest. Robyn wrapped her arms around Quince.

Quince felt safe for the first time since the death of the Erriani Queen.

Quince awoke.

She was lying on her back, staring at the ceiling of the little cavern.

It had been so long since she'd seen Robyn last, on that fretful night before she had taken the two boys and run. So much had changed. She hoped at least one small thing remained the same. She hoped they weren't walking into a trap. She would find out tomorrow.

The night was still, the murmur of the river running by outside the open door the only sound. Something was wrong.

She sat up quietly and looked around. Morgan was asleep, his back to her. At rest, he looked like any normal little boy. She pulled the blanket they'd found in the chest up over his shoulders. Xander was gone.

He must have gone to find Jameson. Her addition to their diet was having its desired effect, apparently, but that meant that no one was keeping watch.

She crept to the door of the cavern, looking into the darkness outside. The moon cast a silver glow across the river valley, and the trees stood still as if frozen by the darkness.

There was nothing to worry about, surely. She was being paranoid, and she should really just go back to sleep.

She'd be remiss if she didn't at least go out and check.

She stepped out onto the terrace and felt something rough underneath her bare feet. She bent down to examine it.

It was a piece of rope.

Something closed around her and she was unceremoniously hauled up into the air. She screamed, but then she was being handled by rough hands, and something was slipped over her mouth.

Everything went dark.

JAMESON LAY nestled next to Xander in the peaceful quiet of the island, their faces just inches apart. Xander's eyes were closed. He looked like a perfect angel.

Not that he'd behaved like an angelic being this last hour together. Far from it. Jameson grinned. He'd waited long enough for this moment.

Jameson felt a sense of peace and contentment that he'd never experienced before, and he wanted nothing more than to lie there forever with Xander. To hell with the rest of the world. Or worlds, as the case seemed to be.

.

He should be analyzing the whole thing. Mortal enemies come together. Literally. The flip side of hate is love. All that psychological claptrap he'd learned during his training. At the moment, he couldn't have cared less.

His old life seemed like someone else's dream, lived in another dimension entirely. He should feel guilty about that. About Jessa. About what he and Xander had just done. But it was just *right*.

He looked at Xander's peaceful face, hungry to try it again.

They kissed, falling from the sky, arms wrapped around each other as the ground raced up toward them. He didn't care.

She was beautiful, fierce, his.

The wind whistled past them as he savored her kiss.

"Now!" she shouted, and they split, spreading their wings and soaring back up into the air, just a few feet above the treetops.

She was reckless, and he loved that about her.

Another memory, this one decidedly not Lyrin's. Still, it made him wonder. *What would it feel like to make love to him in flight?*

His amorous thoughts were cut short by a shout in the darkness.

"Quince," Xander hissed, and they were on their feet, pulling on their clothes as quickly as they could. Xander took off toward the cavern, and Jameson followed, cursing himself for having abandoned his post. He'd neglected his duty, and now Quince might be paying the price.

Jameson could make out Xander just ahead of him, on the pathway in the moonlight as they ran back toward the way station.

Then he was gone.

Jameson stopped and looked around, confused. There was shouting overhead, but he could make no sense of it. He looked up into the darkness, trying to see where Xander had gone.

Then something dropped over him and closed in around him, and he was trapped and hauled into the air. He struggled, but he was caught in some kind of rope net, just as Xander must have been.

He was dumped unceremoniously on the rocky top of the island next to Xander and Quince. Quince looked like she had been knocked out, or worse. Xander shot him a worried look through the netting.

Morgan was nowhere to be seen.

There were five other skythane standing around them. Every one of them had black wings like Xander. Then someone else stepped into Jameson's field of vision.

Jameson looked up to see a woman in a black uniform with short-cropped blonde hair and a sharp, hawkish nose standing over them. She had no wings.

"It took you long enough," she said to Xander, who looked up at her and gasped.

"Dani?"

The woman laughed. It was an unpleasant sound. "It's been a long time, Xander. I wasn't sure you were going to make it."

"Dani, where's Alix? What happened to Alix?" Xander sounded almost frantic.

She ignored him. "Get them ready for transport," she said to one of the skythane. She turned away, and Jameson watched as one of her henchmen placed a cloth over Xander's face.

"Where's Alix?" Xander shouted again, just before he slumped into unconsciousness.

Jameson had just a second to wonder who Dani and Alix were before he followed Xander down into darkness.

CHAPTER 19
CAPTIVE

XANDER'S HEAD WAS POUNDING. He lay on something incredibly soft, and a smell like lavender mixed with sandalwood filled the air.

He opened his eyes. He was in a brightly lit room, on a wide bed covered in hand-woven blankets. Four wooden posters held up a canopy above, covered with a dark blue cloth, stitched with silver designs of stars and the moon.

The temperature in the room was comfortable. A warm fire burned in the stone hearth in one corner, and it was growing dark outside. He could see the sky through the warped glass of two closed doors that looked out onto a wide balcony.

Xander tried to move and realized he was bound at his ankles and wrists to the four corners of the bed.

"I'm sorry about having to tie you up," a voice said. Dani stepped into view, dressed in full enforcer uniform. "I had to be sure you would listen to what I had to say."

So it wasn't my imagination after all. Xander hadn't known Danielle all that well. She had been one of Alix's work friends, and one of the people who had been on Alix's "camping trip." Which he was starting to suspect had been nothing of the kind.

So why was she here? "I don't see that I have much choice." He tested his bonds, but they were tight. He wasn't going anywhere.

Dani sat on the bed, her hand caressing the edge of Xander's cheek, nails scratching lightly over his skin. "I'm sorry about all this. Really I am. You're an important piece of this little puzzle. Alix didn't understand that."

Xander grew alarmed. Since they'd been captured, he'd hoped Alix was still alive, that he was just a pawn in whatever this was. "What plan?"

Dani smiled, but somehow that smile wasn't warm at all. Instead, it seemed cold and alien. "I work for ObersCorp. Just like Alix."

Xander nodded. "What the hell are you doing *here*? Why did you say you'd been expecting me?" *And what did you do with Jameson, Quince, and Morgan?* He didn't say the last part aloud. Better if she didn't know how he felt about Jameson, or the others.

"The company grew tired of all the black-market sales of pith in the Slander, and decided to take over the action. When I discovered there was a Prince of the *Wing Men* among us in Oberon City, we saw the perfect opportunity." She spat out "wing men" like it was a curse word. "Unfortunately, you got away before we had the chance to bring you in. Fortunately, you ran right into us here."

"How did you find us?"

"Simple luck, really. You were spotted on your way to the way station. I'd guessed Quince would try to bring you here, with all the stupid superstitious claptrap these people believe."

Xander's mind raced. He and Alix had been in love once, hadn't they? Alix had rescued him from the Syndicate, after all, and he had been inordinately grateful. Too grateful, perhaps? Besides, he had Jameson now.

Had it been love, or something else? "Did Alix dose me? With pith?"

Dani smiled, and if possible, it was even colder than before. "You always were a little slow on the uptake." She stood, looking out of the window. "No, he didn't. We didn't discover your past until just before you fled Oberon City. You were just his little fling."

"Where is he?"

"Alix is dead." She didn't sound sad. "Poor man was killed by one of these savages when we first arrived."

A knife-blade of pain pierced Xander's heart, and his body shook with anger as he strained against his bonds, pulling the bed half a foot away from the wall. If he could have, he would have wiped that sneer off Dani's face.

He felt so fucking impotent. Whatever they'd had together, he had *loved* Alix. And while he lay here, helpless, the end of the world was coming like the relentless, steady ticking of a bomb.

"It was easy enough to buy the trust of these simpletons." Dani turned to face him. "The King—excuse me, your father—passed away without an heir a few weeks ago, ending almost a year of negotiations to convince him to work exclusively with OberCorp on the pith trade. We've had this town on lock-down ever since."

She looked out the window into the darkness. "We turned to the Queen. Your own mother. She was the one who told us about you, by the way, after much persuasion. Unfortunately, she was unwilling to work with us to calm the Gaelani people. Luckily, I have *you* now." She cupped her hand under Xander's chin. "You're the Prince of the Gaelani, and you're going to help me seal the deal."

Dani had just all but admitted to killing his mother, and he was helpless to do anything about it. He spit on Dani's hand.

The woman pulled her hand away and slapped Xander hard across his cheek. "Your resistance won't matter one whit once I slip you enough pith. You'll fall in love with me instead, and you and I will run this little fiefdom. We've already seen that your heart is… malleable."

Xander's face burned. "What about the flare?"

Dani laughed. "You've got to be kidding me. Is Quince still going on about that? It's simple *wing man* superstition. Oberon's sun has always been temperamental. It'll settle down in its own good time."

Clearly she hadn't been keeping in touch with what was happening back on Oberon.

She knelt down and gave Xander a light kiss on the forehead. "Sleep well, my beloved. We'll get married in two days." She leaned down to whisper in his ear. "I can't wait to get my hands on your beautiful ass."

Then she was gone.

Xander snarled and tried with all his might to break himself loose from the rope that held him down, succeeding only in moving the furniture another couple inches.

How had he ever fallen in love with Alix? If he had been part of this woman's crew, then his soul must have been black as pith.

Xander lay there for a while, cursing his bad luck and wondering what had become of Quince, Jameson, and Morgan. And just after he and Jameson had finally connected.

Fate was a bitch, to bring them together at last only to rip them apart.

At last, he dropped into a fitful slumber.

Alix laughed, throwing another snowball at him. Xander zigged one way and then zagged the other, and then leapt at Alix, knocking him back into a big drift of snow.

They tumbled one over another until they came to a halt against an ice pine, the impact dropping a dusting of snow over the two of them.

Xander laughed in delight. "I never imagined snow could be so much fun." As a city boy in the tropical climes, he'd never experienced this frozen water thing before. Alix had dragged him out to the Rim Forest for a couple days away from work. They'd been together for almost two years, but Alix had still been astounded to find out that he was a snow virgin.

"You like it?" There was a twinkle in Alix's eye.

"I love it." He leaned down to kiss Alix, and licked a snowflake from his lover's nose. "It is kind of cold, though...."

"I know a place where it's warmer." Alix shot a meaningful glance in the direction of their all-weather tent.

"Race you there."

Time shifted.

Xander was a little boy, maybe two years old. He stood on a stone terrace, staring out at Gaelan through one of the House of the Moon's embrasures. The city spread out before him, full of life and light—wing men soaring over the valley and the River Orn far below. He reached out a small hand toward them.

"Hey, get back from there." Warm hands scooped him up and turned him around. "You don't have your wings yet." His mother nuzzled his nose against hers. She smelled fresh, like roses in the garden. "You'll fly with them soon enough."

She carried him back inside the House of the Moon just in time for lunch, but his outstretched hands still reached over her shoulder toward the city.

Xander awoke. He was all alone in the dark. He looked around and remembered where he was, and that Alix was no longer with him. His mother was gone from his life too.

Jameson. He still had Jameson. One thing to anchor him, if they could just reach each other once more.

Xander pulled on his bonds again, but they were expertly tied and the rope was strong. He was well and truly trapped.

· · ·

JAMESON STARED despondently at the sunset. He was locked in a metal cage high on a black stone pedestal, some fifty meters above the ground. The bars were made of iron, and wrapped up and over him in a steel dome. They had chained one of his legs to a metal eye set deep into the pedestal. Try as he might, he was unable to move it a millimeter. It was like he'd stepped into a tri-dee show about the middle ages, but the knights had wings instead of shining armor.

Quince was being held in another cage, some ten meters away.

They had been deposited here in the afternoon by their captors and left alone. They hadn't even bothered to leave a guard.

Xander had been hauled inside what Jameson could only describe as a black castle, perched on the edge of the valley above the city. It was surprisingly compact and squat for a structure built by a race that flew through the air with such grace.

And what had happened to Morgan? Had the boy escaped notice? If so, he was all alone back at the way station.

Or was he being held somewhere in this city too?

Jameson had 360-degree views of the city of Gaelan. It was spread out below him, tall towers built seemingly of the same black stone as the House of the Sky back on Oberon. Unlike those ruins, this city soared above the ground, slender towers connected by arching bridges, with balconies jutting out for what seemed like impossible distances. A river wound through the valley, half encircling a tall hill topped by a single black tower that sat high above everything but the castle.

A few wing men flew past, though not in such numbers as he would have expected from one of this world's capital cities. He tried calling out to some of them, but they all shied away from him as though he carried the plague.

Jameson longed to fly. Instead, he was trapped here like a caged bird.

Where are you, Xander? What were they doing to his… lover? Partner? Jameson's face flushed as he remembered that last encounter. Had he somehow brought this upon himself?

Being with Xander had felt so *right,* but maybe he'd angered some higher power. Was this God's punishment?

Even Quince seemed to feel that gods were real here. Who was he to say she was wrong?

And who was this Dani, the lander woman that Xander seemed to know? Was she from Oberon? Or was she a fallen skythane? Had she lost her wings?

Jameson had no answers for any of these questions.

He longed for his simple life as a psych back on Tander's World. What had seemed so boring and tedious back then now seemed peaceful, and most of all, safe.

Xander was a prince in this city. Quince had told them so, and if she was right, he ought to be able to get things sorted out soon.

He looked over at her. She was staring at the setting sun, her expression unreadable.

Jameson was thirsty, and he needed to take a piss, but so far he and Quince had been totally ignored.

He leaned back against the bars and closed his eyes, willing himself to be calm. He was tired again. Whatever Morgan had done to him to restore his energy seemed to have worn off.

Jameson could just take a short nap. He closed his eyes, certain he'd have a hard time sleeping on the hard rock surface of this cage so high above the ground. He was out in seconds.

Jameson/Lyrin was flying far above the Riamhwood as the sun set in the distance, the sky pink and clear above him. His left hand touched Elyra's, a spark passing between them. The wind tousled her raven-black hair, and her wings beat in time with his.

He pulled her close to kiss her, and their intertwined forms plunged toward the earth far below as he savored the kiss. He opened his eyes, and she was looking back at him, merriment in her eyes.

They let go and swept back up into the air together, spinning round and round each other like two leaves in a windstorm.

They fell again toward the earth, this time hand in hand, alighting on the banks of the River Orn. Jameson pulled her in again, only to find he was holding Xander in his arms.

Jameson woke, staring at the bars of his iron cage.

I've got it bad. Somehow Xander had worked his way into Jameson's head, in more ways than one. Now the skythane man was gone, and Jameson was trapped with only his thoughts and memories for company.

Many of which weren't, apparently, even his own.

QUINCE STARED down at Gaelan, laid out before her in the growing darkness. The Orn flowed down over the rim of the valley behind her in a tumultuous waterfall, kicking up a constant white spray. From there, the river tumbled through the middle of Gaelan, below the black castle—the House of the Moon and the prison cages where she and Jameson were being held.

There was a particular cruelty in locking up a skythane in the sky while denying them the power of flight.

The river wound through the city, wrapping around Founder's Hill and down past the wall that lay at the city's eastern end, hemming in the aeries that filled in the spaces between the river and the valley's own natural walls.

Quince had watched the setting sun go down behind the falls with a growing sense of dread. It was more yellow now than red. She knew the signs. First the storms, then the EMPs, then the change in the color of the sun. Time was getting short, likely a matter of days.

She'd whispered a prayer to Gael and Erro, the gods of the Moon and the Sun, hoping they would hear her and answer her call. It had been a long time since she had last done so. She was willing to try anything that might help get them out of this predicament.

Morgan was lost to them, either left behind or locked up somewhere else in Gaelan.

She'd seen Dani with Xander just before the latter had disappeared into the House of the Moon. *That* had been a surprise. Dani was one of Alix's friends, part of the group that had disappeared with him the year before—it had been in his file. But she knew little about the OberCorp enforcer personally. Not finding out more had been a grave mistake.

It was times like this that she missed Ari, her PA, and her connection to the grid.

How had the OberCorp enforcers taken over the city so easily? Why were the Gaelani deferring to them?

Most importantly, where was Robyn?

The night was growing dark, and the stars were coming out one by one overhead. Quince had lived in Gaelan many years earlier. Back then, it had been a place of great hope and progress. Now it seemed empty and forlorn.

She'd also noticed others like Dani, wearing their black uniforms, on occasional patrol in the city streets below and coming in and out of the House of the Moon—landers. Second wavers. Men and women with no wings.

The occupation was worse than she had believed—the Gaelani had all but been cowed into submission.

If Quince was to have any chance to do something about it, she needed to preserve her strength. There was nothing she could do about the occupation or her own situation at the moment, so she closed her eyes and drifted off.

Pieces of her life drifted past in her light slumber—the night the Queen of the Erriani had been assassinated; her fear and flight after Ballifor had been destroyed; the escape to Oberon with the two children; and her long assimilation into the culture of Oberon City.

She remembered Robyn's warm touch, the long nights spent together under Titania's silver moon. From the first time they had met to the moment the Queen had sent her away because it had become too dangerous to continue their affair.

Those soft lips and that strong embrace.

For a few brief moments, everything was right in Quince's world. Then something brought her awake.

It was cold out. She was still barefoot from being captured in the dead of night, and there was a chill breeze blowing up the River Orn's valley.

She sat up and looked around. The city was quiet, and the moon was almost directly overhead. It must have been close to midnight.

There was a sound, a tapping of something against metal. She turned to find a little pixie face staring at her from the other side of the door to her cage.

"Morgan?" It came out in a loud whisper of surprise. How in the hell had the boy managed to follow them all this way in mere hours, let alone climb up to her cage unnoticed?

The boy put his finger to his lips, and she understood. Then he wrapped his hand around the lock and concentrated. His hands began to glow, and then the metal shone a bright yellow. The latch released as if of its own accord.

Quince's eyes widened. He was no ordinary human, that much was clear, but she ceased caring. He could help them get out of this predicament, and right now that was all that mattered.

She moved backward to make room for him to enter. Morgan swung the grate open silently. Hadn't it made a huge clamor when her captors had opened it earlier? Then he climbed inside. He put his hand on the metal cuff that held her ankle to the pedestal, and after another glow, it too came loose with a small clang as it hit the floor.

She looked over the edge of the cage to the ground below, but sensed no movement in the darkness.

Morgan pulled a pack off his back—it looked like Xander's—and took out her shoes and handed them to her.

She took them gratefully. She had apparently misjudged the little imp badly. "Thank you," she mouthed quietly.

He nodded, and started to climb back down the pedestal. Then he turned back to her and said, "Wait," holding out his palm toward her.

She nodded, and set about pulling on her shoes as quietly as she could manage.

When she was done, she sat and stared in the direction of Jameson's cage. It was hard to make out anything, but after three or four minutes, there was a flash of golden light, and the barely perceptible opening of a grate.

Another flash, and Jameson was free as well.

A minute later, she heard the word "Come." It was so soft she thought for a minute she had imagined it, but then the boy's glowing hand beckoned once.

She pushed open the door as silently as she could, resting it against the outside of the domed cage. Then she stretched and launched herself into the air, her wings carrying her the short distance across the space between the two cages, to where Jameson and Morgan awaited her.

Morgan leaned up and whispered into her ear. "The terrace. Top of the House of the Moon. Take us."

She nodded and scooped him up. Signaling for Jameson to follow, she jumped into the air again, her wings lifting her and the boy up toward the House of the Moon's walls.

It felt so good to stretch her wings in freedom. She only hoped they still had enough time.

Xander slept fitfully, despite the softness of the bed he found himself tied to. He couldn't turn over, and being stuck in the same position for hours on end was straining his arms, legs, and back. He flexed his wings, trying to stretch out his muscles.

His mind was in anguish. His friends—yes, both of them were his friends now, and Jameson was becoming something more—had fallen right into this trap with him, and he had no idea what had become of them. And what of Morgan, the strange boy who had somehow become almost like a son to him?

Never mind that it was Quince who had drafted him into her impossible quest in the first place.

He had vague memories of Gaelan and the House of the Moon, the place where he'd apparently spent his first two years. They were coming back to him now, slowly. He remembered that House of the Stars. In the past, he'd dismissed those memories as the products of an overactive imagination, or wish fulfillment in his darker hours under Rogan's thumb. Now he realized they were simple truth.

The city he'd seen as he was dragged into the House of the Moon, though, was anything but happy. It was practically empty, though he had seen many faces hidden behind the windows of the aeries.

It was like the Slander all over again, only this had been done to his people on purpose.

They were his people, like it or not—they were skythane, like him. That hadn't meant much to him before, but now he felt a renewed connection to this place and its people.

If Dani and her employers had their way, these people would find themselves subjugated and eventually eliminated to satisfy OberCorp's thirst for profits.

In a day and a half, though, it would cease to matter. With enough pith in his system, he'd become a willing accomplice to OberCorp's plan. Would he even remember what had been done to him?

If Quince was right, in a day or two after that, even that would become purely academic.

Xander shivered. He ached to be free, to confront Dani and put an end to OberCorp's plans. So he drifted in and out of sleep, his head full of half-baked plans that dissolved in the firelight when he opened his eyes. He would fight, for as long as he could, however he could. That was all that was left to him.

The doors to the balcony swept open, letting in a cool breeze from outside. Xander started, straining to turn enough to see what was happening.

Surely Dani wasn't ready yet to go ahead with her plan. It had to be close to midnight. He had to have at least until morning.

Instead, it was Quince who strode in, holding Morgan's hand, with Jameson behind her. He had never been so happy to see anyone in his life.

She glanced at the closed door to the hallway, and then knelt next to him. "Hey, are you okay?" she whispered. "I'm not sure how much time we have."

"Yes, I'm all right. How did you find me?" Had they managed to escape their cages, somehow? He'd seen them locked up like animals before he was dragged into the House of the Moon. Had Dani had a change of heart and let them go? That seemed unlikely—and how in three hells had Morgan gotten here?

"It was all Morgan's doing," Quince whispered. "I'll tell you later." She glanced again nervously at the closed door. Then she studied his restraints, frowning.

Morgan handed her Xander's knife from the pack he was carrying. There must be quite a story there.

Quince grinned and set about cutting the ropes that bound Xander's arms and legs.

Freed, he sat up and stretched, massaging the spots on his wrists and ankles where the rope had burned him.

Then he picked Morgan up and gave him a big hug. "I am so glad to see you, little guy."

Morgan smiled. Maybe. A little.

Xander set the boy down.

"Have you seen Robyn?" Quince asked.

He turned away, afraid to answer her, afraid to even look at her. "I'm so sorry, Quince," he whispered at last.

"Sorry for what?" She took him by the chin and forced him to look into her eyes. "What happened to her?"

"Robyn…. My mother's gone. Dani, the Oberon woman… she told me that she tortured her to get information about me."

Quince's face went white. "Oh gods no…."

She stumbled, and Xander took her by the arm to help steady her, guiding her down to the mattress next to him. She looked up at him as if just realizing he'd lost someone important too. He had guessed that they had been more than friends. Quince's reaction was confirmation.

"When?" she whispered.

Jameson came to sit down on his other side, putting an arm on Xander's shoulder.

"I don't know, but it must have happened recently. Otherwise they would have started hunting me sooner, back in Oberon City."

Quince's demeanor changed from grief to burning anger in a flash. "Where is she?" Quince growled softly. "This *Dani*." She spat the name out.

Xander shook his head. "I don't know. Somewhere here in the House of the Moon, I'd guess." He took her hand. "Quince, I'm so sorry. But we can't go up against her, not without a plan."

"We don't have time for a plan. We have the element of surprise—we should go find her now." She fingered his knife blade, drawing a bead of blood from her own thumb, seemingly oblivious to the pain.

Xander shivered. He didn't want to know what Quince planned to do to the OberCorp woman. "We have the occupation forces to worry about too." He glanced out the window. "How many do you think there are?"

She shook her head. "I don't know. Several hundred?"

"Will they know who I am? The Gaelani?"

"With this sigil, yes." She touched the silver quarter moon that hung around his neck. It shimmered in response. "The prince always wears it."

That would make things easier. "You take Jameson and go after Dani. Take out the leader, and the OberCorp forces will be in disarray, at least briefly."

"What about you? What are you going to do?" Jameson asked, his mouth pursed in a frown.

"Rally my people." It sounded right when he said it out loud. Mostly. He'd have to work on that.

Quince nodded. "We can take care of Dani." Her voice had a dangerous edge.

"Don't kill her, Quince. I want to talk to her first." She knew more than she'd told him. He was sure of it.

Quince stared at him for a moment as if she might object, but at last she gave him a curt nod.

"Let's deal with the guard outside first." He stood and started toward the closed door that led to the hall, but Jameson pulled him back.

His warm hands enclosed Xander's face, and he looked into Xander's eyes. "I had some time to think, when I was trapped."

Xander nodded. "Me too."

"Last night with you, I let it all fall away—my walls, my religious superstitions, everything. Oh God, it was difficult. It still is." His eyes were wet. "I'm scared, Xander, about you and me. About this place. About the responsibility we've been given." He glanced at Quince, who nodded. "I was afraid that I waited too long. I'm here now, if you'll have me." He pulled Xander to him and kissed him hard.

Xander's heart *sang*. He kissed Jameson back, and something electric raced through Jameson's hands and into his head. It was like a tidal wave.

As it overtook him, he *remembered*.

A kiss like this one, given without reservation.

A life lived in this city, among his own kind. Scenes that flashed past him in quick succession, memories that weren't his own, but that somehow belonged to him.

He was Elyra, Queen of the Gaelani, and he kissed Daedus, the Erriani King, under a silver moon in a black tower.

They soared over the Riamhwood, and swam in the cold rivers of the Orn.

He was Elyra/Xander—somehow he was both, at once—connected to the House of the Moon and his people.

To Titania.

To Jameson.

. . .

He opened his eyes. Jameson's eyes were full of wonder.

They were connected, to each other and the past, and for a brief moment there was no one else in the world.

Then Quince broke the spell. "Come on." She pulled Xander toward the door. "It's time to set things right."

CHAPTER 20
BATTLE

XANDER CRACKED THE DOOR OPEN, peering out into the hall. Torches lit the stone-lined passageway, and a single man, one of the OberCorp forces, was standing—or rather, sitting—guard. His back was to the door, and Xander could see that he was dressed in a black uniform with the half-circle logo of OberCorp on his sleeve. He was armed with a short knife and a pulse pistol. He also looked half-asleep.

Xander's mind was overflowing with memories of this world, sizzling in the back of his head. They fought for recognition, and it was all he could do to push them back to try to keep some space clear to think.

Jameson's kiss had opened a door, and memories were pushing their way through, things he couldn't possibly have known from his own experience.

In his mind's eye, the drab hallway outside the door was instead filled with tapestries, the pink sun in the sky lighting the hall through narrow crenellations in the walls.

Xander shook his head, forcing his mind back to the task at hand. He signaled silently to the others.

Quince and Jameson nodded.

Jameson swung the door open wide, and Xander grabbed the man from behind, hauling him into the room, his arms flailing, covering his mouth before he could get out more than a grunt.

Jameson closed the door silently, and Xander slammed the man's head down onto the hard stone floor, knocking him unconscious.

Quince retrieved some of the rope that had been used to tie up Xander, trussing the guard up and gagging him with a torn piece of the bedsheets.

She handed the man's pulse pistol to Jameson. She took the knife for herself, handing Xander's back to him. Then she knelt next to Morgan. "Can you help us find Dani? The lander woman?"

Morgan nodded, his face far too serious for his age.

"You trust him now?" Xander asked, surprised. He'd mostly glossed over the boy's presence before in the heat of the moment, but now it struck him how strange it was. "How did he get here?"

"Time for that later. Listen, Xander, there's a bell in the middle of Gaelan on Founder's Hill...."

More memories flooded back. Founder's Hill, the large hillside in the middle of Gaelan, the town square topped by a tower with a huge metal bell, which had been used many times before to signal danger or to call the city together. "I know where it is."

Quince regarded him with a mixture of surprise and resignation. "Of course you do." She gave him a big hug. "Be careful out there, my little sparrow."

Memories, his own this time, flashed through him. His mother, holding him in her arms and calling him "little sparrow." Quince with her, in the House of the Stars, with the little baby who would one day grow into the man who stood beside him.

It was the last time his mother had kissed him good-bye.

"I will." More than the words passed between them. "Keep Morgan and Jameson safe." With one last nod, he turned and ran out the doorway onto the balcony and sprang into the air with a single great leap.

MORGAN LED Quince and Jameson out of the room, following him single-file down the hallway. Huge tapestries decorated some of the walls, though they looked ill-maintained, soiled by decades of soot and general wear. Other walls had wide bare patches that were lighter than the surrounding stone; she wondered where those tapestries had gone.

Torches flickered in sconces every three or four meters, some burned almost down to their nubs. The House of the Moon itself was almost deserted at this time of night.

Morgan led them to a stairwell, and they climbed up to the next floor, pausing in the shadows to be sure they hadn't been seen. They crept down another long hall and up a flight of stairs. Their path was taking them toward the back of the House, where it abutted the valley wall, as near as Quince could tell.

Near the junction of another passageway, they heard noises.

Quince peered around the corner.

A group of four of Dani's lander guards was coming down the hallway together, joking and laughing. They sounded drunk.

Quince seethed at this lander invasion of her people, her home. Though she was from Ballifor, she'd spent more than a little time in the capital, and seeing them here was a personal affront.

There were too many for the three of them to fight, and the guards had pulse weapons on their side.

Quince gestured to the others, and Morgan and Jameson retreated with her to darkened doorways along the hall, pressing themselves back against the shadows.

Fortunately, the party passed by without turning. Quince breathed a sigh of relief.

They followed the boy down another hallway, and when they came to a corner, Morgan stopped them. "There," he said, pointing around the corner.

Quince hissed under her breath. Dani had taken up residence in the Queen's suite. *After she arranged for Robyn's death.* She saw the Queen's face now, as clearly as if she were standing there before them.

She would take care of this one personally. First they had to get past the guard.

They concocted a simple plan in hushed tones.

Morgan looked up at Quince, who nodded. "Go."

The boy ran around the corner, shouting "Guards, guards… the prisoners have escaped." He beckoned the guards to follow him and ran back around the corner toward Quince and Jameson.

One of them did.

Quince tripped him after he rounded the corner, dropping him to the ground. Jameson grabbed him and banged his head hard against the wall, knocking him out cold.

They dropped back into two doorways that flanked the hall, waiting for the other guard to come investigate. Soon enough he popped his head around the corner, and seeing the other man laid out flat on the ground, he ran forward, kneeling to check the man's pulse. "Daro, you all right?"

Jameson knocked him hard on the head with the handle of his pulse pistol. The man fell to the ground with a sigh.

They dragged the bodies into the shadow of a doorway and relieved them of their weapons. Quince tucked one into her belt. It wouldn't be long now before the need for caution was over.

Quince strode toward the doorway with a sense of divine purpose, the others close behind. She turned the silver knob and pushed the door open as quietly as possible. It led into the antechamber of the Queen's suite.

The room was dark, lit only by silver moonlight from the bedroom chamber windows, and it was filled with the shadows of overstuffed furniture. She stood there for a moment, remembering furtive nights spent in this same room with Robyn, having an affair under the nose of the king.

It seemed like so long ago.

Quince took a deep breath and steeled herself. It was time. She pulled out the pulse pistol from her belt.

The sharp peal of a bell rang through the room, clanging urgently. Xander had reached Founder's Hill.

At least, she hoped it was Xander.

XANDER WORKED his way through the dark city, illuminated only by Bandia's light. He leapt from aerie to aerie, soaring between them where the distance between them was too far. He tried to stay aloft only as long as necessary, keeping his exposure to a minimum.

On one balcony, he startled a young skythane girl who had likely just gotten her wings, peeking out into the night in violation of curfew. He alighted on the balcony and she looked up at him, startled. She started to scream.

Xander cupped his hand gently over her mouth. "Listen to me," he said gently. "I won't hurt you." He held up his sigil. "I'm Xander, Prince of Gaelan." Her eyes went wide as she saw the sigil hanging around his neck. It glowed with a faint argent light. "I've come back to claim my kingdom. Do you understand?"

She nodded, and he let her go gently. She bowed and whispered, "Your Highness," shivering.

He gave her a warm smile. "What's your name?" he asked softly.

"Mylin, Your Highness." She tried to bow again, but he stopped her with a hand on her shoulder.

"That's really not necessary."

She blushed. "Sorry, m'Lord."

"Xander will do just fine." He looked around to make sure no one had seen them on the exposed balcony. Far below, a pair of OberCorp enforcers were passing by on the open road, but they didn't look up. "Go inside and spread the word that I have returned. I'm going to ring the bell on Founder's Hill. Tell your parents, your neighbors, anyone you can reach. I've brought friends with me. We're going to take down the invaders. Do you understand?"

She nodded, staring up at him in wonder. Then she reached up and kissed his cheek. "Welcome home, Prince Xander." Then she turned and dashed back into her room and into the hallway beyond.

Xander watched her go, sure now he'd made the right choice to stand and fight. Then he continued toward the heart of the city, slipping from shadow to shadow.

His new memories continued to pester him. In one place in the middle of Gaelan, he clearly remembered flying through the narrow passage between two stone buildings on his way to meet a lover. In another, a sunny afternoon spent splashing in a cool fountain as his mother looked on, amused.

So many memories, one after the next, the whole thing like a reality overlay on the world around him.

Everywhere he went, he saw Dani's guards. There must have been at least a couple hundred of them here in Gaelan, while his people huddled behind closed doors in their own city.

At last he reached the heart of Gaelan, landing in the darkness at the foot of Founder's Hill. He crouched behind a boulder and considered his approach.

The hillside loomed above him, its grassy curve crested by a rocky outcropping and a narrow black tower. There were two people guarding it. He could bypass them, but they would cause trouble when he rang the bell. Best to take them out first, if he could.

He slipped around the back side of the hill, passing from shadow to shadow, looking up to make sure he moved undetected. When he reached its eastern side, where the moon cast a deep shadow, his great wings lifted him up silently to the roof.

Then he dropped onto the two guards, knocking one aside to land hard against the tower, and taking the other one down the hillside with him. They rolled man over woman in a rush to slam against one of the boulders that dotted the hillside.

She kicked him hard and tried to scramble away, reaching for her pulse pistol, but he grabbed her legs and pulled her back. She slammed her fist into his face, knocking him backward, and grabbed again for the pistol.

He got up and hit her back across the face, knocking her out cold.

He grabbed her pulse pistol and spun around, taking down the other guard before he could squeeze off a shot at Xander. The pulse knocked the man back hard, burning his face at such close range. Xander felt badly about that, but it was kill or be killed tonight. He would try to take as few lives as possible, but Gaelan would be freed.

He hoped Jameson was all right—there was no time to check on him, but they had unfinished business between them. If anything happened to him now….

Xander leaped into the air, his wings lifting him up toward the top of the tower. Landing gracefully on the stone parapet, he climbed over it, and took the rope to the big bell and pulled it hard. The heavy metal instrument swung back and forth, setting up a clangor that filled the entire valley.

QUINCE STEPPED into the antechamber. Jameson followed behind her, holding Morgan's hand.

She suffered an attack of déjà vu at this familiar place that figured in some of her most intimate memories with Robyn.

That Dani had taken it for herself was a sacrilege.

She made her way quietly across the room to the bedroom doors of the Queen's suite, looking for the lander woman.

In the moonlight, she could see that the covers on the bed had been thrown back. Dani was nowhere to be seen. "Dammit," she whispered.

Moonrise help her, she remembered that bed too. It was a tall four-poster like the one Xander had been tied to, but grander, its posts filigreed in silver. A great round rug with the sliver of Bandia embroidered on it filled most of the rest of the floor.

Quince stepped into the room.

"You surprise me," a woman's voice said from the darkness of one corner of the room. Dani stepped in front of the window, her form silhouetted.

"Dani," Quince hissed.

Dani stepped forward into the moonlight. "You must be Quince." She was smiling. "Your old lover, the Queen, mentioned you just before she died. Seems she felt… hurt by your abandonment. Especially toward the end." She held something in her hands.

Quince growled. As her eyes adjusted to the light, she saw that Dani had a pulse rifle. "Put it down, Dani." She held her own pistol steady, aimed at Dani's heart.

Dani lifted the rifle into the air and fired, and a big chunk of the ceiling came down between them. "Don't tell me what to do. The Queen pushed me when we first arrived to *counsel* the king. She thought I was some lackey she could order around. When the time came, I pushed back."

I should take the shot. I could end this now. So what if she kills me?

Dani must have read the look in her eyes. She smiled, a cold twisting of her lips. "Maybe you could take me out. But would you be able to do it before I shot your beloved Jameson? Or, should I say, *Lyrin*?" The muzzle of her rifle shifted slowly toward Jameson. "Try me."

Quince paled. "No." It came out as a whisper. Not Lyrin.

She glanced over at him. He was sweating but holding his own, his pulse pistol also trained on the OberCorp enforcer.

Dani laughed. "You won't do a thing," she said with a certainty that made Quince hate her even more. "Not with his life in danger. I'm not sure how you managed to get out of those beautiful little birdcages I put you in, but it looks like I'm still in charge here for a little while longer." She took a step forward. "So this is what we're going to—"

Her mouth fell open and her eyes went vacant, rolling back up into her head. She collapsed to the ground like a puppet whose strings had just been cut, her rifle clattering away into a corner of the room.

"What the hell?" Jameson cried.

Morgan stood behind her, his hands glowing.

"Morgan! What did you do?" Jameson asked the boy, alarmed.

Quince knelt to check Dani's pulse. She was still breathing. "She's alive."

"I made her sleep."

Jameson laughed. "So you did." He turned to Quince, who was still trying to figure out what had just happened. "And you were going to do away with the little imp," he said, jostling Quince in the ribs.

For her response, she pulled Jameson into her arms and hugged him fiercely.

Xander stared out at the city he'd inherited. The moon, the symbol of his people, was before him, edging slowly toward the mountains, casting her silver glow over the city.

The echoes of the bell reverberated across the valley.

Lights were coming on in windows high and low—people looking out from their aeries, up at the dark tower as the bell's sound died down.

Was he ready for this responsibility? All his life, it had been him against the world. He'd never had to take care of someone else, let alone a whole people.

It was a little late for second thoughts, though, wasn't it?

He wished Jameson was here by his side.

"People of Gaelan," he shouted into the silence. "I am Davyn Sléite, Prince of the Gaelani." He'd decided to use his skythane name, hoping it would be more effective. As he spoke, the sigil on his chest began to glow, illuminating his body so that all could see him. "The time has come to overthrow these lander invaders." He held up one of the liberated pulse guns. "They have weapons, but we are many and they are few."

A low murmur filled the city below, but no one dared venture out of their aeries. His speech wasn't enough. They were too afraid.

Xander tried again. "We must stand up and fight—"

He was cut off as a pulse beam hit the tower next to him, showering him with debris and knocking him back hard against the bell, which rang in protest.

He lay there for a moment, stunned, and then shook his head and climbed to his feet. As the dust cleared, he held up the pistol again, blood streaming down his face, and shouted, "It's time to fight!"

A roar went up from the city this time.

Xander had them now. Skythane of all sizes began to emerge from their homes. Men, women, even children old enough to fly.

He dove off the platform and flew down toward his attacker.

All around him the air erupted in a flurry of wings.

Jameson blushed in Quince's embrace. He wasn't used to getting physical attention like this. In his own family, there had always been a formal distance between himself and his parents. His *adopted* parents. That fact still seemed strange to him.

Quince squeezed him one last time before letting him go.

"We should do something about her." Jameson gestured at the unconscious woman.

Quince retrieved the rifle Dani had dropped when she had fallen. "Robyn was my life, and she took that life away." She stared down at the woman's still form and lifted the barrel of the pulse rifle to put it up against Dani's temple.

"Quince, don't." Jameson put a hand on her arm. "You're not like them." He willed her to look up at him. "Don't let her push you into something you'll regret."

"Why shouldn't I?" Her voice was pained, sharp, but she looked into his eyes. "She killed Robyn. She could have killed you just as easily. Then what would I have left?"

Morgan stood to one side, watching the two of them, his expression blank.

"I'm. Still. Here. You risked your life to save me, to save Xander and me, even though it meant leaving Robyn behind for all these years. Do you think she would want this?"

Quince snorted. "Robyn's dead."

"Dani will pay for that, but not like this." He held his hand out, imploring her. "Quince, I'm a professional psych. I've seen what happens when someone hurts someone else for revenge. It eats at your soul."

They locked gazes for a moment, their eyes inches apart. Jameson could see the rage and pain etched in her gaze. Her loss was still fresh, like a deep wound, and Dani had just ground salt into it.

Quince's finger trembled on the trigger. She was balanced on the knife's edge, and a single breath could tip her either way.

He eased his hand slowly down her arm to the rifle. "Trust me, Quince." *Come on.* Xander should be here. She would listen to him.

She closed her eyes.

Her finger relaxed on the trigger, and she pulled the muzzle away from Dani's temple. She handed the rifle over to Jameson, who set it on a windowsill out of the way.

Then he hugged her back. "You still have me," he repeated.

They used sheets to tie Dani up, laying her on the bed. They would figure out what to do with her later.

What would happen if they succeeded in their quest? If Oberon and Titania were one world, once again, with the full power of OberCorp suddenly aligned against them?

He shook his head. Time enough to worry about that later too.

Outside, the sound of a pulse rifle rang out. Jameson ran to the balcony just in time to see chaos erupt in the skies of Gaelan.

Xander....

Then the doors to the antechamber burst open and two enforcers entered.

Jameson was too busy for the next few minutes to think about anything but survival.

Xander zigzagged his way down to where the shot had come from and took out the OberCorp guard there, twisting in midair to shoot the man in the back. He would show no mercy. They were attacking him and his city. Dani had made it personal.

One of his Gaelani screamed and dropped to the ground nearby with a heavy thud as the pulse weapon fire commenced. First blood had been drawn.

The next hour passed in a blur. Xander soared through the darkness of the city like an avenging angel, seeking out the enemy throughout the valley and engaging them. He gathered other fighters around him, liberating the Ober-Corp pulse guns and rifles, and they hunted the byways of Gaelan, bringing down enforcers by the dozens.

As they dove after yet another of the invaders, Xander suddenly felt a terrible heat in his left shoulder. He looked down—his leather vest had been completely torn off his left side by a pulse shot, and his shoulder had a nasty burn.

Pain burned through him savagely. He plummeted to the ground below, hitting it hard on his feet and stumbling but managing not to break anything in the process.

He leaned his forehead against a cool stone wall, closing his eyes and clenching his fists against the pain.

By the Split, it hurt.

Then something slowly eclipsed the pain, a cool wave spreading across his shoulder.

There was someone else with him.

Beside him?

"Who…? Elyra." He saw her now, a Valkyrie who wore the same sigil that hung around his neck.

She nodded. "I'm a part of you now, Davyn, a piece of your past. We have to fight on. We're so close to victory."

He was seeing things. "You're not real."

"No, I'm not." She laughed. "And yet, you're still talking to me."

Xander conceded her point. "How did you make my pain go away?"

"An old skythane trick, lost to your time."

It's official, Xander thought, shaking his head. *I'm talking to myself.*

"Are you all right, sire?" one of his battle companions asked, touching his good arm lightly.

He opened his eyes. Seven men and women surrounded him, all looking at him with concern.

He could read it in their eyes. If he could be defeated by a simple flesh wound….

"I'll be fine. Come on. Let's finish this." He stepped away from the wall and leapt toward the sky, a cheer going up behind him.

A few moments later, they brought down the last of Dani's enforcers together.

Gaelan was free.

CHAPTER 21
AFTERMATH

QUINCE PULLED her knife out of the chest of the OberCorp enforcer who had attacked her, wiping it clean on the man's black shirt. A trail of bodies lay behind them along the halls of the House of the Moon.

She regretted the bloodshed. The poor man had only been here following orders. Someone back home would mourn him.

There was only one way for this to end, though, and the man had fired at Jameson first. She'd had no choice.

She looked up and down the hallway—the fighting here in the House of the Moon seemed to be mostly over.

Once again, the great bell started to ring.

"It's Xander!" Jameson looked anxiously away toward the sound.

"Go on. I'll follow."

He smiled at her gratefully and ran down the hallway toward the Queen's suite and the nearest balcony, where he could fly to Xander's side.

She was proud of her two boys. She had done right by Robyn, had kept her promise from all those years before. The boys—both men now, especially after tonight—were back where they belonged. They knew what they had to do.

She wished them godspeed.

Only then did she look down at the painful, bleeding wound in her side that the enforcer had inflicted upon her when he'd swung around with his weapon. The wound she'd covered with her arm when Jameson had been with her.

She sank down on one knee, breathing raggedly. The pain from the pulse wound was agonizing, and she was having a hard time shutting it out.

The hallway around her grew blurry, and she felt rather than saw the ground hit her face as she fell on her side.

She had done what she promised to do.

Now she could go find Robyn.

XANDER ALIGHTED atop the tower and rang the bell again.

This time, his people came without hesitation.

They flew up to Founder's Hill, landing on the gathering place in ones and twos. Some were bloodied. Others had feathers burned off their wings. Children too young to have their wings ran up the hillside, laughing at their own sudden freedom.

Soon they surrounded him, a virtual army of the young and old, staring up at him.

Xander suffered a bout of double vision, remembering another life when he had stood here to talk to his people. He shook his head to clear it and held his arms up in victory.

"Gaelan is free!" he shouted, and a ragged cheer went up from the gathered throng.

"Davyn!" one man called out. "King Davyn!"

Soon the crowd took up the chant. "King Davyn! King Davyn! King Davyn!"

Xander surveyed the crowd, chanting his skythane name. He shook his head. "Listen."

The crowd kept on chanting.

He shouted "Listen!" and his sigil glowed. His voice boomed out over the crowd, and they went quiet.

"I'm just a man, not a king." His shoulder was throbbing again, but he could manage the pain. "I was only a child when I was taken from here. I don't know you, and you don't know me. You don't owe me anything."

Talking to them from high upon the tower was wrong. These people had come at his call, and they had fought for him. Some had died for him.

Without pausing to think, he leaped from the tower, his wings lowering him to stand in front of them. "I am humbled by you all. You risked your lives for me, for this city, and some gave them up for that fight. Gaelan belongs to you once again."

The crowd let loose a cheer.

Where was Jameson? Had he been hurt in the fighting?

A young girl pushed her way to the front of the crowd. He remembered her. Mylin, the girl from the balcony. He knelt before her. "I remember you. You're Mylin, right?"

She nodded. "Yes, sire." She looked very serious. "You told me your name was Xander, but you told the whole city that it's Davyn. Which is it?"

Xander laughed. "A little of both. My birth name is Davyn. But on Oberon, everyone called me Xander."

"King *Xander*, then. If you don't like 'King Davyn,' I mean."

"Wait… I'm not a king…."

"King Xander!" another said, and soon the whole gathered throng took up the call.

She was right. He *was* the rightful heir, though how a street kid from the Slander had ended up here…. He'd certainly never asked for it. And maybe he was more comfortable with Xander than Davyn.

Give them what they want, Elyra's voice whispered in his ear.

He looked out at his people, the men and women who had fought for the city at his call, and nodded. "King Xander it is, then." He raised his hands in the air.

The crowd cheered even louder.

"You've become quite the celebrity." The crowd parted again, and Jameson was standing there grinning up at him.

Xander pulled him forward into his arms and kissed him hard. He was a sweaty, bloody mess, but at the moment he didn't care. Jameson's lips met his and set his libido on fire. "Are you good with 'Prince Jameson'?"

Jameson laughed. "Yeah, that works." He squeezed Xander tightly.

When they parted, he held up Jameson's arm. "This is Jameson, my… companion, and a prince of the Erriani."

The cheer this time was more muted. People looked at one another, and several whispered "An *Erriani*?"

"We'll work on it," he whispered into Jameson's ear. To the crowd, he called out, "We have much to do. Gather the wounded and dead. Tonight we honor them, one and all. Tomorrow, we have important things to do."

The crowd began to disperse, but many of them passed by him to touch his wings or shoulder softly.

A man with black wings silvering with age appeared out of the crowd, one of the Gaelani who had fought at his side. He was a little older, but still handsome, with a firm jaw and short salt-and-pepper hair. His mouth was set in a thin line. "I'm Kadin, sire." He held out a hand to Xander. "I was the King's Chamberlain, sire, before the landers came and took advantage of the old man." Kadin looked like he was probably into his sixties, his silver beard neatly trimmed, his gray eyes as full of life as a man half his age. "I would be happy to offer you my services."

"Xander Kinnson," he said, shaking the man's hand. "That's an offer I'd be hard-pressed to refuse at the moment. We still have a lot to do, but if you could help organize a crew to start cleaning the filth from the city, that would be a big help."

Kadin nodded. "I'll get it organized right away, sire. I can come find you at the House of the Moon afterwards?"

Xander nodded, though that "sire" thing was going to get old fast. He put a hand on Kadin's shoulder. "Glad to have your service. Just call me Xander."

"Yes, sire… Xander."

Xander watched as the man turned to start organizing people to clean up the city.

It had been a short but hard-fought battle; having someone who knew the city inside and out would be a huge help in sorting out the aftermath. He doubted there would be much sleeping in Gaelan tonight.

XANDER TOOK charge of things, ordering a table brought into the King's quarters so they could start organizing their expedition to Deireadh an Domhain, or the Mountain, as Kadin called it—the closest gate between the worlds, and one of the places where the *shift* could be accomplished, as they were now calling it.

Shift. What a simple word for such a mind-boggling idea.

Dani had been strapped to a chair in a corner of the room. Jameson sat in another chair across from her, watching her for signs of life.

Morgan sat by the fireplace, staring into the flames.

Xander had gone into a mad rage when he'd seen her, and only the combined efforts of Kadin and himself had kept Xander from strangling the lander woman with his bare hands. Strange…. When had he started thinking of the wingless ones as landers? Or himself as skythane?

Not that Jameson blamed Xander. Or Quince.

Where the hell was she?

He'd gotten distracted by their hard-won victory and the rush of activity afterward, but now that things were taking on some sense of order, he missed her brusque, no-nonsense presence.

Dani was still asleep. He'd have to trust Xander to leave her alone for a few minutes.

Jameson stepped up to the table, where Xander was examining a paper map—strange to see such a thing. He missed his connection to the grid.

He put his hand on Xander's shoulder. His lover looked tired, his eyes rimmed with red. "Have you seen Quince?"

Xander looked around. "Last time I saw her, she was with you."

Jameson nodded. "I left her to come find you. We were fighting in the halls."

"I'm sure she's all right." He looked less certain than he sounded. "Quince is tough." Xander turned back to the map. "Why don't you see if you can find her? We could use her advice on the *shift*—she knows more about it than any of us."

"All right…. Just promise me you won't kill Dani while I'm gone?"

Xander glanced over at her. "I promise, I won't kill her. Not yet."

"Fair enough." He kissed Xander's cheek and went out to search the halls for Quince.

KADIN SUPPLIED maps of the surroundings and the Mora, and ordered in refreshments for everyone, including keff, the local equivalent of coffee. Two sips, and Xander's eyes were wide open. *Damn, this stuff is strong.* It tasted nothing like coffee. More like a sharp herbal tea, with maybe a hint of coconut? "Do we know if the lander men are in Errian as well?" he asked the Chamberlain.

Kadin shook his head. "We've had little to no contact with the… Erriani… in months. Relations between the Erriani and the Gaelani have been tense for years."

"That ends now. But we can't worry about it just yet." Xander rolled out one of the maps. "Quince brought the two of us here to shift Oberon out of harm's way, but we have to do it quickly, or there won't be an Oberon to worry about anymore, and maybe not a Titania either." He looked up at Kadin, searching the man's face. "Do you know anything about this?"

Kadin's brow furrowed. "Some. The queen was a believer in the old tales, and had me do some research through our oldest records." He looked up at Xander. "What did you want to know? I brought a copy of the prophecy…."

"Prophecy?" More of these people's… his people's silly superstitions—but maybe it held a grain of truth. "Can I see it?"

Kadin handed him an old piece of cured hide, written in longhand.

Tempest comes with clash and thunder,
Skies alight with rainbow's blood,
When the sunlight runs to red,
Comes the reaper for the dead

One with wings as black as night
One with wings of golden light
Spin the worlds back into one
To save them from the murdering sun.

Xander's hand shook as he read it. *Rainbow's blood….* The auras that had occurred when the shuttle had crashed. *Sunlight runs to red. Wings as black as night, wings of golden light.* "When was this written?"

"Near as we can tell, Queen Elyra wrote it herself, more than seven hundred years ago."

Xander sank down in his chair. He closed his eyes, and he could see her face. Part of his memories now. He was so unprepared for any of this. "Dammit, we need Quince here. I hope Jameson finds her soon." She was fine. She had to be. "All right. How long do they have to stay in phase once they are joined?"

"It's hard to say for certain. In the last cycle, reports say the solar activity lasted for ten days."

Xander scratched his chin. "Ten days. We'll have to figure out how to keep both sides away from each other's throats until we can send them to their separate corners again. Maybe for good." He put his finger on the map. "So how long will it take for us to get from here to the Mountain?"

Kadin considered. "Less than a day, if the weather holds."

"Quince mentioned something. A… key?"

"The rocthane." Kadin nodded. "It's in the royal armory."

"Can you bring it? I'd like to see it."

Kadin nodded. "I'll bring it to you, sire."

Xander looked at the map. The distance didn't look very far, but the air would be thin at the altitudes they'd have to fly at to reach Deireadh an Domhain. The Mountain.

They'd need a couple days' worth of supplies.

The doors burst open. Jameson rushed in, holding Quince's limp form. Her face looked deathly white.

He was at Jameson's side in a heartbeat. "What happened? Is she…?"

"She took a pulse blast to the abdomen. And I don't think so." Jameson laid her body down gently on the bed in the adjoining bedroom.

Xander leaned out the door, finding one of the guards Kadin had left there. "Get me a doctor. Or healer. Or whatever the hell we have here."

The man nodded and ran off.

Xander returned to Quince's side. She lay on the bed, looking ethereal and pale, as if the living, breathing part of her had been washed away. Jameson had pulled her shirt back gently from the injury on her stomach. The pulse blast had left an ugly burn on her stomach with an open wound in the center, and it looked like she'd lost a lot of blood.

What he wouldn't give for an honest-to-God OberCorp medic at the moment.

He brushed back a stray lock of Quince's hair, tucking it behind her ear. "Hang in there, Quince," he whispered. "Help is coming."

She showed no signs of consciousness.

At last, the healer arrived, an older woman with gray hair and feathers and startlingly green eyes. She took one look at Quince and set Jameson to work. "Go put some hot water on the fire," she ordered him, shooing him away from the bed. "You, cut her shirt off."

Xander pulled out his knife and started to cut away the cloth as gently as possible.

The healer took out a pouch of dried herbs. At his concerned look, she smiled. "Fennow root. It's a natural antiseptic. I'm not as much of a witch doctor as you might have feared."

Xander chuckled softly. She had him nailed.

She sprinkled the herb into the pot of water heating above the fire. When it was warm enough, she dipped a clean cloth from her satchel inside, and gently dripped the water over the wound. "Nasty bit of work, that," she said. "It's going to start to bleed again once I clean it out. Wash your hands in the hot water."

Xander did as he was ordered.

"Here, take this." She handed him a small cloth pouch. "It will help absorb the bleeding and start the healing process." She gently cleaned out the wound, which did start to bleed again. "Okay, lay the poultice on the wound, gently, and then keep pressure on it."

Xander did so. Quince didn't respond at all.

She placed another clean cloth over it, and he put pressure on that too.

"You." The healer pointed to Jameson. "Come help me pull her up."

Together, they managed to get Quince up into a sitting position and wrapped a length of cloth around her waist to make a bandage. Then they laid her back down gently on the bed.

Looking satisfied, the healer washed her hands and held one out to Xander. "Essra Nessaí."

"Xander—"

"I know who you are. Welcome home, *young* prince." Her tone suggested she didn't exactly trust his experience. "Now you'll need to change the dressing twice a day. I'll leave you some extra poultice packs, and will check back on the patient tomorrow."

"Is she…. Will she be all right?" Jameson asked, shooting a concerned glance at Quince.

She looked grim. "Honestly, I couldn't tell you. Only the gods know for sure."

Jameson and Xander sat on either side of the King's bed, where Quince lay still as death. Morgan sat in a chair by the window, staring out at the sky. Xander had ordered Dani taken out to be held elsewhere—Quince did not need to see her when she woke up.

If she woke up.

Her breathing was shallow, almost undetectable.

Jameson caressed her arm gently. "Come back to us," he whispered, regretting now all the mean thoughts he'd harbored about her when they had first met.

He caught Xander's eye. His lover nodded at him, and returned his own gaze to their sleeping friend.

Out there, the world was coming to an end, and yet being here at this moment seemed more important than anything else.

Jameson glanced over at Morgan. He wondered what the strange little boy was thinking. The boy had done something to him back at the way station—touched him and made him feel better. "Do you think he could help her?" he asked Xander softly.

Xander looked at the boy. "I don't know. He helped you."

"I can ask him."

Xander nodded.

Jameson approached the boy. Morgan sat as still as Quince, not acknowledging Jameson's presence in the least.

Jameson knelt before him, putting himself between the boy and the window. "Morgan, I need your help."

Morgan's gaze shifted to look into Jameson's eyes, and Jameson thought there was a flicker of recognition there.

"Morgan, Quince is sick. She was hurt in the battle. I don't know if she's going to make it." It was at least partly his fault. He had left in a rush to find Xander. If he had known that Quince was injured, maybe he could have done something.

"She's not part of the plan," Morgan said flatly, and turned his gaze away again.

"What plan?"

The boy ignored him.

"Morgan, what plan?" He took the boy by the shoulders and shook him. "Tell me."

A normal child would have cried. Morgan just stared back at him, his eyes empty of emotion. That frightened Jameson even more.

"Only you and Xander are necessary for the plan."

The plan.

He was talking about the *shift*. He had to be. Or else there was a whole other grand plan Jameson didn't know about? "Do you mean the plan to bring Oberon and Titania back together? *That* plan?" He searched the boy's face for some sign of humanity, but found only that impassive stare.

Morgan nodded. "Only you and Xander are necessary for the plan."

He had some leverage, then. "What if I refuse to go along with the plan?"

Xander stared at the two of them from the bedside, his brow creased.

"That makes no sense. You must do your part for the plan."

Jameson shook his head. "Not without Quince." He glared at the boy. "She was like a mother to me when I was a child. She protected me and sent me off-world to keep me safe. She saved my life more than once." He squeezed Morgan's hand. "No Quince, no plan. Look at me—see how deadly serious I am."

Morgan looked at him again.

Jameson kept his gaze steady and open, drawing on his psych training to evoke the boy's trust, his agreement.

He had no idea if he was reaching the boy. Time stretched out as they stared at one another. Then at last, Morgan looked away. "Quince is necessary for the plan," he said softly.

"Yes. Yes she is!" He'd finally gotten through to Morgan, whatever the boy really was.

Morgan let go of his hand and stood, padding barefoot across the floor to Quince's bedside. He pushed Xander aside and leaned over, putting his hands on her stomach and closing his eyes.

Those hands began to glow, a golden light suffusing them and then sinking into Quince's body.

For a minute, nothing happened.

Then Quince took in a huge gasp of air, her body lifting up off the sheets and her eyes opening.

Morgan stepped away, and Quince settled back onto the bed.

Jameson and Xander looked at one another, and then back at Quince.

She was fast asleep, and breathing normally now.

"Thank you, Morgan." Jameson swept the boy up in a hug. He didn't care what Morgan was, not at the moment. He had just saved Quince.

"She's a part of the plan" was all the boy said. When Jameson set him down, he went back to the chair by the window and recommenced watching the stars.

Xander shrugged. "She seems to be all right now." He put his hand on her forehead. "The fever is gone, and she's breathing normally."

Jameson nodded. "Thank God."

There was a hesitant knock from the doorway.

"Come in," Xander called.

It was Kadin. He held something in his hands. "I'm so sorry to interrupt…." He glanced at Quince. "Is everything all right?"

"She's an old friend who was injured in the fighting. It will be now."

"She must have been here before my time. I'm glad to hear that, but I'm afraid I have bad news." He held up two pieces of a broken black sphere. "The treasury was pilfered, probably by Dani and her enforcers. I'm afraid the key is broken."

Xander swore.

Jameson took his hand. "Look, we're all tired. Why don't we get what rest we can before morning? Then we can look at this all with fresh eyes."

Xander frowned, then nodded. "Kadin, can you find me a place to sleep?"

The man nodded. "Follow me. There's an empty room close by. I'll have to roust up some sheets. We'll find a place for the little one too."

Jameson watched him leave, feeling suddenly forgotten.

At the door, Xander turned.

"Aren't you coming? The King doesn't want to sleep alone."

Jameson laughed for the first time in days. "Does the King always get what he wants?"

"Let's find out."

Jameson let himself be led to the King's temporary bedroom. They didn't wait for the sheets before getting reacquainted.

CHAPTER 22
AWAKENING

QUINCE ARRIVED IN THE CAPITAL, *her Royal Letter in hand. She had been invited by the Queen herself to become a part of the royal retinue.*

Why, she had no idea. Destiny, she supposed. Her encounter with the nimfeach had her thinking about fate and destiny, and the arrival of the letter from the Queen, coming so soon afterward, had the feel of fate.

She stood before the Queen's quarters while a guard announced her arrival. Her knees shook. She had no idea what the Queen wanted from her. Something about an offer of employment.

The door swung open. "Come in."

Her voice sent a shiver up Quince's spine. She'd always been attracted to women, but she'd never found anyone in her little village who was attracted back.

"Hello?"

"In the bedroom."

She crossed through the antechamber and entered the Queen's sleeping chamber. It was a wide room with a four-poster bed. A cheery fire burned in the fireplace and soft rugs warmed the stone floors.

The Queen stood by the window, turned away from Quince.

"Hello?"

She turned, and Quince stifled a gasp. She was beautiful, her long dark hair cascading over her emerald-green gown.

Her black wings were tucked behind her.

She was at least seven months pregnant.

"You were recommended to me by a... friend. I have need of a nanny to help me with this child. Are you interested?" Her green eyes fixed on Quince's.

"I'm here, aren't I?" Quince said, surprising herself.

The Queen laughed. She put an arm around Quince's shoulder. "I think you're going to do all right here."

Quince's eyes flickered open. She felt a moment of pure and utter peace. She lay on a soft surface, more comfortable than anything she had slept on in years. She was surrounded by a warm pink glow.

Robyn.

Was this heaven? Or some other version of the afterlife? Was Robyn really waiting for her?

She remembered dying. Being wounded—a pulse shot to her gut—and lying in the darkened hallway on the hard stone floor as the world dimmed around her.

Her hand reached reflexively to her side. The skin there was smooth and whole.

Her eyes adjusted to the light. She was lying on a large bed.

She sat up and looked around.

If this was heaven, it was a very particular one.

She was in a wide stone-paved bedroom chamber. There was a chair by the one window that looked out on a pink sky. Morgan sat in it, staring out the window.

So, *not* heaven, then.

She felt a strange mixture of relief and disappointment. It seemed she wasn't quite ready to die, but the pain of losing Robyn was still fresh.

Now they would have to wait a little while longer to see each other again, and she would need to face the possible end of the world, after all.

She sighed.

She stood and made her way to an old wooden armoire against one wall. Opening it, she found a selection of fine robes. This had been the room of someone important. The King? She'd never been in his rooms before.

She chose the smallest one, and though it was still far too long, she supposed it would do for now.

"Good morning," she called to Morgan, who ignored her. If she had to bet, she'd guess the little imp was responsible for her miraculous recovery.

He wasn't the little boy he seemed to be on the outside, but she'd been wrong about all the rest. If she'd had her way....

She shuddered. Nothing else would have mattered.

Nothing to do about it now.

It's been a long journey back here, she thought as she stared out the window at a city at once familiar and strange. One that had started twenty-five years before. She closed her eyes, trying to remember every detail of the charge that had been given to her, that day when her life had changed.

She still didn't know where the nimfeach had come from, or how it had found her in the woods all those years ago, but it had sent her off to meet the woman she would fall in love with, and one of the children who would redirect the course of her life.

The sky outside was already getting brighter. She stared across the Orn at the cages where they had been trapped just the night before. She wondered how the battle had gone. Was it truly over?

A sharp knock brought her back to the present.

"Quince, are you up?" It was Jameson.

"Yes. Come on in."

Jameson opened the door hesitantly, as if afraid of what he would find. He had something in his arms. When he saw her standing by the window next to Morgan, a big smile spread across his face. "Oh it's good to see you on your feet." He hugged her with one arm, his wings fluttering with emotion.

"I thought we taught you how to control those things," she said with a sardonic smile.

"Still learning." His wings settled down. "Xander sent me to get you if you were awake. You and Morgan." He frowned at the boy seated silently in the chair. "He was like that last night too."

"Did he…?"

Jameson nodded. "Hands and glow and everything. Glad he's on our side."

Quince had her suspicions about that. Just because their motives seemed to be currently aligned, it didn't mean the boy was "on our side." She decided to keep those doubts to herself for now. "Are those for me?" she asked, indicating the bundle he held.

"What? Oh, yes. Here you go. Xander had Kadin—he's the Chamberlain—roust some clothes up for you." He handed them over.

"How soon are we leaving?"

"You can't…. It's not a good idea for you to travel just yet." He looked nervous.

"I'm perfectly fine, and I'll be the one who decides if I am fit enough to travel. Now, a bath?"

"I'll ask Kadin to arrange it. Quince… are you sure? Just last night, you were at death's door." Poor boy looked white as a sheet. "I was afraid we'd lost you."

She heard the ache in his voice. It was hard to remain unmoved by it, and yet they *needed* her with them. They were like children—useless without her, her dying thoughts to the contrary notwithstanding, and she really *did* feel fine. "I'll be all right, but thank you."

He started to say something, then stopped, seeing her determined look. "Fine. I'll come back for you in an hour. Xander is planning the expedition to the Mountain, and he wants your input." He kissed her, and she blushed, her cheeks flushing hot. She wasn't used to such solicitousness. "Glad you made it back to us," he whispered into her ear. "Come on, Morgan. Let's get something to eat."

The boy got up dutifully and took Jameson's hand, and they left her to get herself together.

XANDER LOOKED over the map once more. It was a fairly straightforward journey, but he still didn't know what they were going to do about the shattered key.

He turned to his Chamberlain. "Jameson and I should leave at first light. Kadin, I'll need three others to accompany us, as well as supplies for three to four days." He'd turned the dining hall into his impromptu war room to plan out the expedition, with Quince ensconced in the king's rooms.

A steady stream of citizens was coming through the hall. Most of them were there to just lay eyes on the new king, but some had petitions as well.

"I'll go," Kadin said, "and I'll choose two others who I trust."

"Anyone else have anything to add?" Xander looked around the room.

"You might tell me how you plan to pull this off without the key," a woman's voice said from behind him. He spun around to find Quince standing there, dressed in her new clothes and holding the broken pieces of the rocthane.

"By the Split it's good to see you." He swept her up in a hug.

"Yeah, I got that from Jameson earlier. Put me down already!"

He set her down and took the broken pieces of the round key from her. "We think Dani ransacked the treasury after the King died, and destroyed whatever she didn't take."

"How did they get such a large force here in the first place?"

"They had help. Dani Black and her crew apparently knew someone on this side who smuggled them in, a few men at a time. This thing was planned for years." He turned back to the maps.

"Dani… Black?"

He nodded. "We have her locked up, for the moment. I plan to question her before we leave. Why?" He glanced over at her.

Quince's face had gone pale.

"Hey, are you all right? Jameson, grab her a chair!" They helped her sit. "I knew it was too soon to get you out of bed."

She shook her head. "It's not that. It's the name. Dani…. Danielle?"

He nodded.

"Danielle Black. The man who killed Jameson's mother, the one who tried to kill me and both of you, was a skythane man named Danner Black—remember?"

"Barely. That's… interesting." It was all starting to make sense. If she was Danner's daughter…. "Would you like to join me when I question her?"

"Damned straight." She stood again, her face locked in a determined scowl. "What's the plan, then?"

"There's not much of one, I'm afraid. We take Morgan and head to the Mountain. I don't know what he is, but he has a part in this. He's saved our asses at least three times." He traced the route on the map. "And I'm not leaving him behind. Poor kid has been through too much."

He glanced over at the boy, still sitting quietly by himself. He sighed. "Once we get there, I suppose it's up to fate. Do you know anything else that might help us?"

She shook her head. "I'm not sure. All I know is that we need the two of you and the key. Without that… we'll just have to figure it out when we get there."

Xander laughed harshly. "That's hardly comforting, with the fate of two worlds on our shoulders."

"Nevertheless, that's all I can give you. I have the key Robyn gave us, but it's only tuned to the gate that links the House of the Sky to the House of the Stars, where we came through." She seemed shaken by the revelation about Dani and Danner Black.

Jameson put his arm around her shoulders, and she looked up at him gratefully.

Xander rested his hands on the table palms down, and looked over the maps once more. "It'll have to do."

• • •

KADIN HAD selected the room where Dani was being held. There were no windows, and only one door, which was guarded by two of his men. Both standing up.

"Is she secure?" he asked one of them.

"Yes, Your Highness. We just checked on her five minutes ago."

Xander wasn't used to people calling him "Your Highness." He wasn't sure he'd ever be. He didn't feel like a king, just a man who'd been forced by the course of events into a position of responsibility he hadn't sought or wanted.

Quince followed him into the room. Dani was on the bed, her hands and legs tied to the posts. She glared up at them as they entered.

"This looks familiar." Quince flashed her a wicked grin.

Xander pulled up a chair and sat on it backward, with his arms crossed on the back. "I'm sorry about having to tie you up," he said. "I had to be sure you would listen to what I had to say."

She sneered at him. "Very funny." She turned away. "I don't have *anything* to say to you. You may as well do whatever it is you're planning to do to me."

Xander could *feel* Quince behind him. She had tempered her earlier rage, but it still burned like a red-hot coal behind her eyes. He regarded his prisoner. He'd have been lying if he didn't say he enjoyed having their earlier positions reversed, at least a little. "Dani, where is your father?"

That got her attention. "I don't know what you're talking about." Her gaze went nervously from one of them to the other. "My father's dead."

Quince sat down on the bed next to Dani and ran a hand along the woman's exposed thigh. "Danner Black's dead too? That's quite a trail of casualties you've left behind."

From the brief shock in Dani's eyes, Quince had scored a point, but it was covered up quickly. "My father was Anthony Black, and he died on the Split ten years ago."

Xander picked up the narrative from Quince. "I don't think so. Your father is Danner Black, and he's been working for a quarter century to undermine the royal families in Gaelan and in Errian too." Dani looked away, but Xander took her by the chin, forcing her to look into his eyes. "Quince was there when he killed Jameson's mother. Did you know that? She saw it all. Your father took a knife like this...." He pulled out his own knife and held it up to her neck. He could feel her shaking. "Then he slashed it across her throat. Like this." He whipped the blade past her neck, missing the skin by a whisper.

She shuddered and tried to reach her neck with her hands, but she was tied too securely.

"I said I hadn't decided what to do with you yet. You're unharmed."

She spat in his face. "Screw you, Xander. Screw you and that redheaded bastard you're fucking and calling it love."

Quince slapped her. "Enough out of you." She got up, staring down at her nemesis. "She's not going to tell us anything."

Xander wiped the spittle off his cheek with the back of his hand. "You're right. We'll throw her in one of the cages until we return. Then you can see what else you can get out of her."

He stood and returned the chair to its corner.

"He's alive, you know," Dani said as they were leaving the room.

Xander kept walking.

"Alix is alive and my father has him. Live with that, you bastard."

Quince followed him out the door, and they closed it behind them without another word.

"She's lying." Quince put her hand on his shoulder.

"Probably." But he couldn't put it out of his head.

"He's alive, you know."

What if she was telling the truth?

He shivered at the thought. What if Alix had been alive this whole time, maybe suffering at the hands of Danner Black, just waiting for Xander to come find him?

How would he live with himself if that were true?

Kadin found them in the hall. "Xander, Quince, you have to see this." He led them along the hall and then down several long flights of stairs.

At the end of another hall, two guards were posted. At a wave of the Chamberlain's hand, they stepped aside. Kadin pushed open the door.

They were in a small room filled with wooden crates. The top of one of them had been pried off. Inside were hundreds of little glass vials, packed in hay.

Xander picked one up and stared at the dark liquid inside. "It's pith," he said, trading a glance with Quince.

"They were stockpiling it all along."

Kadin nodded. "There are years of production in here. It predates the arrival of the OberCorp enforcers, though they apparently took it over and accelerated the program once they arrived."

"They were creating an artificial shortage." Xander set the vial back down inside the crate.

Quince nodded. "To prime the pump." OberCorp had come to Titania to exploit its resources, just as they had on Oberon. And they were starting with pith.

It all made sense now. Dani and her father had failed to get what they wanted from the skythane, so they'd switched tactics and left the Syndicate to work with OberCorp instead.

So what would the company do once it learned its gambit in Gaelan had failed?

The list of things he'd have to deal with later was starting to overwhelm Xander.

"One thing at a time," Quince said, putting a hand on his shoulder.

He nodded. *One thing at a time.*

CHAPTER 23
SHIFT

THEY DEPARTED at dawn as planned—Quince, Jameson, Xander, and Morgan, along with Kadin and his chosen guards, a man named Venin and a woman named Alia. Both carried crossbows as well as medium-length swords, strapped to their waists. Not that they expected to encounter any opposition in the mountains, but Xander wanted to be safe.

They needed to travel light, and quickly.

Jameson wished he'd taken fencing in school. His hand-to-hand combat skills were also sorely lacking, and he had never used a bow and arrow or crossbow. They had confiscated a bunch of pulse rifles and pistols from the captives, though, and each of them carried one. He had practiced with his a few times before they had departed.

Jameson was determined that he would not need rescuing again.

Before they left, Xander had knelt next to Morgan to explain what they planned to do. The boy nodded, and Xander gave him a big hug, enveloping him with his wings. The sight gave Jameson a lump in his throat.

The morning had dawned cool and foggy. The worst of the fog had burned off, but it promised to be a cold flight through the mountains. The sun above was almost yellow, a shocking change from the rosy pink it had been when they had come through the waygate. Jameson imagined he could see giant flares coming off the sun's surface. He shivered.

Kadin had outfitted them all with protective thermal clothing. As Jameson was discovering, the skythane society was a strange mix of hand-made items and modern conveniences imported from Oberon, probably in trade for pith.

Gaelan sat in the foothills of the Mora, the mountain chain that defined the western edge of Titania. Jameson tried to picture the two halves of the world combined—the Pyramus Mountains and the Mora Mountains as one big mountain chain, back to back.

He looked around at his companions. Their society seemed blatantly incapable of having devised whatever machinery or method had ripped the world into two, and his knowledge of human expansion and technology certainly supported that.

If not their ancestors, though, then who had?

They climbed to an altitude high above the valley floor, following it up into the mountains. Quince had warned them that it would be cold, and already Jameson was feeling the chill, but the steady exercise seemed to help.

Morgan was once again strapped to Xander's chest for the flight. The boy remained an enigma to them all. He and Xander had talked it over the night before, after Jameson had told him the things the boy had done. They were still mystified about his origins.

Even Kadin had seemed shaken by the boy's powers and unsure of what he was. Jameson had asked him if the boy was a sneach, a wood spirit, as Quince had first suspected. Kadin had never heard of a sneach helping a human being. They were little tricksters, according to legend.

Xander and Jameson flew side by side, and every now and then Xander would shoot him a private smile. Jameson had come a long way in the last nine days, both physically and emotionally. He looked back on that previous version of himself and wondered why he had ever been so scared to let his real self out.

The mountains ahead were covered in a dense blanket of clouds. "We'll need to fly wing to wing," Xander said as they approached the mist. "Kadin, you take the lead."

The Chamberlain nodded, and they arranged themselves in a V shape as they entered the clouds. Jameson was reminded of flocks of geese on Beta Tau.

The air was cold and clammy on Jameson's exposed face, and he wished this whole thing would just be over. Not for the first time.

What would he do when it was? Assuming he survived, would he stay with Xander? Would Xander even want him? What would he tell his parents, if he ever made it back home? He had changed fundamentally since they'd met, and he had no desire to go back.

They had a deep connection, something they hadn't explored fully yet, but that was literally in the past. Just because they were linked from an earlier time, did that mean they were meant for each other in this one?

Was he more Lyrin, or Jameson?

So many questions with no answers.

They flew on through the blank white sky, and his thoughts were as nebulous as the clouds.

The journey gave his mind lots of time to roam, and his subconscious time to work a few things out.

After an hour or two, he decided he wanted to stay with Xander and see where this thing would go. If Xander wanted it too.

After another couple hours of slow going, they broke out of the cloud cover at last.

Jameson gasped.

Below them was a wide, verdant valley, filled with purple trees. A long, diamond-shaped lake sat in the middle of the valley, its waters the deepest turquoise blue.

The sky had taken on a cascade of colors. Just like it had when the flare on Oberon had brought down the shuttle.

Time was running out, and fast.

At the far end of the valley, a mountain rose up and up into the sky like a granite tower.

The Mountain, as Kadin had called it—or the end of the world.

KADIN LED them in flight up the side of the Mountain.

Xander "remembered" it. His borrowed memories were no match for the impressive scope of the thing in real life before him. They rose on air currents from the warm valley below, drifting in circles higher and higher for half an hour, and still it seemed as if they were no closer to the top.

The lake below was now little more than a puddle.

It was *freezing* up there. Although there were no clouds around the Mountain, the air was colder than ever this high above sea level. Xander wondered how close they were to the stratosphere.

"The entrance is on the other side," Kadin called, gesturing for them to follow him. He led them around the back side of the Mountain, which was much narrower at this elevation. Jameson gasped.

The Mountain's slopes on this side trailed off into nothing, straddling the Split, and there were stars above and below them.

"It's quite a sight," Kadin said. "We're almost there, Your Highness." The Chamberlain pointed to a dark patch in the rock above.

They swooped toward it. It was a terrace jutting out from the rock wall of the Mountain, with a cavern entrance hollowed out behind it, which looked too symmetrical to be natural.

Kadin alighted first, followed by the others. "Welcome to the Mountain," Kadin said with a theatrical sweep of his arm.

They hurried inside the cavern, out of the chill wind, and Xander ran his hand along the walls, marveling at how smooth and warm the stone was. Something must be warding off the chill—that suggested machinery of some sort. It was a tunnel, not a naturally occurring cave.

The tunnel led straight back into the Mountain, running slightly downward. Xander could see his breath in the air, and the cold seeped through his gloves and under his flight gear.

He loosened the ties that held Morgan to his chest, and the boy dropped to the ground.

Kadin pulled a lantern from his pack to provide them with light. Before he could ignite it, however, Morgan strode ahead into the darkness, holding a hand in the air that began to glow with a soft golden light.

Xander and Kadin exchanged a glance, and Xander shrugged, setting off after the boy. They'd trusted him this far.

They followed the passageway down into the Mountain, and as the entrance receded behind them, the air itself began to warm. After a few moments, Xander took off his cap and gloves. After a few more, he shrugged off his jacket, leaving them all to be picked up on the return trip. He wondered once again who had built this place.

Soon, he noticed that the tunnel walls were lit by some other external glow—something ahead was providing illumination. Morgan put down his hand, and the golden glow faded, replaced by a faint silver light.

Xander took Jameson's hand, and they proceeded toward the light.

It grew stronger, bit by bit, and at last Xander could see the end of the tunnel, an opening into a much brighter place.

He gripped Jameson's hand tighter, and together they stepped into the light.

They found themselves in a wide circular room. The stone here had been polished to a reflective luster, and the ceiling soared overhead in a high dome, decorated in fine lines of silver filigree. The lines gave off a soft hue, lighting the room, reminding Xander of a circuit board writ large.

On the far side of the room was a rock archway big enough for three people to walk through, side by side. Like the gateway at the House of the Stars, it was filled with stone.

Xander looked around. "Is this it?" he asked Quince, frowning. It seemed anticlimactic.

"This is the place," Jameson said. He walked around the room, running his hand along the wall; wherever he touched one of the silver lines, blue sparks flew into the air, but didn't seem to hurt him. He turned to Xander. "We were here, you and me. In another life. You with your raven hair and black wings...."

"I've never been here before in my life." And yet.... Xander touched the archway with his free hand, and his vision splintered into a thousand shards as his mind was flooded with memories. It was like someone had connected a firehose to his brain and opened the valve, like the memory flood before, but even stronger.

They stood side by side, hand in hand, and stared through the portal. On the other side was a world like this one. Half a world.

Xander/Elyra turned to Daedus, pulling him to him/her for a last passionate kiss. There was no guarantee this mad plan would actually work. Just because the nimfeach had prophesized it....

They might be torn from one another's arms forever.

Their lips met, and he was Hesies and Damella and Virgo and many more besides, a door opening up in his mind to his long line of ancestors. Jameson was Davos and Thera and Lydia and many other iterations of his own, each connected to Xander's own past incarnations.

Then he was Elyra and Jameson was Daedus once more, standing in this very room seven hundred and fifty years before their present.

Though his features were very different, his essence was still Jameson's, and Xander knew him.

The vision fell away, and it was just the two of them, Xander and Jameson, standing together in the cavern with their friends and companions arrayed around them. Everything had changed.

"We're supposed to have the rocthane," Jameson said. "It's the key."

Xander nodded.

Jameson reached out to knock on the wall beneath the arch. It was solid, unyielding rock.

"I have an idea. Do you trust me?" he asked Xander, holding out his hand.

Xander frowned again, and then nodded. "I do." *Damned if I know why, but I do.* He took Jameson's hand and pulled him forward in front of the archway.

"Stand here, and look through the arch."

Xander did as he was told.

Jameson held his hand out… to Morgan. Without a word, the boy stepped forward and took Jameson's outstretched hand.

Morgan put his other hand in Xander's. Somehow, it made sense.

"Are you ready?" Jameson asked.

Xander nodded. "If you are."

Holding Morgan's hand, Jameson stepped backward through the rock wall as it dissolved.

JAMESON STEPPED through the arch, holding Morgan's hand tightly, and the rock flowed around him, dissolving into nothing as he passed through it.

Something the boy had said about *the plan* had resonated in his mind, and when they had reached this place, it had come to him. This was the reason Morgan was here. To help them see this event through to its end.

He'd been fairly certain, but it wasn't until Morgan had taken his hand that he'd been sure.

Morgan was the key.

Jameson glanced around the room; it was the mirror image of the one he had just left, but empty.

When Morgan reached the midway point, held by the two of them, blue lines appeared on his neck, running down his back and up over his head like lightning. A sound came from the boy as well, a low hum that grew and grew in power and volume, until it drowned out everything else.

Suddenly Morgan shone with a silvery blue light, which quickly shaded over into gold and red. Jameson watched, fascinated and then with growing horror, as the boy was consumed by fire. From inside the cascade of light, Morgan looked up at him and smiled.

The whole room flashed silver and there was a pulse of energy that knocked him backward onto his ass, momentarily blinding him, tearing his hand away from Morgan's. He opened his eyes, but he could only see the vaguest outline of the shapes around him.

Slowly Jameson's vision cleared. There was a deep rumbling beneath his feet. He could see the others through the gateway.

"It's happening," Quince said.

Morgan was nowhere to be seen.

. . .

"It's happening," Quince said.

Somehow, Jameson had known Morgan was the key. The boy, the creature she had tried to snuff out. Only dumb luck and the intervention of Xander and Jameson had stopped her.

She shuddered at how close she had come to ruining everything.

As the boy started to shine like a miniature star, the circuitry in the ceiling —if that's what it was—began to glow, electrical charges running back and forth across the dome faster and faster, a hum building to a crescendo.

The flash, when it came, left her momentarily blinded, but her vision was coming back.

Jameson stepped back into the room with them as the shaking increased in tempo.

"Is it supposed to do this?" she asked.

"I don't know," Jameson shouted over the tumult. "I don't think it did the last time." He looked around. "Where's Morgan?"

Quince shook her head. The boy was gone.

Bits of the ceiling were starting to fall now as the smooth surface began to crack and split. Dust and small pebbles were shaken loose, along with pieces of the silver inlay.

"I think we'd better get out of here."

Xander nodded. She hustled everyone back into the tunnel. If anyone else was going to die here, it would be her.

The roar continued to increase. Quince ran along the tunnel after the others, feeling the grinding shudders as the Mountain groaned all around them. Her ears were filled with the moaning, crushing sounds, and the floor jerked back and forth underfoot. It was like being in the maw of a giant beast, and Quince had never been so aware of her own mortality and insignificance.

The illumination Morgan had provided was gone, but there was only one way to go, so they ran on ahead through the darkness.

One minute, the boy had been there, and the next he'd been gone.

Quince had no time to mourn him.

There was sunlight directly ahead.

Now larger parts of the tunnel's ceiling were starting to fall, and twice she had to detour around a chunk of rock as it crashed to the ground. The small party pushed on toward the light.

They reached the terrace at last, emerging into the open air. Quince followed Jameson out and took a big gulp of the fresh air.

"Look!" Jameson was pointing to where the edge of the world had been.

The stars were gone. Now mountains stretched out ahead of them for miles. The mountains of Oberon. *We did it.*

"I don't think we're safe yet," Xander said, looking down the mountainside. The rumbling had reached a crescendo and parts of the Mountain itself were collapsing behind them.

Their terrace began to split away, a crack running along the base where it connected to the mountainside.

"Fly!" Quince shouted, leaping into the air and away from the disintegrating peak. One after the other, each of her companions followed, swooping away from the ongoing destruction.

When she looked back, the tunnel mouth had vanished.

They flew together, away from the collapsing Mountain and back down toward the valley on the other side. The rumblings slowly began to subside.

They soared over the valley. The upper half was buried under the debris from the Mountain. On the eastern side, large swaths of trees had been flattened. Others were relatively untouched.

All the atmosphere on the split side of both halves of the world must have been forced out in the shift, flattening the forests for miles.

Quince alighted on a purple hillside at the valley's lower end. The shaking finally stopped, but the atmosphere was unsettled, a line of storm clouds marking the line where the worlds had been rejoined.

Quince wondered what had become of the miners who had been on the Split when their world had been forcibly reattached to its missing half. Hopefully the end had come quickly. She closed her eyes and said a prayer for their souls.

She wondered about the denizens of Oberon City, looking up to suddenly find themselves living under an alien sky.

As the dust clouds from its collapse began to dissipate, what was left of the Mountain reappeared, a cracked shell of its former self.

The gateway was lost, along with Morgan and his secrets.

She had no idea how they were going to send Oberon back to where it belonged.

As if on cue, it started to rain.

XANDER'S HEAD swam with the memories of a hundred selves, each one his ancestor, and somehow himself as well. How had Jameson managed to hold it all together with so many selves inside his head?

The two of them alighted safely on the eastern edge of the lake with their companions, and turned to see what they had wrought.

The Mountain was in shambles. It had collapsed, filling the western half of the valley with rubble. Beyond it lay the Pyramus mountains of Oberon. Storm clouds were rushing down upon them, sure to clear the dust out of the sky.

"We did it," he whispered, taking Jameson's hand.

Jameson nodded. "Against all the odds." He grinned. "I always wanted to save the world."

They'd have to deal with the implications of what they'd just done—the tens of thousands of Oberon's citizens who would now find themselves in a changed world.

They'd have to find another way to send them all back when the crisis was over.

They would figure it out tomorrow.

Morgan was gone. Whoever or whatever the boy had been, he had vanished into thin air after he'd opened the gate. He left a hole in Xander's heart, but there was nothing to do for it. Jameson was alive, and the world wouldn't end today. So instead, they would savor their victory.

Xander took Jameson in his arms and kissed him, and the echoes of the others in his head faded away.

EPILOGUE

VASSIR HO STARED at the order in disbelief.

"Abandon camp," the note said. It had come across the telegraph line, the only way to get messages from OberCorp quickly to the Split. "Disaster imminent."

The Prison Master of Alpha Camp, one of the two OberCorp amalite mining operations on the Split, called in his crew. The camp had three escape balloons, not nearly enough to evacuate all its personnel. Only its company officers.

"Come on, boys, we're evacuating camp," he told the gathered crew.

"What about the prison labor?" Jason Onns, his second in command, asked. The man seemed to have a soft side for their prisoners, which Ho didn't approve of. They'd all been sent out here for a reason.

"Let 'em loose. They'll have to fend for themselves." Even criminals deserved a shot, he acknowledged to himself, poor though it was. He threw the man the keys. "But be quick about it. We launch in ten minutes."

HE WOKE in the pitch-black darkness. He'd gotten mostly used to it these last two weeks, but he still woke up screaming some nights.

There was a clack, and the door to his cell was unlatched. He sat up, groggy. It couldn't be time again for his work shift. He'd only just lain down.

"Run while you can," Jason Onn's voice called out. "We're evacuating the base, but there's not enough room in the evac balloons for the prison labor." Then he was gone.

He pulled on his clothes and work boots and pushed the door open cautiously. The hallway was filled with other prisoners who had been pressed into labor in the camp. Most were running down the hall.

Two of them were staring at him, a woman and man. The man was Tucker… something or other. But the woman….

He gasped.

"No time for that," she said. "Where do we go? It's happening soon."

"What's happening?"

"The shift."

He frowned. Not that skythane superstition again. Still… something was clearly happening. He'd never heard of the mining bases being evacuated before.

"Follow me." He led them out into the open air.

Three balloons were lifting off from the north side of the camp, blown by the steady wind from mid-Split up toward the rim. "Fucking cowards."

"It's this way." He led his companions away from the camp, heading south. Most of the other inmates had run away to the west, hoping to reach the edge of the world and flee into the Pyramus Mountains. He had another destination in mind.

They followed an old mining trail for about half an hour. The sky above was full of stars, clearer than he'd ever seen from the other side of the world.

Off to the east, the Storm spun around the planet's center of gravity, a vast bank of clouds like a silver wall.

They turned off into a broken valley filled with black rock, at a point marked only by a pile of stones, following his memory. At the back of the valley, there was a dark gash in the stone.

One of the miners had discovered it a decade before—a tunnel that pierced the veil between the two worlds. OberCorp's own little secret gateway.

He'd been through it twice.

"This is it?" she asked, frowning at the narrow passageway.

He nodded. "Have anything for a light?"

Tucker grinned. "I have this." He held up a butane lighter.

"Thanks!" He took it and used it to light their way.

They followed the tunnel through its twists and turns, climbing over sharp ridges and under heavy overhangs that looked ready to collapse and crush them all. Finally, they reached a place where the air shimmered like water.

"Ready?"

His companions nodded.

They stepped through, one after another, into another cavern on another world. His skin tingled as he made the transition.

In fifteen minutes, they reached Titania's side of the Split. In another half an hour, they were up over the edge of the world, standing at the base of the Mountain.

The world began to shake.

He looked around in alarm.

"We have to get to shelter," the woman said. "There, behind those big rocks."

The rumbling grew louder and stronger, threatening to throw them off their feet. He decided not to argue. They ran.

As they reached the outcropping, there was a terrible roar, and the whole world shook. They threw themselves behind the rock as a sound like a thousand jet engines sounded off behind them.

Water vapor gushed into the sky from the split like a wall, and a huge gust of wind passed over them, knocking down trees and pulling rocks and soil into the air. Clouds mushroomed above them, manifesting thunder and lightning.

The three of them held on to each other, huddled against the rock, waiting for the terrible wind to pass.

At last it did, and things calmed a little.

That's when he saw the fliers, far above, outlined against the angry clouds.

"Hey! Down here!" He waved and shouted.

One of them must have seen them, because a figure descended while all the others flew away.

The skythane woman alighted right in front of them. She saw him first. "I'm Alia. What are you three doing here?" She looked at their black OberCorp uniforms and her eyes narrowed. "It's not safe." She shot a look up at the mountain. A third of it was gone—thank God it had fallen the other direction and not down upon their heads.

Alia turned to look at his companions, and immediately went down on one knee. "Your Highness! I didn't realize...." She looked confused. "You're Robyn Sléite. The Queen!" Her eyes widened even farther. "What happened to your wings?"

Robyn put her hand on Alia's cheek. "We can talk about that later. For now, we need your help to get home. Alia, this is Tucker."

The man bowed. "Pleased to meet you."

"And I'm Alix."

GLOSSARY

Alia: Guard in Gaelan
Alix Preston: Xander's ex, a lander man missing for a year
Amalite: Raw ore found only on Oberon that serves as a Common Worlds power source
AmSplor: Exploration division of the Northern American Union
Andra Madainn: Queen of the House of the Sun, Jameson's mother
Angela Havercamp: Jameson's adopted mother
Angie/Angela: Jameson's PA
Arcatus: Interstellar ship Jameson came in on from Tander's World
Arco: Vast buildings where most of Oberon City's citizens are housed
Argent Sea: Titania's sea
Ari: Quince's PA
Arracha Grain: Native grain grown as a staple on Oberon
Ballifor: Small Titania village where Quince is from
Bandia: Titania's silver moon
Beta Tau: Jameson's home world
Blackware: Illegal apps/software/code
Blueoak: Native Oberon tree
Boxcorn: Genetically modified square corn ears used as base for foods/fuels on Oberon
Cafflite: Oberon equivalent of coffee
Chit: Portable cash chip

Christianist: Throwback religious sect that hearkens back to conservative "Christian" values

Cirq: Bio-interface in the temple that allows users to access the Grid

Citrone: Native yellow fruit that grows on vines on Oberon

Colifir Tree: Red native tree that grows by rivers

Common Worlds: Loose-knit government of human worlds

Conjunction: Alignment of one of the moons of Oberon with the planet and sun

Creeper Vines: Native silver ground vegetation on Oberon

Crits: Credit/money

Croyol: Fungus that burns without smoke

Daedus Madainn: Prior King of the House of the Sun

Damella Sléite: Prior Queen of the House of the Moon

Danielle (Dani) Black: One of the lander enforcers in Gaelan, daughter of Danner Black

Danner Black: A skythane pith trade runner who helped instigate civil war between the skythane

Dark Market: Black market on Oberon, run by the Syndicate

Daro: One of Dani's lander guards

Davis: Zefron's son

Davos Madainn: Prior King of the House of the Sun

Davyn Sléite: Xander's Gaelani name

Dawson: Rogan's henchman

Dax: One of Rogan's enforcers

Deca: Oberon's tenth month

Deireadh an Domhain: The Mountain

Demetrius River: Southern tributary to the Theseus

Deterrent Field: Rope that is used to create a field to deter the local wildlife, especially wereveren

Dillan Farrai: Quince's brother

Distortion Field: Shield generated by a small device that blocks electronic surveillance

Distortion Zone: Zone of electronic interference at the edge of Oberon

Earth-Standard: Timekeeping based on Earth's clock/calendar

Egeus: City on Oberon

Elyra Sléite: Prior Queen of the House of the Moon

Enforcers: Men who work as the "muscle" of the Syndicate

Errian: City of the Sun (as in House of the)

Erriani: Citizens of the House of the Sun

Erro: Sun God

Ethilium: Growth hormone that stimulates the development of wings in the skythane

Farris: Assistant to the Prison Master

Feather Trees: Trees native to Oberon

Fennow Root: Natural antiseptic

First Wave: First human colonists on Oberon, also called skythane

Gael: Moon God

Gaelan: City of the House of the Moon

Gaelani: Moon (as in House of the)

Galaxion Hotel: Interstellar hotel chain

Gildensea: Oberon's sea

Glow Sphere: Portable light source

Governor: Governmental head of Oberon

Governor's Residence: Vast estate where the Governor lives

Great Division: Period after skythane refugees were chased out of Oberon to Titania

Great Retreat: The flight of the skythane settlers before the landers and OberCorp

Grid, The: Oberon's data and communications network

Gridcode: App, programming code, etc.

Gumba Tree: Tall, leafy native tree often used as a windbreak for farms on Oberon

Hachmoss: Yellow moss native to Oberon

Heart Fungus: See Croyol

Hermia: One of Oberon's two moons – red-colored

Hesies: Xander's past life

High Slopes: Northern district of Oberon City, where the Spaceport is

Hippolyta: City on Oberon

Hoarberries: Little berries covered in a sweet white "frost"

Honey Ale: Titania alcoholic drink

House of the Sky: Ruins in the center of Oberon

House of the Stars: Royal retreat in the center of Titania

Hoverplat: Transportation platform used to move small amounts of goods

Hoverbike: One of the main methods of personal transport in Oberon City

Hoversport: Hover craft used for human transport

Ice Pine: White tree native to the northern climes of Oberon - the Rim Forest

Imprean: Carrier pigeon–like bird used to carry messages

Jameson Havercamp: Psych from Beta Tau who comes to investigate pith shortage on Oberon

Jessa: Jameson's fiancée on Beta Tau

Joseph Havercamp: Jameson's adoptive father

Kadin Tamain: The Chamberlain of the House of the Moon

Keff: Titanian equivalent of coffee - tastes like herbal tea and coconut.

Knacks: Oberon insect pests

Landers: Second-wave human settlers

Lydia Madainn: Prior Queen of the House of the Sun

Lyrin Madainn: Jameson's birth name

Lysander: One of Oberon's two moons – golden-colored

Midcity: Heart of Oberon City

Mikelos: Miner on Tander's World

Morgan: Mysterious child Xander finds on Oberon

Morgan Kinnson: Xander's foster father

Mora Mountains: Titania's mountain chain

Mountain, The: Location of one of the gates between the two worlds, close to the House of the Moon

MRE: Meal Ready to Eat

Mugjuice: Oberon beverage made with pith

Mylin: Young skythane girl who helps Xander

Nimfeach: Butterfly-like creatures on Titania

Northern Glacier: At the North Pole on Oberon

OberCorp: Corporation that controls most of Oberon - The Oberon Mining Corporation

Oberon: Also known as Split - the half world where the story takes place

Oberon City: Capital of Oberon, with about one hundred thousand residents, most living in arcos

Obieberry: Native red stippled fruit on Oberon

Orn: Main river on Titania

Outland: Desert and wilds beyond Oberon City

Philo: City on Oberon

Pith: Psychoamoratic drug derived from the sap of the púca tree in Titania

Plas: Versatile artificial material with the hardness of diamond and the malleability of plastic

Plascreet: Variation of plas used in heavy construction; a concrete analogue

Pocans: Edible white fungus that resembles a string of pearls and tastes like chocolate and bread

Psych: Therapist

Psych Guild: Association of psychs

Psychoamoratic: A drug with aphrodisiac qualities

Púca Tree: Tree that pith comes from

Pulse Laser: High powered blast-pulse weapon used on transport ships

Pulse Pistol: Small pulse weapon

Pulse Rifle: Large pulse weapon

Pyramus Mountains: Mountain range along the Eastern edge of Oberon

Quince Farrai: Xander's skythane friend who joins the quest

Ravi: Xander's PA

Red Sands: Desert covering the southern part of Oberon

Redfruit: Fruit native to Titania

Redoak: Tree native to Titania

Rentz Class Cargo Carrier: Heavy lifter that carries amalite ore up from Oberon to interstellars

Riamhwood: Forest on Titania

Riding Armor: Body armor Xander wears when riding

Rift: The split that divides Oberon and Titania

Rim Forest: Forest on the northern half of Oberon

River Apples: Native Oberon water fruit

River Cat: Small scavenger the size and temperament of a raccoon

Robyn Sléite: Queen of the Gaelani and mother to Xander, and Quince's former lover

Rocthane: Access key to bring the worlds together

Rogan: Syndicate boss who has history with Xander

Second Wave: The second set of human colonists, also called landers

Seven Weeks' War: War between the Erriani and Gaelani twenty-five years before

Shift: Moving Oberon into Titania's space

Silverbark: Tall, thin tree with silver bark, leaves, and a dark stripe on the northern side, native to Oberon

Skythane: First wave of human colonists, who have wings

Slander, The: Slums of Oberon City

Sleeper: Sleep drug patch

Slit: Transfer funds or information electronically

Sneach: Skythane term for orphan - mischievous spirits who cause trouble or death

Split: Nickname for Oberon; also used for its broken side.

Stim: Stimulant

Swamp Bear: Harmless forest creature

Syndicate: Crime ring that controls the Slander

Synth-Meat: Meat grown in a vat from a cellular culture

Tander's World: Mining colony where Jameson was stationed

Tartanga Tree: Oberon riverside trees with broad, tripartite silver leaves

Tharsis: Home to one of the Tander's World miners, Mikelos

Thera: Prior Queen of the House of the Sun

Theron Sléite: King of the Gaelani, Xander's father

Theseus River: Main river in Oberon

Titan Station: Receiving space station for visitors to Oberon

Titania: Half of the planet on the other side of the rift

Tubers: Native Oberon edible plant - can be eaten cooked or raw, like a jicama

Vassir Ho: Prison master on the Split

Venin: Guard in Gaelan

Virgo Sléite: Prior King of the House of the Moon

Water Cane: Native Oberon edible plant

Wereveren: Birds that transform at night into lethal pecking machines

Wetreeds: Native plant with numbing properties

Wing Man: Slang for the skythane

Wrenwood: Bush from Titania whose wood burns without smoke

Xander Kinnson: Skythane who works in Oberon City, embarks on a quest with Jameson

Zefron: Stranger on Titan Station

ALL OF J. SCOTT COATSWORTH'S BOOKS

Liminal Sky: Ariadne Cycle

The Stark Divide | The Rising Tide | The Shoreless Sea

Liminal Sky: Ariadne Cycle Box Set

Liminal Sky: Redemption Cycle

Dropnauts | Coredivers (Fall 2026)

Liminal Sky: Oberon Cycle

Skythane | Lander | Ithani

Liminal Sky: Oberon Cycle Box Set

Tharassas Cycle

Tales From Tharassas | The Dragon Eater | The Gauntlet Runner | The Hencha Queen | The Death Bringer

The River City Chronicles

The River City Companion | The River City Chronicles | Down the River

Chaos and Order

Office of the Lost | Searching for the Lost (Late Summer 2026)

Other Sci Fi/Fantasy

The Autumn Lands | Cailleadhama | Flawless | The Great North | Homecoming | Wonderland

Short Story Collections

Spells & Stardust | Tangents & Tachyons | Androids & Aliens | Love & Limitations

Non-Fiction

Suck a Little Happy Juice

Audiobooks

Cailleadhama | The Autumn Lands | The River City Chronicles | Skythane | Lander

ABOUT J. SCOTT COATSWORTH

Scott lives with his husband of 25 years in a leafy Folsom, California suburb, in a little Italian-style house, just outside of Sacramento. He has always inhabited the space between the *here and now* and the *what could be*. Indoctrinated into fantasy and sci fi by his mother at the tender age of nine, he devoured her library. But as he grew up and read the golden age classics and more modern works as well, he began to wonder where all the people like him were.

After he came out at twenty-three, he decided that it was time to create the kinds of stories he couldn't find at Waldenbooks. If there weren't many gay characters in his favorite genres, he would reimagine them himself, populating them with a diverse universe of characters. He would subvert them and remake them to his own ends. And if he was lucky enough, someone else would want to read the things he wrote.

His friends say Scott's brain works a little differently – he sees relationships between things that others miss, and gets more done in a day than most folks manage in a week. Although he was born an introvert, he learned to reach outside himself and connect with others like him.

Scott writes stories that subvert expectations, that seek to transform traditional sci fi, fantasy, and contemporary worlds into something new and unexpected. His writing, whether romance or genre fiction (or a little bit of both) brings a queer energy to his stories, infusing them with love, beauty and power and making them soar. He imagines a world that *could be,* and in the process, maybe changes the world *that is,* just a little.

He was recognized as one of the top new gay authors in the 2017 Rainbow Awards, and his debut novel "Skythane" received two awards and an honorable mention.

He runs Queer Sci Fi, QueeRomance Ink, Liminal Fiction and Other Worlds Ink with Mark. He also runs the Queer Sacramento Authors Collective (QSAC) and the Sacramento Book Festival, along with the 2026 Nebula Con for the Science Fiction and Fantasy Writers of America (SFWA).